BEARNSHAW

Book One
Legend of the Whyte Doe

N. S. Rose

ISBN: 150023916X
ISBN-13: 978-1500239169

Dedication

This book is dedicated to the real Lady Sibyl, Lord William and Robin, whoever they were. If they did exist, I hope they're not too put out by their portrayals here...likewise everyone else depicted!

Also to my grandparents who always urged me to be a writer. Now here I am, writing proper stuff; I finally buckled down and did it! I'm only sorry Granma didn't live to see it but I like to think she's 'looking down' on it all.

CONTENTS

1   The Whyte Fawn   Pg 11

2   The Rising Sunne   Pg 13

3   Waberthwaite   Pg 35

4   Recovery   Pg 63

5   Mother Helston   Pg 91

6   Capturing a King   Pg 105

7   The Whyte Doe   Pg 135

8   Loss of All   Pg 155

9   The Curious Miller   Pg 181

10   False Promise   Pg 207

11   The Hand of Fate   Pg 225

Acknowledgements

Most thanks must go to my husband who, as always, reacted calmly when I came home from my work milking cows one day with the announcement that I'd thought of a way to adapt the legend of Bearnshaw Tower into a novel and I felt I should write a book and write it quickly before the muse left. Our workload at the time was such that most husbands would doubtless have dubbed the idea ridiculous and told me to concentrate on the real world for another year or two, please.

Instead Rob allowed me to go to work at 4am, get home and catch up on sleep before achieving as much work on our farm as I could and then spending the evenings writing late into the night. The house didn't get cleaned very much, our diet suffered, everyone else had to look after my daughter most of the time and although it began to feel like we were drowning as a family, we were committed by that point and the pressure was on me to make this book worth the effort!

Not only did he have to take up the slack with our farm and daughter, he also had to listen to the story as I went along - he's not much of a fictionlover and has no qualms about not sugarcoating his feedback for me, so I felt it was an important test for the story to pass. If it entertained an indifferent Yorkshireman, it would likely excite other readers for sure! Not only did he patiently listen, he also surprised me by helping me through 'sticky patches' in the story and providing some good 'fixes' for problems which actually enhance the story.

I'd also like to thank my gang of test readers who have provided excellent, invaluable and *real* feedback which has likewise enhanced the book and given me the courage to press the 'publish' button...

The talented Frances Quinn's artwork adorns our tale here

wonderfully; a far more fitting design than what I originally came up with, so thank you Frances! Thank you to Tom Proctor for stepping in at the last minute without fuss to expertly design the cover, too.

Final thanks go to Sharon Kay Penman for her glorious work 'The Sunne in Splendour' which ignited my passion for all things Wars of The Roses. Her book opened my eyes to all the unbelievable bloody drama of this period of my country's turbulent history, which had somehow been reduced to a dull footnote at school.

Legend of the Whyte Doe

1

The Whyte Fawn

Seeding grasses waved lazily in a circle all around the young fawn. Above, the white clouds were tinged with grey, mirroring the coat of the fawn perfectly. It was a beautiful creature, its pale coat almost shimmering, the nose a delicate pink. The large eyes were shut tight against the world as it lay curled in a ball, waiting for its dam. The craggy hillside stretched away from it in all directions, the little scrap of white clearly showing against the summer green.

Suddenly the eyes blinked open at a distant sound, showing their blue-grey colour. The large ears swiveled towards the sound and then flicked back and forth uncertainly as the fawn struggled to decide what course of action to take in response to the sound. It quivered as the sound formed into the clearly discernable bark of a dog. The fawn had not heard this sound before, but instinct told it to be frightened, and it was torn between the urge to run and the urge to stay quiet and hidden.

The decision was made, Sibyl saw, when a fine little bay pony ridden by a young boy cantered into view. Now Sibyl saw the world from the fawn's point of view, the boy's head peering over the ring of seed heads around her field of vision, directly at her. His eyes were large as saucers and she watched passively; sure it was too late to run, as his hand reached slowly for an arrow from his quiver.

Just as he was carefully notching his bow, a man appeared in the ring of vision above her, his large bay horse snorting and making her jump.

"Well, would you look at that..." the man breathed in wonder, his arm reaching out and coming to rest authoritatively on the boy's. "Don't shoot; it's far too young. We must let it grow into a worthy opponent!"

The boy seemed happy with this and lowered his bow. Neither could take his eyes from the fawn's pearlescent coat.

"It's special, this one. I've seen white deer before, but never one like this, with a real silver shine to it. Well done for finding it lad, it will be a joy to hunt in future years!"

With that, the man hauled on his horse's reins and the animal beneath him wheeled around out of view. Sibyl watched as the boy struggled to take his eyes from hers, even as his pony danced beneath him, eager to be away with its fellow.

"I'll be back for you one day." He said, "you and I share a destiny, you are my prize, I'm certain of it."

Then he was gone, the drumming hoof beats quickly dying away leaving only the sighing of the grass, all of which began shimmering and melting away around her.

"Sibyl!" A voice penetrated the darkness. "Sibyl, awake girl! You have gained a brother.....but lost a mother."

Sibyl's eyes snapped open.

2

The Rising Sunne

1461

"Lady Breckley thinks it would be best for me to return to court soon..." Sibyl mentioned over the meal. Her father slowed his chewing in a thoughtful manner. She could sense he was irritated.

"What about the wedding, dear?" He asked politely.

"Lady Breckley thinks this is a critical time for me, and she needs my help with all the changes taking place." Sibyl replied with nonchalance, taking another bite of the meat. Losing patience would not help in these situations. Her father snorted.

"Your help? There is no shortage of girls to serve Sibyl."

"And we should give one of them the opportunity instead? Given the current...climate?" Sibyl looked him in the eye.

"The new King you mean." He said with a scowl.

"Of course!" She replied. "I realise my marriage is important to the future success of the family, and I realise the old King is still at large and we should be loyal but....I cannot help but think that this new King will be at an impressionable stage, and it would serve our family well to put ourselves under his nose. Everything is changed at court - new, hopeful. It is a critical time and it could be the same for our family." Sibyl reached out and placed her hand on her father's tenderly.

Lord Bearnshaw was loyal to the Lancastrian cause, but above all else he was striving to save his family. Sibyl and her younger brother Thomas were his only children, only family indeed, and since their mother was dead and his health was failing; he had to be sure of making the very most of opportunities for them. Thomas was too young to be much of a presence at court and he himself was busy and ageing, so yes, it was down to Sibyl to fly the banner.

This plan of hers meant that he could stay quiet in Lancashire and his position would be ambiguous until either a successful rebellion from the old King or the event that the new King showed favour to the Bearnshaws. His daughter was a clever one he thought as he regarded her now.

"And when does 'Lady Breckley' think you should go back to court?" He said at last.

"As soon as possible....I could go tomorrow?" Sibyl said casually, pushing her food around with her knife. "I hear the King is currently in York, so I wouldn't have far to travel alone. It is a good time to go."

"Very well. Go forth, for at least a short time, and woo this new King for us. Maybe see if there is a chance young Thomas can be found an advantageous bride..." He grinned. Sibyl gave a small satisfied smile and bowed her head.

~

The very next day after a frustratingly long morning of packing, Sibyl was happily seated on her little grey palfrey 'Belaud' and the party was pulling away from Bearnshaw Tower. The journey to York would be a fairly long one and once she was away from home any number of letters could be sent back to delay her return, as had been the pattern for the last few years.

She had built up a great rapport with the strong Lady Breckley as the two women seemed cut from the same cloth, though Sibyl was a great many years younger than Catherine. Fortunately Catherine had sympathy with Sibyl's plight and had subtly hindered the plans for her for as long as she could, though Catherine explained, it was unlikely anyone could undo the betrothal altogether, so warned Sibyl she may have to resign herself to her fate one day.

Sibyl did not want to leave her home this spring, or ever, truth be known. She adored it: the craggy, brooding landscape which was bleak and harsh in winter had its own beauty then, just as much as during the green and busy summer season. With such a placid father and no mother at all after the age of eight she'd had more freedoms than most girls such as she. She regularly took her ponies out onto the moors completely alone, jumping them over ditches and logs, exploring every inch of her family's lands, receiving only a scolding and empty threats from her father upon her return each time. He was a busy, distracted man with no kinsmen to help him in his affairs and could spare little time for constantly reining in his wild young daughter, or cash for staff to do it for him.

After her mother had died giving birth to Thomas, the responsibility of the years of family heritage had seemed to flood into Sibyl, perhaps because of the lack of an older son and the certain knowledge of no more boys from then on? Her father was ageing and had been in poor health for years so Sibyl felt, even at such a young age, that it was up to her to preserve this little corner of Lancashire. Solid old Bearnshaw Tower and all the local people who relied on the wealth of her family. She had a duty to keep that going, to not let her generation be the one who failed after all those years of tradition.

For some reason, her marriage to Lord William did not seem to be the fulfillment of those wishes. The man was vain, ignorant, and Sibyl could name many other unflattering characteristics if pressed on the matter. On the surface of things of course he was a good match - a similar age, strong, tall, handsome and richer than her family. Many girls would feel lucky to have a husband such as he. Loyal to the Lancastrian cause, he would also be a good local ally.

Sibyl was not so trusting however, Lord William had plagued her throughout her childhood because they were neighbours; he was the boy from her fawn dream and over the years she had got to know his arrogant, greedy character very well. She was convinced that if he got anywhere near the Bearnshaw lands he would grind the lot beneath his boot heel and nothing would be left for Thomas when he came to take it. She therefore saw it as her duty to avoid William until her brother was a man at the very least.

His attitude rankled her as much as anything. He looked at her as he had the fawn in her dream, barely able to contain himself, almost licking his lips! He treated her like a hunting trophy and ever since the news of the betrothal had strutted around like her owner, always poking his nose into her business, wanting to know what she was doing and more importantly, who she was with.

Sibyl could think of few things worse than sharing a bed with this man and rearing his little rats. She had imagined the inevitable wedding day with dread for years, already able to feel the constricting gown scratching at her skin, the tight tension in her throat as she fought to stay calm...

However, Sibyl thought, she had found a way to get around this problem and her heart sang as she rode along in the fresh spring air. The new King, Edward, offered her a beacon of hope. She had seen him before, although she did not feel she 'knew' him as such because he came from a far higher family than she, but she did know that he was a vivacious young man who was not afraid of change. He seemed pleasant and was known to be fond of women. His new reign seemed to throw everything up in the air and she felt she had a chance of influencing which way the dice fell.

~

Sibyl knelt at the door of the room, went halfway in and knelt again in greeting and submission to Lady Breckley, who nodded approvingly and ushered her in.

"Sibyl my dear, it is good to see that you got away!"

Sibyl gratefully sat down, tired after her journey but relieved to be among friends once again.

"Father saw the sense in my plan." She said simply. A corner of Lady Breckley's mouth curled.

"This cannot go on much longer Sibyl...you are most definitely of marriageable age now, a youth, not a child."

"Yes." Sibyl agreed, looking to the floor.

"Think you perhaps it would be better to get it over and done with? After all, Lord William fights often, there is a good chance he would be killed and then you would be in my enviable position!"

"Until the King decided to marry me off again." Sibyl said gloomily. "No, I cannot stand the thought: anyone but him." She scowled, feeling safe to do so in the company of her Lady who was also a friend. Lady Breckley considered for a moment.

"I can't see how you can get out of it. You certainly cannot afford to buy your freedom, and your father is keen to strengthen the family bonds...I think you may just have to accept it, my dear?" The older woman looked down tenderly at the younger, hoping to soften the blow. Sibyl had been obsessed with avoiding this marriage for years; she had hoped that by now the girl would have resigned herself, but apparently not. She had to admit, although she liked Sibyl, she was losing patience. Sometimes women just had to accept their fate.

Sibyl shot a look at Lady Breckley before she could check herself. At first it was full of indignation, as she thought her only ally was suddenly changing sides, but she managed to temper it into a good humoured, wry smile.

"No, I won't." She said simply. Lady Breckley didn't

overtly roll her eyes at the girl but Sibyl was clear that Lady Breckley didn't think any 'plan' would work.

"He's here you know." Lady Breckley sat back and resumed her reading, or at least made a pretense of doing so. She felt Sibyl's expression sour even though her gaze was averted.

"I suppose he will track me down." She said with a sigh.

"He heard rumours of your return and I think yes, he is eager to catch up with you. He left this for you as well" Lady Breckley turned a page, and motioned for one of the other girls to bring the small silken bag Lord William had left for her. Sibyl took it with silent interest and looked inside. Though she didn't want the other girls to see, she knew they would be dying to know what her gift was so there was no getting out of showing it to them. She lifted a beautiful pendant, complete with a brilliant royal blue jewel, out of the bag and all the girls gasped.

~

There was no sign of Lord William that day until the evening dance and meal. All of Lady Breckley's girls were turned out to perfection for the occasion, including Sibyl. She had picked out her best dress in her favourite dove grey, which brought out the blue grey of her eyes. Her hair was midway between blonde and brunette just as her eyes were midway between blue and grey. Tied up fashionably in ribbons to be incorporated into her headdress, the light caramel provided a nice contrast against her pale dress and skin.

They followed their lady in an excited gaggle into the hall where they were to eat and instinctively Sibyl swept the faces in the room and immediately spotted Lord William, watching their entrance over the rim of his goblet with an excited smile upon seeing them. Sibyl looked down modestly. In a way it was almost comforting to know that there was someone here so eager to see her above all others. She had lived with Lord William lusting over her for so long, what would she do without it? That was a real possibility at this moment in time.

Sibyl knew the younger girls would be eager to fulfill their duties and be dismissed to dance. She had no wish to be intercepted by William so she volunteered to accompany Lady Breckley all evening in the hope that the presence of the higher ranking older woman would put him off trying to commandeer her.

Sibyl eagerly snatched glimpses of the King. She had of course seen Edward around court whilst growing up but had not paid particular attention to him before - he was just another highborn lad like all the rest. Now though, he looked nothing short of glorious bedecked in jewels and finery. He was nineteen years old, fit and fresh from his victory at Towton. He was the new, young King of England having claimed victory for the Yorkists against the odds and there was a general feeling in the air that this was a special time. It was impossible to look at him and not be taken in by the sense of opportunity; it, or he, was quite intoxicating.

She needed to speak to him. Alone. It would be difficult to achieve; he had so many people of far more importance than her making demands on his time. A formal appointment was simply out of the question. No, it would rely on her feminine charms unfortunately. Now was not the time to be annoyed at how nature worked, she simply had to work with what she had.

She was torn away from her thoughts because, as predicted, as soon as the food was cleared and the music began Lord William was politely greeting an amused Lady Breckley and trying to steal Sibyl away.

"May I steal Lady Bearnshaw away from your good self Lady Breckley? Just for a short time, I promise." He said in an exaggerated manner, his dark hair falling over his face as he bowed.

"Whatever for Lord William? You know I am lost without her..." Lady Breckley replied with a wry smile.

"I am well aware of that my Lady," he said, trying to hide an obvious resentment, "I merely wish to dance with my betrothed for a little while." He smiled widely at the two women. Sibyl remained stony faced, knowing she did not really have an escape route from this situation, no real reason not to dance with her future husband.

The two women looked at each other in silent dialogue for a second, then Lady Breckley gave a nod of approval. In a trice, Lord William was around the table and holding out his arm for Sibyl to take, whereupon he steered her towards the dancing. Sibyl knew this was a formality; Lord William wanted to press her on the marriage issue, not enjoy a dance. They were both fair dancers and performed one round before William lost patience and guided her into a darkened alcove.

"Sibyl, I've missed you." He said tenderly, his gaze flickering to her lips in a way that would have been most welcome from someone she liked in return. As it was she was simply annoyed and frowned as she looked back to the activity out in the room. All those people happy, enjoying themselves and here she was, constantly hounded by this man!

He quickly switched from tenderness to annoyance himself when Sibyl ignored him.

"Don't be so rude, my love." He said stroking a finger down her neck. She reached up impulsively and slapped his hand away.

"Inappropriate!" She said.

"Your behaviour towards me is inappropriate!" He replied, catching her hand. "You will have to get used to me Sibyl, it is that simple." He growled.

Sibyl pouted. He released her hand and took a swig of wine.

"I am a good husband for you, Sibyl! I can provide for you, strengthen your family, I'll give you children, I'm well proven on the battlefield, I'm not disfigured, or aged, and yet you..." He trailed off as his voice grew strangled.

He wanted to talk of his love for her, but that seemed silly. Few noble marriages were made on the basis of feelings for each other. He hated how Sibyl made him feel so small like this. Most girls would love a man reducing himself to this tangled mess over her but the more he contorted himself before her, the harder she seemed to scorn him. Even though they had been betrothed for years he felt the situation would be unstable until they were married. Then he would have his prize at last and would feel secure. Then she would be dancing to his tune.

Sibyl felt she should say something but struggled to find the words, knowing that the concept of not liking one's husband was a pathetic reason to be against a marriage. She was also not quite brave enough to mention how the thought of being 'given children' by him made the bile rise in her throat. She merely hurriedly mumbled an ill-thought-out stream of thoughts.

"I...I don't want any of your property, or children, or battle victories!" She winced as soon as she'd said the words; she could see the sneer already forming on William's flushed and shining face above her.

"Then what *do* you want Sibyl? What is your plan that is such a preferable alternative to me? Sitting alone in your draughty tower? Someone else?" He leaned far too close to her face.

"I just want to be left alone, William!" She shrieked as quietly as she could, mortified at the thought anyone would be looking at them and associating her with making a scene with William.

At that moment a third voice interjected. A mature, authoritative voice.

"Is this man bothering you my Lady?"

William and Sibyl both shot a look to the origin of the voice and tried to mask their shock and embarrassment as they both recognised Richard Neville, the Earl of Warwick. William was horrified that his superior had caught him in this situation and seen fit to reprimand him - keeping one's wife under control was one thing, but upsetting maidens quite another. Sibyl was simply shocked that the high ranking mastermind behind the new King's reign had noticed her and stepped in to save her. Her mind was quick enough to seize this chance before it slipped away however.

"No, but I am ready to return to my duties serving Lady Breckley now." She said firmly but with a note of gratitude, brushing past William who was caught between his indignation at having his betrothed taken away from him and his need to show respect. He opted to stay silent and take another swig of wine with a terse nod.

"How can I thank you my Lord?" She said to the well groomed Earl in a low voice once they had left William behind.

"Oh, no need, a maiden should not be harassed by men who should know better is all." He waved his hand dismissively, evidently in a good mood. Sibyl felt emboldened enough to speak fairly bluntly with him.

"What is your view on maids hassling men, my Lord?" She said. Warwick immediately came to a halt and faced her with a bemused look on his face.

"Whatever do you mean girl?" He said.

"I need a meeting with the King." She said hurriedly and earnestly, searching his eyes for clues on how he would react to her brazen talk. She guessed that although she had been taught that women should always be modest and polite, men, actually, were not at all and would not be shocked at such open words. She looked up at Warwick with wide, pleading eyes and awaited her fate, wondering if anyone was watching this exchange. A half smile played on his lips and she began to relax.

"A...private meeting I suppose?" He asked with a cocked eyebrow.

"Yes." Sibyl nodded. Warwick considered.

"We leave for Durham shortly, but I'll see what I can do." Warwick bowed slightly, kissed her hand and propelled her over to Lady Breckley. Sibyl seated herself and folded her hands in her lap, her chest fit to burst with excitement and shock at what she had done, avoiding the curious and knowing gaze of her older friend.

Warwick went and seated himself close to Edward who was laughing and surrounded by other laughing men. Warwick wasn't sure what the joke had been and politely sipped his wine and waited for the next topic of conversation to begin. The laughing died down and the men began chatting again, but Edward, like a hawk, had homed in on Warwick's subtle but unusual exchange moments ago.

"What was your business over there Warwick?" He said quietly, leaning close to avoid anyone overhearing as he wanted to judge whether he would want anyone else to know the information before they heard it for themselves.

Warwick gave Edward a look with a smirk and said no more, taking another swig of his wine. Edward frowned fleetingly in a way that asked Warwick to divulge more, but Warwick did not budge and Edward made a mental note of it.

~

"Gentlemen! I'm done, please, out...for tonight." Edward shook his head tiredly as he spoke, feeling the effects of the good food, wine and late night as well as all his organising and planning and the aches and pains of recent battles. He patted shoulders as men left the room.

"Not you Richard." He said as Warwick made as though to leave. Edward thought Warwick's evasion earlier might be something worth investigating.

"I was going to say one last thing before I leave, Edward." Warwick was informally permitted to use Edward's name rather than any title, given their close relationship. Edward smiled.

"Oh good!" He said.

"The young lady I rescued earlier - Sibyl Bearnshaw - she would like to meet you. Seemed very keen. Nice grey eyes." He said, one corner of his mouth lifting. Edward raised his eyebrows; that was not what he had been expecting.

"Well Warwick, you'd better show her in! Can't have maidens with nice grey eyes going wanting for a meeting with their King, can we?"

~

There was a knock on the door. This was most unusual at this hour and all the girls looked at each other. Lady Breckley settled her gaze on Sibyl, who had frozen with the brush in her hand halfway through a stroke of the older woman's greying chestnut hair. Despite her hair being uncovered and being dressed only in her nightdress, Lady Breckley called for the knocker to come in from her chair. She cocked an eyebrow when a young man in Warwick's livery entered and cleared his throat nervously upon seeing the scene.

"I assume this is for you Sibyl?" Lady Breckley said to end the awkward silence.

"Yes, my Lady," the lad came to his senses, "I am sent to search for a Lady Sibyl Bearnshaw? And I apologise for the intrusion at this hour, but discretion was preferred." He said pointedly, recovering from his embarrassment.

"Well girl, off you go. We can manage without you." The older woman said guiding Sibyl forward, who was struck dumb with shock and nerves.

Sibyl's heart pounded alarmingly as she walked towards the man, and she saw he had a pile of fabric over his arm and was now shaking it out and holding out a hooded dark green cloak for her to put on. She obediently stood for him to drape it around her shoulders.

"It is cold tonight and the hood will maintain your anonymity, Lady Bearnshaw." He explained. She nodded gratefully, still unsure of what to say. Etiquette training did not cover such things. It was good that somebody had thought of this though as a maiden being led around when everyone else was in bed was sure to set tongues wagging if spotted and this way, none would know which maiden it was.

The heavy door to Lady Breckley's chambers was bolted shut behind them and Sibyl could hear the whispering starting before they had even fully closed it. Then she blindly followed Warwick's man, staying within the golden orb of the lantern light as he led her to who knew where. She was assuming this was all in relation to her request to meet the King but didn't really know for sure. Would this be a further meeting with Warwick, or someone else, for further clarification, or was she just about to actually meet the handsome young King of England in person, right now? She didn't want to seem affected as that would be undignified and she felt she had already acted in a fairly undignified manner in front of Warwick. She now needed everyone involved, especially the King, to think well of her, not just dismiss her as some excitable young girl. She made a special effort to gather her wits and give the appearance of calm despite the intense fluttering in her stomach and chaos in her head.

The young man seemed unwilling to talk. Maybe out of embarrassment. Maybe because this was a usual occurrence for him and he was bored? Sibyl was grateful for his silence however, even though she had many questions. Presumably all would be answered soon anyway.

Sibyl had only a vague idea of where the King's chambers were sited but she knew that that was where they had arrived now because a cluster of men were outside the chamber which included Thomas Burgh, recently made a Knight of the Body by Edward, which Sibyl had heard about upon her arrival back at court. He politely acknowledged her and the other men followed suit before returning to their conversation as some prepared to bed down on their pallets or return to their chambers nearby. Warwick was nowhere to be seen.

Sibyl was not surprised at the lack of reaction to her presence. It confirmed the rumours she had heard about Edward's penchant for women and although she had not wanted to earn herself a reputation, she was relieved that she would at least not be the first or last and she was prepared to do what had to be done for the good of Bearnshaw. The young man she had been following nodded to the assembled men who seemed to give some kind of approval and then knocked quickly on the door.

A voice was heard inside and the man opened the door

and entered. Both then knelt and knelt again, Sibyl then remained kneeling, hardly daring to look at the man himself, while the squire introduced her.

"Lady Sibyl Bearnshaw your Grace, as requested." He said.

"Very good!" The King replied and Sibyl could hear from the tone of his voice that he was happy, if a little bemused. This emboldened her and she chanced a brief look at him.

There he was in a magnificent large bed, propped up on cushions and wearing only a nightshirt, fingers knitted together on his stomach and eyes bright as he beamed at the other man.

"Now I'll just talk to the Lady and then I might get some sleep!" He said with a wink, upon which the other man bowed and backed out of the door, whereupon the King transferred his smile directly onto Sibyl, who had forgotten to look away. She hurriedly redirected her eyes to the floor when she realised her mistake. Edward laughed a little.

"Please, rise, and then sit down again, near me. So we can talk." He said and she saw with a sidelong glance that he was patting the bed next to him. This felt incredibly informal. In truth, she was completely unaware of how anyone would act when alone with a man, let alone the King. She decided to follow his lead and sat herself down on the bed, placed her hands in her lap and looked down again. The King seemed to know he would have to lead proceedings and patiently started the conversation for her.

"My good friend Warwick informs me you needed to speak to me but he could not tell me why, so you will have to do that." He picked up his wine from the small table next to the head of the bed and took a sip in anticipation. Sibyl cast around for the right words.

"I...appreciate your Highness enormously for bestowing your time on me this way; I know you must be so busy!" She gushed. "Especially at this time, so new to your wondrous reign - there must be many things for a King to deal with...things I have no comprehension of!" Sibyl had decided to play the damsel in distress, hoping to appeal to the protective side of his male nature.

He nodded and blinked slowly, irritated in a good natured way with this procrastination. Edward did have sympathy with his subjects who were not in regular contact with their King. They may well know how to interact with him in a public setting but how would they know the protocol in a situation such as this, which no one would ever prepare them for? In any case, he did not really care how people did or did not interact with him; he merely wanted to get things done.

"I am busy, but I have made time for you." He took another sip. "A little time. Kings do get tired." He said pointedly, urging her on.

"My matter is a little delicate and not of great importance to a King but I hope you will have some sympathy with my plight and see fit to help me." She looked into his eyes, eyes the colour of a horse chestnut. He nodded with a small, indulgent smile and waited for her to say more. He was giving little away, Sibyl decided, while taking in his curls: brunette with a blush of gold around them. His hair was carefully styled to be straight but after a long day the natural curl had broken through, giving him a disheveled look.

"You see, I am betrothed." She said, looking up at him briefly to check his reaction. There was none, he was merely listening intently. "To a man I do not like." She checked again. He blinked confusedly.

"You and many other girls, I think?" He said.

"Yes," Sibyl nodded. "Only, in my case, I feel especially strongly about the issue. My match is not old, or ugly, or beneath me. Quite the opposite. On the surface, he is a fine match. I have known him since a child though, and I feel that rather than acting as custodian to our ancient family, he will steal it before my younger brother comes of age. He will rape the lands and our people until it is worthless. He cares only for himself, and sees me as a means to an end. He-" She was getting carried away and stopped herself lest she bored the King.

"This is all fairly normal, Sibyl." The King said, a look of kindly pity in his eyes. Sibyl looked back despairingly, unsure of what to say. Edward reached out a hand and placed it on hers. "Many women are used as a way to further the fortunes of men, I'm afraid it's just the way it is." He waited for her reaction. She hung her head.

"Just as I must fight for my place in the world, risking my very *neck*." He continued. "I may enjoy my spoils as King, but always with the knowledge that I must be looking over my shoulder for the next usurper. Enjoy your spoils, Lady Sibyl. Bear this man fine sons who will inherit all he has, including your family's land, and you will have the last laugh, no?" He raised his wine glass to her.

"Where are my manners?" He exclaimed, "You have no wine!" And with that the King himself took up the jug on his bedside table and poured her a small measure of wine, handing her the cup. She took it but did not drink, as she was swallowing hard trying to keep from tears, which men hated and would win her no favours.

"Yes." She choked. "You are of course right, my King." She took a sip so as not to appear ungrateful and the King said nothing, but continued watching her. The silence stretched for a while.

"Of course," she went on, brightening a little at her thought, "there is another element, which may be of interest to your Grace?" She shot him a coy glance.

"Go on?" He said, an amused smile spreading on his lips as his eyes narrowed in mock suspicion, enjoying this cunning little creature who evidently was not willing to accept her fate yet.

"Lord William, my intended, has traditionally been loyal to the Lancastrian cause. As has my family though I know father could easily be swayed. It could not hurt to marry me to a Yorkist instead and break any remaining Lancastrians bonds. Father would be delighted with any marriage for me and my younger brother Thomas who will inherit all is young, and impressionable, and in the wake of our mother's death I raised him so I hold great influence over him." She stopped gabbling and awaited the King's verdict.

"So you have a tactical mind Sibyl." Edward mused, looking into his wine. He was thinking now and Sibyl knew not to interrupt. He looked her up and down, taking in her unusual grey dress and piercing eyes intent on him, her golden brown hair's ribboned plaits poking out under her headdress.

At that moment he felt the intoxicating power he now had. His next words would decide this young woman's entire future. And her betrothed's. It would decide which families and their lands would join. Based on his words children, who would in future fight, conspire and wed and die would be born, or would not be born.

He weighed up the possibilities and decided that this was really a minor matter. William's family at Hapton and Sibyl's at Bearnshaw were virtually unknown to him and the decision would be inconsequential. This idea that it was somehow a threat to him for these two minor Lancastrian families to join was not truly too worrying for him, but he admired the girl for having shown so much game, when most of her sex just accepted whatever the world handed to them.

He could now send fate spinning one way, in which Sibyl now leaves the chamber disappointed, crying and fully clothed. Or, he could bat it off in another direction entirely. He swilled his remaining wine around his cup, then downed the mouthful and smacked his lips.

"You're right Sibyl. Wherever I can I should break up Lancastrian alliances and sow Yorkist seeds." He said as he took her barely-started wine and placed it on the table.

Sybil gave a gasp of joy and her face broke into a genuine, beaming smile which she did not have occasion to practise often. The King had leant back on his pillows and returned the smile, waiting for that tide of feminine joy to bubble over and sure enough within moments Sibyl had forgotten herself and sprang to his side, planting a kiss on his lips.

Sibyl felt the King of England's arms rising to encircle her and suddenly what she had meant to be a quick kiss was being returned and lengthened far beyond her intention. With his arms firmly pulling her towards him and his lips eagerly parting she had little choice but to go along with it. It wasn't that she hadn't expected this, but she had been carried away by her joy and only now remembered that she had no experience with this, only snatches of information gleaned from the other girls and the farm animals. She found however that his stroking, seeking hands were not unpleasant. She was only worried that she would not please him and the deal would be off. She broke away.

"Highness, I...I am not experienced-" She tried to explain with a frown.

"Call me Edward." He said with a smile, pulling her gently but firmly back onto him and silencing any further talk with a kiss to match.

Sibyl was shaking with nerves but relaxed onto Edward and copied what he was doing with his mouth. She could feel him smiling through the kiss and when he playfully flicked his tongue across her top lip she returned the gesture and he laughed. They broke apart to look at each other and then Edward reached up and carefully tugged off her headdress. Sibyl helped him pull the ribbons from her hair and it fell over her shoulders in waves.

Edward's fingers combed through it with wonder and Sibyl suddenly thought of William. By rights, this moment was his - a woman's tempting hair was only for her husband. She saw Edward's bewitched face and realised that she had robbed this moment from William forever, no matter what happened from now on. She felt a pang of guilt and shame at having spat in the face of her father and a man she was supposed to obey, but that was washed away by a realisation of the power she held.

On the surface she meekly allowed the King to stroke her hair with one hand as the other found her calf and made its way up her leg, but inside she felt she was bursting, like all of life had just flooded into her. Here was she, Sibyl Bearnshaw, enjoying the undivided attention of the very King of England and blasting the marriage she did not want into tiny pieces.

With renewed confidence she presented her kirtle lacing to the King and with fumbling fingers he pulled it off.

Once she was knelt on the bed in only her chemise, hair tumbling around her face, Edward threw back the bedclothes and removed his own shirt in one suspiciously well practised move. Then they were knelt opposite each other and he reached forwards and pulled her shirt over her head, throwing it to the floor and grasping her waist before her arms had even come down. Suddenly his face was buried between her shoulder and throat, kissing and sucking and licking, his stubble scratching in a way that would have been unpleasant against her delicate skin in other circumstances, Sibyl thought, but which was strangely exciting now.

His hand moved lower, brushing over her buttocks and then gripping her thigh and hauling it up above his hip as he pushed her back on the bed. Sibyl felt his weight pushing down on her and her breath came in gasps, the hair of his chest and belly was soft against her own. His face was still hidden against her throat but suddenly there was a hardness pressing insistently between her thighs and her heart began to thump against her ribs.

She didn't know if she should do anything in particular now and Edward seemed to sense this. He propped himself on one elbow and ran his free hand down her side, trailing his fingertips over her ribs, following the curve of her hip before stroking a single finger over her belly towards the triangle of hair, which she realised with a twinge of embarrassment that she had not plucked as gentlemen liked....but it was too late now.

Edward seemed unconcerned and she felt the finger softly part her lips and continue its downward journey. She looked away at the ceiling, knowing that Edward was watching the frown of confusion and apprehension she could not hide with amusement. Very carefully he pressed a finger into her and she tensed. He grinned.

"That was just a small taster I'm afraid!" He laughed.

Sibyl smiled uncertainly in response, unsure of what to say, and readied herself as he propped himself on both elbows and resumed the pressing. Her mind was soon taken away from that when he began kissing her again and his kisses muffled her sharp cry at the stab of pain when he had finally gained entry.

A short while later Sibyl was glad when Edward had stopped his thrusting and flopped onto her, now sticky with sweat and breathing heavily and hotly against her ear. She felt raw and was wondering how she would ever do that again. But at the same time, she felt the deal was now sealed and her marriage to William would never happen. Now she could only hope Edward chose a nice replacement, someone who would be a good mentor for Thomas and protect and guide them until the day he could inherit and start producing heirs for Bearnshaw.

She absent mindedly stroked Edward's back as she thought and felt the sweat cool and begin to chill them both. Goosebumps prickled on his skin and he shivered and rose off her, throwing himself down by her side and gathering her to him in his arms with a happy grumble as he closed his eyes. It felt cosy and somehow normal, so Sibyl relaxed against his large, comforting form and drew the covers over them both, savouring this moment that was unlikely to occur again - she had no delusions. It was by now very late, so with a last yawn she closed her eyes.

Just before dawn she was woken by somebody very noisily scraping at the fire grate in an attempt to restart it. She shivered in the chilly spring air and dimly saw Thomas Burgh marching in.

"Good Morning your Grace...my Lady" He said with a bow. "I hate to break apart this happy party but I'm afraid we have much work to do."

He carried on talking in this loud, bright way as he handed Sibyl her clothes. She dressed hurriedly with the help of the girl who had been preparing the fire. With a last look to the King, who smiled and bade her farewell as Thomas fussed around him, she almost fled from the chamber, her mind spinning with how she would handle the other girls at Lady

Breckley's.

BEARNSHAW

3

Waberthwaite

"Sibyl!" Alice shouted despite herself when Sibyl hurried through the door, shut it behind her and leant on it, holding her breath as she looked at the girls all looking at her.

"Where have you been?" Shrieked Jane. "What was all that about last night? ...Are you well?" She added, with meaning.

"I'm perfectly fine thank you." Sibyl said, dusting herself off and settling into a chair for lack of anything better to do. "I was....arranging my future."

"The Lord William issue?" Asked Alice.

"Yes." Said Sibyl. The girls were clearly unhappy with this tiny little bit of information.

"Were you with the King?" Jane blurted, then clapped a hand over her mouth. Sibyl glared at the younger girl, but Alice leapt in to help her.

"We saw you talking with Warwick, we know the King's the only person who could end your betrothal Sibyl, we're not stupid." She explained. Sibyl sighed and frowned crossly, as much with herself as with them.

"Yes. I managed to persuade the King to wed me to another man." She said. Both girls gasped and widened their eyes.

"How!" Alice demanded.

"I simply asked Warwick when the chance came up. He must have taken pity on me?" Sibyl shrugged.

"Who?" Asked Jane.

"I honestly don't know yet, you know as much as me. I don't know who and I don't know when and I don't know how I will be told, please stop pestering me!" Sibyl ranted. Both girls quietened down, remembering their manners. At that moment Lady Breckley breezed into the room, seeming hard and cold somehow.

"Of all my girls, Sibyl." She murmured to Sibyl, taking up her kirtle which the other two girls rushed to help her with. "I think as soon as your new husband will take you you should leave my service." She added sadly.

She would always be friends with Sibyl but had lost a little respect for her, it was high time the girl should move on and become a wife before any more trouble occurred in Lady Breckley's revised opinion. Sibyl seemed a nice, polite, straightforward girl, accomplished and beautiful. But she was also intelligent and could not accept the way the world worked apparently; Lady Breckley's days of drama and excitement were over.

Sibyl was greatly embarrassed but could not help but be elated and eager to find out who her new husband was to be. She did not know how this would happen, and did not feel like she could approach the King herself again, so she could only wait. When the announcement came a few days later it was surprisingly public. The entire court was dining in the company of the King and enjoying a dance afterwards when Edward himself came across the room with a man at his side and introduced himself to Lady Breckley's party.

"Ladies, this is Viscount Arnold of Waberthwaite, Cumberland. He is betrothed to Lady Sibyl of Bearnshaw, by order of the King!" Edward raised his voice so that all around could hear and all heads turned in their direction as he took Sibyl's hand and joined it with the tall, blushing youth's beside him.

Sibyl took in his height, his plain brown hair and fine clothes. She was thankful he was young, not some dried up old man, although she chided herself for being so fussy having already had more than her share of luck. He seemed nice, pleasant. He also seemed as uncomfortable as her in the gaze of all the onlookers. It was down to Lady Breckley to break the silence.

"Wonderful news Sibyl, your father will be delighted with your new match!" And she rose to kiss Sibyl and curtsey to Viscount Arnold, who bowed and kissed her hand.

At that moment, a commotion broke out nearby - Sibyl heard a familiar male voice wail a 'no' which twisted into a yell of enraged pain before it ended. She winced, knowing that Lord William knew rather earlier than she had hoped he would, thanks to Edward's public announcement. The music had stopped and the crowd nearby parted untidily, Lord William bursting through.

"Sibyl!" He boomed, red and snarling, his fists clamped to his sides, obviously being very careful not to let rage get the better of him and let his hands stray to a weapon. "Waberthwaite?!" He bawled when Sibyl merely stood in mute shock.

"Yes. By order of the King." Waberthwaite himself growled. Edward was now nowhere to be seen and Sibyl was grateful and impressed that Lord Arnold was willing and able to stand up for them both. He had given the impression of being young and soft before but she supposed he had been as much on the back foot as her at that moment and she had mistaken his quietness for shyness. In fact he was bold, just careful. "Please do not speak to my wife to be in that manner." He added levelly.

Lord William was clearly struggling to control his rage and his friends rushed forwards, grasping at him and pulling him back out of view into the crowd. Sibyl looked him right in the eye, a worried expression on her face. She then looked down to the floor rather than meet the gaze of any of the shocked onlookers and felt Arnold's arm nudge her own in a request for her to take it. She did.

"I think we should leave." He said. Sibyl followed his lead out of the hall, out of Lady Breckley's service and Lord William's shadow.

~

In a few days the entire royal court was on the way to Durham. Sibyl and Viscount John Arnold rode together, chatting freely. Both thought the King had shown incredible good judgment and kindness as they were a good match, a good looking couple. Many of the party smiled and congratulated them as they passed or were overtaken on the ride North. Sibyl rode her grey Belaud in her characteristic dove grey kirtle and John rode a shining black hobby in a striking dark green doublet. Sibyl felt that this was how marriage should really work; both parties at ease with each other, not the constant struggle and awkwardness between her and William.

William had fled court the night of her betrothal to John. He had ridden North ahead of the main party, unable to face the King or Sibyl or anyone but close friends, yet unwilling to miss any important events. The King had written to Sibyl's father and she had yet to hear back from him but the gold sent by John would please him no doubt. John was not one for flamboyance; he promised a small wedding as soon as they had chance. This suited Sibyl, as things were still a little uncertain all the while she was still unmarried.

"Were you at Towton, John?" She asked as they rode along a stretch that was a little quieter than others, as the waggons were far behind and the faster riders had pulled ahead.

"Of course!" He replied.

"How did you find it?" She asked, having heard the other men talk of it for some days.

"Brutal." He replied. "Gruesome business. Edward was brilliant though, a lot of the others were losing confidence, but Edward was unafraid and made a speech, saying to them he'd live or die alongside them, and he was true to his word. It gave everyone courage, and of course, we won." John said with evident satisfaction. "I'd follow Edward anywhere."

At that moment the peace was shattered and a commotion could be heard behind them. Both horses started at the noise and both riders craned around to see what was going on. They could see a number of figures falling out of the doorway of an inn they had just passed, holding up the procession of the King's party behind them. At the head of the group the leading figure stumbled drunkenly towards them, the others desperately scrabbling to catch him and hold him back. Every time someone laid hands on him however, they were pushed off. It was William.

"Sibyl!" He bawled in the fashion that was fast becoming a habit, Sibyl thought angrily. "Waberthwaite!" His cries were like a wounded animal's; pain and anger in one. John was clearly furious and embarrassed, his jaw working as he glared down at William.

"Sir, contain yourself please, you are drunk!" He commanded.

"You might own *her* now, but not me Waberthwaite! You can't tell me what to do!" William slurred back, scrabbling at his scabbard for his sword. His men all saw the move and descended on him, grabbing whatever bit of him they could so that the blade stayed covered.

"Will, it's not a good idea..." One tried.

"I'll kill him!" William snarled.

"I'll choose to ignore that if you leave us." John replied. "Otherwise I shall be forced to report your threats to the King."

"To the King? You will hide behind him will you?" William sneered back.

"Yes." John said with finality. "He would be most interested to know about any who defy his express wishes."

William merely pulled a face in response, clearly not so drunk he would run the risk of treason. Sibyl was torn between verbally tearing a strip from him and not wanting to make John feel like his wife was fighting his battles on his behalf. Up until now she had never thought twice about speaking her mind and dallying on the edge of good manners, but now she had her husband's reputation to consider and she truly did not want John to think badly of her.

"*You!*" William turned his attention to Sibyl. "You will regret this Sibyl! I'll make sure of it, you think you've escaped me but-"

At this John's sword flashed out of its scabbard, his horse jumping and dancing at the sudden movement, the hooves clashing on the stones, but John's head was level and trained upon William. Sibyl saw his knuckles white on the reins as he held the creature steady.

"You make threats against a woman, sir? My woman, no less!" He cried, eyes fierce. "Get a hold of yourself man!"

"She was *mine*!" William called as he finally gave in and allowed his men to drag him away.

There was silence for a few moments. Then the party behind John and Sibyl started to move along again and John sheathed his sword and whirled his mount around. Sibyl slowly followed suit and they were on the move once more. Sibyl was entirely devoid of ideas on what to say, she had no idea just how passionate William felt about their marriage. She knew he would be furious of course, but to become a drunkard? Staggering out of inns and shouting on the road, threatening people and disrespecting the King's orders? She had not seen that coming. John turned to her.

"Don't fret over him, he will not harm a hair on your head if I, or the King, can help it." He said, his voice thick with anger.

"Thank you." Sibyl said, worry still etched on her face. John's face suddenly brightened.

"He was bound to be sore Sibyl, after losing a jewel such as you." He reached out and took her hand. She smiled back, taking in the scene of her husband to be in the spring sunshine proclaiming her a jewel from the back of his shiny black steed, resplendent in his green finery and ready to protect her from

William. From anything.

~

Unfortunately once they were settled in Durham Sibyl received an unwelcome shock. Her monthly bleed had not arrived and she knew full well what that meant. This held the potential to ruin completely her newfound stability as the baby was clearly Edward's and she had no idea how John would react. She recognised her only course of action could be complete honesty however and she would simply have to accept whatever fate had in store for her now. She hurried to John's quarters to tell him and threw herself down on her knees before him.

"John, my flow has not arrived." She said unhappily and bowed her head. She was terrified. He sat down in the nearest chair.

"Then you are with-" he said quietly, "..the King's?" He asked. She looked up at him.

"Of course." She replied. John's jaw worked. Everything now hung in the balance for Sibyl once again. Eventually John sighed and nodded to himself.

"I will sort this out. I will talk with the King's people. You will have to go away for a time. I have friends in Leicestershire, you will have to go there until the babe is born, then it will be Edward's problem and I wish to hear no more of it." He looked her in the eye.

Sibyl nodded quickly and eagerly. She was overcome with shock and just wanted rid of the problem growing inside her that threatened to ruin everything she had aimed for. She was so unbelievably grateful to John for not casting her out that she threw her arms around him and kissed his cheek lovingly.

"We shall have to get married quickly," John said, "and then I will concentrate on serving Edward and my military career until you are ready to join me again at Waberthwaite." He patted her back.

"I cannot wait John, I really can't...you are all I ever

dreamed of." Sibyl replied earnestly. "I was terrified this would ruin everything for us."

"I suppose you won't need my gift now." He said after a moment's thought.

"Gift?" Sibyl replied. John gently turned her off his lap and rose to his considerable height. He crossed the small room and disappeared for a moment. When he returned he was carrying a basket with a cloth tied around the top. The basket was squeaking and mewling. Sibyl gasped and waited for John to hand it to her, even though she wished to snatch it away immediately.

She set it down on the floor and knelt beside it, carefully untying the ribbons. Inside she found a tiny puppy, which was overjoyed to be released and leapt into her waiting arms. He was pure white, with little flopped triangular ears.

"I could not find a grey one to match your horse for love nor money!" John said.

"Ah John, he's perfect, I love him, thank you!" She jumped up and hugged him joyfully again, her worry turned to happiness in the blink of an eye.

"There was me thinking you'd need something to practice on and instead you'll be rearing the King's pup." He said. The words jarred Sibyl and she instantly calmed and looked downcast again. "Sibyl, don't worry. At least I know you are proven and I know how Edward is.....this bastard will be a good thing for you, as Edward will always provide for it, I know him well enough to know that he always cleans up after himself."

It was an unfortunate turn of phrase, and made Sibyl feel dirtier and more unworthy of John than ever, but she reminded herself that she was not the only one and this must actually be a fairly common occurrence. Though as a nice young lady she would not have been expressly told about it, which made it seem the worst thing in the world. Though she was sure she was lucky that John had taken it quite so well.

~

They were staying in the magnificent Bishop's Palace of Durham, guests of the Bishop Lawrence Booth. He had been known as a Lancastrian so Edward was keen to visit as soon as possible to see how deeply that ran given Booth's strategic position on Scotland's doorstep at a time when the Lancastrians had gone to ground up there. Edward had hopes of manipulating the situation in Scotland in order to winkle them out. He needed to know he had the loyalty of the man on his border though and luckily, Bishop Booth had proven himself a highly adaptable man and had welcomed Edward well.

It was not necessary to have a churchman at a wedding but there was no doubt that having the word of one to speak in your favour should it be needed did prevent a lot of the 'he said' and 'she said' arguments that could occur without. John was keen to lay to rest any disputes over who Sibyl was promised to and could think of no firmer way to do so than ask Bishop Booth himself to officiate. Booth himself saw it as a good opportunity to build on the goodwill between himself and the new King, to marry such a nice young couple of his party, so he made space in his day to say a few words for them in the cathedral itself.

Sibyl found herself stepping out of the warm April sunshine into the cool interior of the cathedral and hearing the echo of her shoes on the stone floor and the whispering rustle of Booth and John and John's party waiting for her. She had brushed out her hair and gathered some little spring flowers to make a wreath for her head and as she approached she could see that John could not tear his gaze from her. Neither of them paid much attention to what Bishop Booth said in the end but it did not matter, what mattered was that Sibyl belonged to John now, indisputably.

Upon arrival back at the Great Hall Sibyl immediately made discreet enquiries as to William's whereabouts as she was worried he may appear at their celebration. She was surprised and relieved to hear that he had retired from court and gone back to Hapton. It was not too conspicuous an absence as many had done the same thing, leaving only those closely associated to the Yorkist cause to continue the pursuit of the old King. She related the news to John, who seemed gratified, and they were able to enjoy the food and dancing that night. Edward dedicated the evening's festivities to them and everyone seemed happy for the handsome young couple.

Sibyl was deathly tired, but forced herself to stay awake and smiling; terrified that anyone would spot that she was with child. She and John had an unspoken agreement that they would keep up the charade of consummating their marriage so when their friends began to bundle them off to John's bedchamber, singing and joking all the way, they both went along with it. Just when Sibyl thought they would never leave, she heard John bawling over the racket:

"Can you please leave me to enjoy my wife?!" And the resulting cheers from the crowd, who immediately began to filter out through the door. Then John swung the thing shut and leant against it, tipping his head back with a sigh.

The comparative calm and quiet was like a balm. Sibyl gratefully slumped onto the bed and lay stretched out, the room slightly swimming with all the wine and tiredness. After a time she became aware that John was stretched out beside her, running his hand up and down her torso with a feather-light touch.

"You're not asleep already are you?" He asked.

"Hmmmno." Sibyl replied, dragging herself out of her sleepy state to look at him. There was a pause.

"May I kiss you?" He asked. She nodded, and John leant forward and placed his lips tentatively on hers. She returned the kiss and wrapped her arm around him, stroking his rough, dark hair. Then they lay still again for a while, unsure of what to say or do. In the end Sibyl began to undress, worried she would fall asleep in her day clothes and John helped her to do so. Then Sibyl helped him to undress, her fingers brushing against his long limbs and they climbed into the bed. It was the most luxurious Sibyl had slept in for a while - so much nicer than the pallet beds in Lady Breckley's chambers - and they quickly fell asleep, entwined together in comfort.

~

All too soon the arrangements for Sibyl's stay in Leicestershire were made, her things had been packed and a team of people assembled to transport her South safely. Sibyl was not particularly keen to stay in the King's entourage now, in his pursuit of the Lancastrians into the North. She felt her scheming and monitoring of the machinations of court were done for now and she had a great urge for some peace away from it all, time to reflect on the stressful ordeal of pregnancy. She either wanted to return to the familiarity of the wild fells around Bearnshaw or to be with John, properly.

John had made a great show of sending his wife to his friends 'for safety' while he continued with the King's campaign - the story was feasible. He kissed her hand goodbye as she sat on her grey once again, Pierre the puppy in a little satchel at her side.

"I'm not sure what to say..." He admitted in the courtyard. They both knew that childbirth was an extremely dangerous time and this could easily be the last time they saw each other. The knowledge settled in Sibyl's stomach like a cold stone and she shivered.

"Neither am I." She replied, looking into his eyes with her own pale grey ones. Each was trying to reassure and gain reassurance from the other somehow. After a moment or two of this, his hand still on hers which balanced on her thigh in the saddle, she straightened her back and took in a deep breath through her nose, attempting to banish the fear and negative thoughts.

"We will be together again John." She said confidently.

The look of concern didn't leave his eyes however, he merely nodded once and stepped back, allowing the party to move off.

As her steed swung towards the gates and began its ambling pace she turned in the saddle to watch John as he stood mournfully in the courtyard watching her go.

Sibyl wondered how it was possible that a few short weeks ago she had been a mere girl, repulsed by the thought of marrying William. Yet now she was a woman, truly, who had spent a night with the King, was carrying a child, and was inexpressibly, surprisingly sad to be saying goodbye to the husband she had only known for a matter of days.

The journey was predictably tedious and tiring and when they arrived at John's friend's place in Leicestershire, Lord and Lady Westcote were not there having gone to visit relatives elsewhere at short notice. They had left instructions for Sibyl to treat the place as though it were her own and she saw that she would enjoy a handsome standard of living during her pregnancy, with her own chamber, bed and maid.

She immediately sent off a letter to her father to let him know her whereabouts and that she was now married. She urged him not to risk the journey to see her however, as no doubt his health would not take it. She promised to visit him instead when she could and perhaps to bring John, too. Then she sent a letter to her brother Thomas, chastising herself for having forgotten him in all the recent events.

In the days following her arrival Sibyl decided to make the most of this stay - it was nice to have the place to herself and she was keen to get back to what she enjoyed doing, which was riding or walking through the world documenting the plants and insects she found. Her aim was to produce a full work, detailing every species of each in the country. An ambitious aim, but one she had stuck to since her very early teens. She periodically sent the completed pages back to Bearnshaw to be added to the master collection and now she had a golden opportunity to examine what Leicestershire could offer.

Over the morning meal she mentioned this to her attendants and they immediately offered to alert the horse keepers of her intentions and arrange for someone to go with her. She was about to dismiss this as unnecessary but quickly closed her mouth again when she remembered she was not at Bearnshaw now and it would not be the done thing for her to go off alone like she did at home.

For the first few days she was able to go on some delightful rides and her attendants were fairly good company who indulged her strange requests and patiently waited while she observed and sketched. Soon though she began to feel exhausted by even short rides, constantly yawning and longing to crawl back into her bed. Then the nausea started, just a little unpleasant at first, but it soon grew until she did not feel she could stay on the horse or drag her own feet around.

"Try eating some plain biscuits my lady, 'tis all perfectly normal." A kindly maid told her as she offered her the platter of freshly baked biscuits. Sibyl, propped up on her pillows looking pale in the early summer sunshine streaming through the small window, obligingly took one and chewed. It did ease the nausea and she came to rely on these biscuits, although soon she began purging them as soon as she'd eaten and then nothing could help.

News of Edward's lavish coronation reached them and Sibyl felt a pang of jealousy and longing. John would have been there, celebrating, dancing with other girls, while she was here feeling grim and useless. Pierre was there to keep her company, but the kennel men had to exercise and train him for her. He was good company in the evenings though, curled up on her lap while she endlessly rubbed his little silky white ears, much to his joy.

She received a letter from her father. He was pleased for her and said that the Viscount of Waberthwaite was a fine man, but he was grieved that they had upset Lord William so and it was going to be difficult for him to attend social events locally now. To her profound relief she read that his joints would be too bad for a journey to the Westcote's estate but he looked forward to seeing her when she came back to Bearnshaw.

Shortly after that a letter from John arrived, but although it contained courteous flourishes such as 'my dearest wife' there was not much personal content. Merely details of the campaign in Northumbria as they hunted the Lancastrians and attempted to flush them out of Scotland.

As summer wore on she took to her bed full time and various physicians and wise women were called. By this time Sibyl was so tired and weak from the constant vomiting that she couldn't really tell who was who and why they came. She gathered John's friends Lord and Lady Westcote had returned and she thought she remembered Lady Westcote looking over her worriedly perhaps on one occasion. It all became a blur of discomfort and as the shutters of her window were closed one last time for her confinement she relished the descent into the darkness. Then the shattering pain began and all Sibyl was really aware of was that.

A few hours later and Sibyl awoke, feeling a little cold as it was now Christmas. She frowned and screwed up her eyes against the bright white light coming from the window and pulled the covers around her. Then she became aware that although she felt sore, bruised and still tired and weak, she did not feel sick and she knew she would not vomit. What this meant dawned on her and she immediately began to cry softly to herself with relief and confusion.

A hand was placed on her shoulder and began to rub gently up and down.

"There there my Lady, you're back, you've made it through the worst now....we all prayed for you!" A female voice said. It was Bess.

"What did I have?" Sibyl groaned in reply, her throat raw.

"A boy! A very healthy boy! We found him a fresh wet nurse and he's being sent off to the care of the King, so you need do nothing my Lady." Bess replied. Sibyl nodded with satisfaction.

"I can go to John now." She said.

~

Sibyl had tried to heal as fast as she could but it took a full month before she was fit enough to sit a horse for a prolonged period. She wrote back to her father explaining that she was rejoining John in the North for a while and would probably see him soon. She had not heard from her brother, but then, young boys were very busy and forgetful of their older sisters she supposed. Now here she was, back upon Belaud in the stabbing cold February air, waving goodbye to Lord and Lady Westcote who had come out in their furs to see her off.

"Thank you! Goodbye!" She called. The Lord and Lady nodded graciously. They had been perfectly polite, civil and generous but Sibyl was not quite sure what they really thought of her; she felt an edge to some of Lady Westcote's comments. Certainly no true friendship. Although, Sibyl reflected, she hadn't had many true friends if she examined the matter. Lady Breckley was as close as she'd come - other women seemed slightly wary of her and Sibyl had never been one to dwell on it.

She tired and became saddle sore extremely quickly and clung to the reins with a deathly grip as her hands froze. One of the men travelling with her noticed her condition and kindly threw his cloak around her and rode extremely close - manners forgotten in the worry of the Viscountess coming to harm. The man was warm enough to keep her thawed until they reached their staging post at an abbey, where she gratefully rolled into a bed and shivered her aching bones to sleep after some rich broth.

Two days later she had to call a halt to the journey so that she could rest for a day. As eager as she was to see John again, she was simply too weakened from the near starvation she had suffered. As she lay in the bed, for the first time she allowed herself to think about her son. She hadn't even seen his face, or named him, or thought to ask what they had named him. She was not worried for him; he was to be looked after extremely well and given land and his own title. Sibyl felt her part was done, though she would have liked to have seen whether he looked like her or Edward.

~

John waved with his whole arm above his head, a huge gesture that could be seen from a distance. Sibyl urged her grey into a canter and her accompanying party did the same, surprised at the sudden burst of speed. John had done the same too and in moments they were clattering to an untidy, snorting halt in front of each other. John then spurred his mount forwards a few steps and embraced her.

"Glad I am to see you wife." He said with real feeling, kissing her before she had time to respond. Sibyl beamed with happiness as she hugged him back, feeling his tall, solid form beneath his layers.

"How was it?" He said, holding her back by the shoulders so that he could scan her face. "You look, forgive me, dreadful." He was clearly unhappy with what he saw.

"It was unpleasant." Sibyl said simply, shaking her head as if to rid herself of the memories. "But I'll be fine John, really. I'm so glad to be back with you." John frowned but accepted her words.

"Let's get back inside then, it is certainly far too cold out here!" He said, turning his mount back towards his quarters in Durham.

Within the hour Sibyl had shed her heavy travel clothes and was sat in bed with a hot drink, her hair loose about her shoulders and John sat respectfully on the bed, a hand on one of hers. Having dismissed everyone else they were alone at last. She was tired and cold but relieved to be back and see that John's feelings had not waned while she'd been away. She looked at his large nose with its prominent bump and shaggy, bedraggled hair from the ride.

"I trust Lord and Lady Westcote looked after you well?" John enquired politely.

"Oh, yes, wonderfully. I was not a good guest really. I was extremely ill most of the time, but when I was well it was lovely." She replied.

"You do look so terribly thin Sibyl." He said worriedly.

"I didn't manage to eat much. I feel so much better now though, it's only a matter of time - with some good food and rest I'll look much more pleasing!" Sibyl laughed off his concern. It was true; nothing could compare to the misery she had been in just a few weeks previously, and although she was ravaged by it, she could feel she would recover.

"Oh you still look pleasing." John complimented her, before completely changing tack. "I have organised some leave and I'd like to personally escort you to Waberthwaite next Sibyl...when you're well enough?" He announced tentatively.

"We're going to Waberthwaite?" Sibyl was genuinely surprised; she had expected to be trailing after Edward's army for the foreseeable.

"Yes. I think it's a peaceful, healthy atmosphere for you, far away from the troubles of court and any fighting. I'd like you to see my home, it's beautiful. And I'd like to be the one to show it to you." He admitted. Sibyl nodded with a smile over the rim of her cup.

"That sounds delightful."

"...Besides, we have work to do." He added. Sibyl cocked an enquiring eyebrow at him. "We have to get work on my heir, do we not?" He said, looking up at her from under his fringe, his blue eyes sparkling. Then in a trice he had lunged forwards up the bed and was kissing her.

"John!" Sibyl was pleased but a little surprised at how forwards the usually polite and mannerly John was being. Then she remembered that they were married and this level of intimacy was probably normal for married couples, and of course after eight or so months away and giving birth to a King's bastard John was probably eager to consummate his marriage and claim her as his own at last.

She lay back on the pillows, replacing her cup on the table next to the bed in the same movement, feeling that nose pressing against the side of hers and returning the pressure with closed eyes. John held himself still for a few moments.

"I'm sorry. You're tired, and you've been ill. I'm running away with myself." He said at last without looking at her, pulling away and settling himself beside her.

"I *am* tired and still suffering the effects John but I'm not offended. I too cannot wait to make your heirs and I'd love to see Waberthwaite. My body isn't allowing me to do the things I'd like to yet though." She explained, stroking him and adding little kisses for good measure. "I can play the dutiful wife now, if that's what you really want," she added, "but although I don't know much about these things I think it would be better for both of us if I had a little time to rest before seeing Waberthwaite, and to heal before...I enjoy you." She added the last to emphasise that laying with him would be a joy, not a job. He seemed pleased with the thought.

"You're right; of course I would not rush you. It's all just unfortunate." He said, hugging her to him. "Your lips still work though?" He asked, looking into her eyes.

"Yes!" She said with a little smile, and gripped his hand tightly as he moved in for another kiss.

~

After a few days of doing very little but resting in front of the fire in John's chambers, Sibyl's aches and pains from the ride began to subside and she moved a little free-er. Everyone around her strove to ensure she ate enough and she began to feel like she was putting on weight and gaining strength. John busied himself hunting and making arrangements for what would be a difficult journey across mountainous terrain in early March, which would likely offer cold and unpredictable weather.

The night before they were due to leave Sibyl lay in bed curled up against him, feeling warm and full from their delicious meal, reflecting on this probably being the last time they would enjoy such peaceful comfort for a while. Although their lodgings would probably be of a good standard, the travel during the day would be so tiring and cold they would be unlikely to be able to enjoy it. Indeed, Sibyl thought, she would be likely to arrive at Waberthwaite in worse condition than she left Durham....so perhaps it was now or never for the consummation of this otherwise perfect marriage? They would have to be quiet as some of their party shared the room or adjoining ones, there was only a curtain between them.

She looked at John. He appeared to be on the verge of sleep.

"John." She said softly.

"Mm?" He replied without opening his eyes.

"I'm ready." She whispered in his ear.

John took a second to allow the statement to sink in, and then his head sprang up from the pillows and he stared at her questioningly. She smiled in response.

"Are you sure?" He mouthed. Sibyl pouted with mock annoyance.

"Does the stallion question the mare, John?"

He rolled onto her with an imitated horse's snort, suddenly full of energy and pleasingly heavy, his skin burningly warm through the thin linen shirts they were wearing. Sibyl listened to the fire crackling as they kissed, running her hand up inside his shirt to stroke his smooth back. She felt his own rougher hand reaching down to her calves and running up her leg, savouring the feel of her thigh with a subtle groan of pleasure.

"At last, Sibyl." He whispered. Sibyl did not reply but raised a leg, inviting him into an embrace that couldn't be closer. He hopped between her legs and she gripped his hips joyfully with her thighs and his shoulders with her arms. His arms also wrapped around her and there was no gap between them, everywhere they were pressed together and Sibyl thought about how a married couple became a single entity. This felt a lot more 'mutual' than it had with Edward, which stood to reason, she supposed.

They savoured it for a long time, with Sibyl slightly concerned about when the rubbing would start as she remembered how it hurt last time. At least this time she was prepared and that automatically relaxed her more. John also took things very, very slowly; partly out of a wish not to hurt her but also partly because he wanted something to remember about this night, not the work of a few seconds.

He was of course a typical young man and had spent time with the other young men in the cities they travelled through, sampling the local women; sometimes paid and sometimes not. Having a wife was different however, it was somehow more exciting knowing that she was only his and was altogether in a different class - unmarked by the hard work of the lower women, beautiful and accomplished. He didn't want to do her a disservice.

Sibyl actually found the sensation pleasant and felt herself urging John along a little, pressing against him with her hips, hoping that was acceptable behaviour from a wife. Unfortunately this brought things to a close a little quicker and he went slack in her arms. Sibyl felt tightly wound and panted quietly as John did, letting the tension fall away with each breath.

"Hopefully that will do the trick!" John whispered with a grin through his sweat-soaked fringe when his head rose out of her hair.

"Good luck with that John!" came the clear voice of John's man Edmund, with accompanying stifled giggles through the curtain.

John's face flopped back into the pillows with a theatrical groan and Sibyl silently laughed and patted his shoulder.

~

Sibyl awoke the next morning in the darkness, hearing the others stirring around her and the sounds of a fire being poked back into life. She drew the covers tightly around her with a shiver in the chilly March morning air and quickly took stock of how she felt. She didn't remember feeling the moment of becoming pregnant before but she wondered if this time would be different somehow, as she felt so much more for John. She felt no different though and her thoughts flew towards the journey.

She was desperate to see Waberthwaite, but how she wished she could simply be magically transported there rather than clambering back into that saddle again and having the wind whip around her and possibly freezing rain soaking her. She wished they could take the easier route south, wend their way over the comparatively gentler Pennines back to Bearnshaw instead and flop down on her own bed in her own familiar chambers.

She was dragged away from her reminiscences about the spring flowers budding on the moors near Eagle Crag by John surfacing from sleep next to her.

"Ohhh is everyone getting dressed already?" He croaked.

"Yes, time to go over the mountains." Sibyl replied.

"Yes!" Said John, leaping out of bed in his shirt. "To Swallowhurst!" He bellowed in a mock battle cry, evidently in a wonderful mood. Sibyl peeped around the curtain and saw his men all cheer and laugh.

Hours later they had eaten, the pack ponies had been laden and already started on their way and the riding horses were being held ready in the yard for the higher ranking members of the party. Pierre had been packed into his travelling satchel and his little wiry white head was poking out. He seemed to sense the excitement of the occasion and indulged in bouts of yapping at the horses as Sibyl stood close by.

John helped her forward and she was hoisted into the saddle.

"I had some extra padding added for you, as I know this journey will be tough for you." He said with a smile from the ground.

"So I can feel!" Sibyl said, shifting in the saddle to feel the softness of an extra layer of sheepskin. "Thank you." She bent and gave him a quick kiss and with that he whirled around and strode away towards his horse, mounted easily in one swift movement, throwing his cloak out to cover its quarters.

He gathered up the reins from his squire in one gloved hand and pulled the animal's head around to face the gate. He adjusted his green hat while the others mounted and then the party moved off out of the gateway and onto the muddy road, with the jangle of bits being mouthed at in eagerness and hooves beating on the ground, fabric swishing and voices murmuring or laughing.

The party set a good pace and Sibyl held up well with the aid of favourable, if cold, weather. She was energised by the simply breathtaking terrain of the Cumberland and Westmorland mountains, which she had never seen before. So far her travels with court had been between Durham, York, London and Bearnshaw for the most part, on roads well-travelled and quite 'genteel'. She had thought Bearnshaw was wild and remote but Cumberland took things to a whole new, almost frightening level of wilderness. She was in awe of the majesty of those mountains and could not believe John's tales of wilder places in Scotland.

They began to descend towards the gentler country where Swallowhurst Hall sat and John started to point out places along the route that were familiar to him for some reason. Sibyl fantasised about doing the same for him one day, and perhaps their children. It then struck her that her children would probably not know Bearnshaw as she did. They would grow up with Swallowhurst as the familiar and Bearnshaw as just another part of their outlying family estates, a place to be visited briefly.

She consoled herself with the beautiful views - children raised around here would be every bit as independent and canny as children raised on the Bearnshaw moors no doubt; this was a good place for them. Swallowhurst Hall itself came into view and the party trotted on with renewed vigour, eager to be home and warm at last. It was a modest structure, simple in construction, quite obviously well used for holding off the Scots and therefore functional. Sibyl was not particularly taken with decoration anyway and the lack of a lavish grand dwelling was no problem for her.

"Here it is," John said proudly, "The centre of my world - Swallowhurst and I are what stands between the Scots and

England! She's not pretty, but she's comfortable and safe."

"Yes, I can see that!" Sibyl replied, "Luckily I'm not one for ostentation!"

"I knew you'd like it." John replied with a slight smile, his eyes fixed ahead.

~

John had stayed at Waberthwaite with Sibyl for an idyllic couple of months. They rode together, hunted, danced and ate together and enjoyed each other at every opportunity. The resident people at Swallowhurst seemed genuinely delighted to have life in the castle again and Sibyl was treated with courtesy, even spoilt. It was truly a magical time but unfortunately John's career had to come to the fore again and he had to return to the King's army and show his face at court.

He wanted Sibyl to stay behind and rest, holding Swallowhurst for him as wives were expected to and, he hoped, grow a baby. Unfortunately Sibyl's monthly bleeds had arrived on time and she held out little hope of that happening before he left this time. It would have to wait until he returned. It was extremely hard to let him go and she physically clung to him as he mounted ready to leave. He patiently returned the embrace for as long as she was willing to give it, equally unwilling to leave.

Sibyl was not the crying kind but had to work hard to stifle her urges at that moment.

"You come back safe, and soon John." She mumbled into his cloak, smelling his scent one last time.

"Of course I will." He smiled kindly and they mutually pulled back.

Sibyl watched as he left, her mind flying back to that spring day in 1461 when she had been the one riding off to Leicestershire, watching John's receding figure for as long as possible. Now it was the other way round, and was likely to be so for the most part for the rest of their lives.

His leaving did however provide her with an opportunity

for a quick visit to Bearnshaw in the favourable summer conditions. She found everything delightfully the same, her father not deteriorated much and thoroughly accustomed to the idea that she was a Viscountess. He quizzed her about John, his income and military achievements. She got updates on Thomas, how he was fit and well and making a name for himself in all his sporting exploits. She was proud and hopeful for him and the Bearnshaw name - he was a good boy.

She delighted in feeling well enough and having the freedom to go riding over the moors alone as she used to. Just as John had to leave to pursue his military career though, so Sibyl had commitments at Swallowhurst now and she felt the tug of responsibility pulling her back North. Her father nodded her off with pleasure and gifts as she rode back to take the reins of her hall and await her husband's return.

John did return periodically over the next two years, but frustratingly they were never blessed with a baby. This cast a cloud over their relationship, to the deep unhappiness of both. Each sought remedies from physicians and wisefolk, but to no avail. The most hurtful thing was that both knew Sibyl was capable. She had bourne the King's bastard and although publically it was known never to be the man's fault when a woman could not bear a child, how could this be explained? Sibyl had no clue what to say or do to remedy the situation though, so they retained a wall of silence on the matter.

~

"John I've received word about Somerset's whereabouts." Lord Montagu, Warwick's brother and an equally formidable character said hurriedly.

John had been waiting for orders as he was part of Montagu's force now, tasked with bringing the Lancastrians to heel in the North on behalf of the King. Montagu was a good man to serve under and John felt confident of success, particularly following the victory at Hedgely Moor just twenty days hence.

"He's camped down by Devil's Water." Montagu continued, giving John time for that information to sink in. John said nothing; it wasn't his place to tell Montagu what the best course of action was. "I don't know about you, but I think that would be the perfect place for us to meet him. He's intending merely to camp there and fight on ground of his choosing no doubt."

"Yes." John nodded, plans forming in his mind. Montagu could see him thinking and was pleased with his promising young Viscount's quick mind, as per usual. "They'll have a river at their back there..." John mused.

"I know it would be a push, but if we race over there we could catch him. The men would be tired, but we'd be guaranteed victory if we surprise them there: it'd be a quick thing to finish the job and we can have that bastard's head off by sunset!" Montagu rubbed his hands together with grim satisfaction.

"We can do it....easily!" John said with a grin. "My men are virtually fresh, let's not waste another minute." He said, hoping Montagu would not take the suggestion of heading off immediately wrongly. He didn't.

"Very good!" Montagu said, clapping John on the shoulder before heading out of the chamber with his men around him, leaving John to discuss things with his.

The men were armed within the hour and on the march immediately. The air of the May night was cool but not cold, the perfect temperature for the men to keep up a good pace John thought with satisfaction. He was mounted on his heavy bay courser, trotting up and down the line of marching men, explaining how easy it would be to catch Somerset's army and promising them a great meal and extra money when they won. The atmosphere was jolly, excited, and they covered the ground quickly.

Soon the men inevitably began to tire and the noise died down as they concentrated on their destination. Speed was their main hope and they all focused. John fell to a slow trot alongside the column, thinking it would look aloof to simply ride in a group with his higher ranking mounted men and he liked to keep morale as high as possible. He had seen many battles where the men of unfair Lords who pushed their men and did not reward enough simply refused to fight, or did not fight with enough heart to secure victory.

Montagu called a halt and related the news that scouts had been spotted who had undoubtedly noticed their arrival. As soon as the back of the column had caught up, they had to rush the camp ahead. John took his men forward and arranged them according to orders, looking down on the Lancastrian army with satisfaction, seeing the camp in complete panic at their sudden arrival. His horse flung its head up and down, pulling on the bit with anxiety.

Just as the Lancastrians had assembled themselves untidily below, Montagu's order came to charge and the Yorkist men surged forwards, a great cry going up for the King. John's mind emptied of everything except the drumming of hooves and the roaring of the men, the clanking of armour and weapons and the rush of his own blood in his ears as he charged right along with his men.

He kept his eyes trained on the small army below in the dawn light and saw that already it was beginning to break in fright, one end drifting away before them. John felt anger at such cowardice and fell upon the remaining ranks with fury, his sword flashing at any body he saw with Somerset's portcullis badge sewn to it. Frustratingly little resistance was given, the Lancastrian men backed away as they fought, the whole battle quickly drawing closer and closer to the river.

Men began to slip as they reached the riverbank, and many chose to stop fighting at that point throw their weapons clear and make a jump for it into the water. John was so intent on punishing the cowards that he hadn't looked up ahead and was unaware of the riverbank until the men directly in front of him fell away and his horse began slipping in the churned mud of the bank.

Instinctively he hauled the animal's reins back towards dry land and the horse did try for him, he felt the lurching beneath him and the animal managed to turn around, but he also could see that they were sliding downwards regardless. He looked up into the eyes of the ranks of Yorkist men grinding to a halt as he felt himself toppling backwards.

Both man and steed landed heavily and immediately began writhing to free themselves in the sticky mud below, but there were so many suffering the same fate that every time they gained a foothold they seemed to be knocked back. John began desperately to fight with his armour, aiming to free himself of the weight, but then his horse gave one mighty leap almost vertically with its great powerful hind legs. Due to the slope of the bank however it fell into John as it did so and landed fully on top of him.

With horror the men still on the bank who had managed by now to stop themselves saw the animal gain its feet and scuttle away into the river, but that John lay still in the mud and showed no signs of moving.

~

"We lost the Viscount of Waberthwaite sir." Edmund had been chosen to break the news to Montagu as the second in command.

"No!" Montagu replied, his joy in victory tempered by the loss of that promising young man. "How?"

"His horse fell upon him in the mud of the riverbank." Edmund said with a slight break in his voice. Usually his freckled, slightly chubby face looked jovial under a mop of wiry ash-blonde hair, but today there was no amusement, no jokes, no winks.

"Ach, such a waste!" Montagu grimaced. He then addressed the men assembled behind him. "Make Somerset and any other Lancastrian leaders you can find pay for this. Such an easy victory over such cowards should not have cost us that man!" He barked.

BEARNSHAW

4

Recovery

"My lady! My Lady!" A girl rushed into the chamber where Sibyl sat at the window, looking up occasionally from her sewing to admire the distant glittering sea. "There is a messenger here with a letter for you, from court!" The girl gushed.

"Oh, excellent!" Sibyl said happily, expecting a letter from John. She almost threw down her sewing and hurried after the girl to the hall, where the messenger was waiting. His back was turned to her but he turned around and bowed as soon as he heard her footsteps.

Sibyl took the small folded letter from his outstretched hand and could not fail to notice the royal seal. This note was not from John. Immediately she was flooded with a sense of concern and foreboding, not seeing why the King could possibly want to see her. There must be some kind of problem. Perhaps a problem with the marriage? Or maybe their son, she thought with a jolt. With a frown she opened it and quickly scanned the words. It was a summons, requesting she immediately join the King at York. Her frown deepened with annoyance at such vague information. It would be days before she reached court! All that time she was supposed to live in suspense and worry?

"Do you have any further information for me?" Sibyl questioned the messenger. He immediately looked uncomfortable.

"I'm afraid not, my Lady." He said, his eyes travelling to the floor as he spoke.

Sibyl was no fool she knew there was something here she was not supposed to know, but clearly this man had been told not to divulge more, and Sibyl did not want to try to weasel her way around the King's wishes so she resolved to leave it at that and wait until she reached court. Her heart pounding, she rushed off to make preparations for the journey and order some food for the messenger.

They had ridden at a hard pace and flew into the courtyard where Sibyl almost flung the reins at the waiting boy. Then she waited impatiently while her man dashed off to find someone to attend to her. Shortly he reappeared with John's man Edmund who she could see was uncomfortable and had to make an effort to be bright and breezy around her. Sibyl scrutinised him openly.

"What is it Edmund, what's happened? Have I done something wrong? Where's John?" She asked in a torrent.

"Uhhh..." Edmund played for time, his eyes flicking back and forth as he sought the right words. Sibyl felt enraged and crossed her arms, giving him a warning look.

"The king did say he would see you as soon as you arrived; he's out hunting right now but will be back shortly no doubt. Please, Sibyl, come with me and wait for him." Edmund looked at her pleadingly and proffered his hand and Sibyl began to feel a little sick. Whatever was going on here was serious, and what of John? She followed him to a chamber to wait in in silence and sat down on the chair, her mind spinning over the possibilities.

It seemed to take Edward a long time to arrive. It was already late afternoon and Sibyl occasionally got up to pace before sitting down again, chewing her lip anxiously. When the door finally creaked open, it took her a moment to remember herself and deliver a halfhearted curtsey as she scanned Edward's face for clues. He looked strained and waved his hand impatiently at her curtsey.

"Don't bother yourself Sibyl." He said with a slight shake of his head.

"I came as soon as I received the letter...." Sibyl began.

"Yes." Edward said, an uncomfortable look on his face.

"Look, I won't beat about the bush for your sake Sibyl. John is dead." He awaited the reaction.

Sibyl stood stock still for a second, looking through Edward rather than at him. Once the news sank in she let out a choking sob, cried "No!" and dropped onto her knees. The King knelt down before her and placed one of his hands firmly on her shoulder, to hold her steady more than anything. Almost unable to breathe, she at last dragged in a deep breath and wailed, her hands coming to her face.

"I'm desperately, truly sorry Sibyl," Edward said, "he was a good man, he served me excellently. It is unjust that he is gone so soon! He and Montagu were ahead of me at Hexham and went after Somerset. They beat him easily, but conditions on the field were difficult and his horse fell upon him. There was nothing anyone could do Sibyl, believe me he would have had the very best care otherwise...I know you two were fond of each other." Edward bowed his head.

Sibyl was still sobbing, not really taking in what Edward was saying. She felt him haul her by the shoulders into the chair behind her and rubbing her back awkwardly. She felt she should say something.

"We have no children! I have no piece of him!" She blurted accusingly, knowing he had died fighting for Edward but also that it was a dangerous game to speak and act like this around a King, no matter what your history with the man. Edward sighed.

"There are some things outside of a King's control, Sibyl." He said with genuine sadness. "I know it's not much of a consolation to you now, but you're my ward now and I hope you know that I will look after you as John would have wanted." He knelt and kissed her trembling hand as her crying started afresh involuntarily. With that he had swept from the room, stooping slightly to fit his tall frame through the door, and then he was gone.

Within moments Edmund and a gaggle of girls entered to pick her up and take her to her quarters for the duration of her stay. It was all a blur for her.

"Is there anyone you'd like me to send for?" Edmund had asked tentatively. For a moment Sibyl almost instinctively said John, but stopped herself with a tragic half-smile through her sobs.

"...No." She managed, "I want to go back to Bearnshaw. My Bearnshaw." She said before she had to break off again. Then she cried for a long time, until her throat felt like it had dried out and she literally had no more tears left. Then she sat up on the bed and, ignoring the solemn looks of the girls around her, thought about John; all the memories she had of him and just the thought of never *once* seeing him again. The children they would never have. Swallowhurst sat virtually empty. Never receiving another letter updating her on his latest military successes or losses. Him never brushing the hair out of her face and smiling at her so tenderly, not saying a word but her knowing nonetheless how he loved her.

Each loss stabbed at her like a physical pain, her face contorting. The girls looked on at a loss as to what to do. Sibyl didn't seem to hear them when they asked her things or offered her things and they themselves had no experience of the loss of a husband. They could only sit in silence.

A figure appeared in the doorway. Sibyl glanced that way and saw only a blood red dress through her swollen eyes. She knew who it was though.

"I suppose you've come to gloat at the mess I made for myself through my immoral acts." She coughed unhappily.

"Come Sibyl, this is hardly a mess for you. You have the protection of the King, and freedom. You and your son will never starve no matter what befalls you." Lady Breckley said matter-of-factly. Sibyl was upset enough to challenge the older woman.

"I actually *liked* my husband." She replied, disgusted.

"I never implied you didn't. I can see you're upset. I simply dispute that I came to gloat over any kind of 'mess', in your words." Lady Breckley said patiently. "I came to see if you would like to live with us for a while?"

Sibyl saw how cold hearted she had been, so quick to assume that everyone was judging her. Despite her anger and sadness at her loss, she reminded herself to be kind to the true friends she still had.

"Where was he laid to rest?" Sibyl asked, fresh tears springing from her eyes.

"Near Hexham dear." Lady Breckley, usually aloof, hugged the young woman as though she were her own daughter. In many ways, she supposed Sibyl was like a daughter to her, and like it or not she did play the role of mother for the girl who lost hers so young.

"You could lend me your litter. I must see him one last time, then I must get back to Bearnshaw, where I will stay, and never meddle again. But I don't feel I can ride all the way." Sibyl croaked into Lady Breckley's fur trimmed collar.

~

The atmosphere in the abbey was cool and quiet compared to the bright, hot June day full of sunshine outside. There was no one else around - she had specifically asked for the quietest time to be picked and everyone else was now hard at work out in the sun, she presumed. Her guide wordlessly indicated the plaque in the floor which Sibyl immediately recognised was freshly engraved with John's passant ram.

Fighting tears, Sibyl handed the other person a few coins and waited patiently for them to leave. Then she dropped to her knees and began to chokingly pray for John's soul as the warm tears streaked down her cheeks. When she had finished her prayer she slumped forwards and traced the cold stone of the ram with her fingers, then carefully laid her cheek on the stone. Her mind's eye dropped through the stone and imagined the soil below and travelled deeper until she imagined John's corpse there, the worms already at work on his handsome but pale and lifeless face. His hands crossed on his chest, never to touch her or raise a sword again...never to cradle his son. What she felt was a mix of anger and sadness. She badly wanted to blame and lash out at someone - Edward? God? John himself?

She lay there on the slab, aligned with his body below for some time, chewing over these thoughts of anger and stabbing sadness until she began to shiver with the cold. She then heard movement outside and self-consciously rose to her feet, dusting off her dress and roughly smearing away the tears on her face with her palms. With an ache in the core of her being she looked at the slab one last time to seal it in her memory along with the other moments she'd stored and then turned and walked briskly out into the warm sunshine.

Outside the men and women travelling with her looked at her face anxiously but she didn't make eye contact with them. She hitched up her skirts and climbed straight into the door of the litter with the aid of a helping hand which was offered by one of the men. Closing the curtained side behind her she cried out "to Lancashire!" clearly and firmly and the litter jerked into motion as the ponies set off in unison. She gathered Pierre into her lap from the basket at her feet where he had been waiting and hugged him to her.

The party barely stopped, travelling late into the night and setting off as early as was possible. Nobody ate much and the pace was quick but Sibyl promised all time off and hearty meals once they were at Bearnshaw and that was enough to keep spirits up. With grim satisfaction Sibyl saw that they were passing Burnley and would soon be travelling along the paved road known as The Long Causeway, which they would soon leave and drop down into Cornholme, her village.

Then things would get hard for those doing the carrying and walking as they would pass onto Tower Causeway, the road up the other side of the valley which took the pack trains over Todmorden Moor. It rose steeply, winding up the craggy valley side in the shadows. When travellers reached the top, where the view suddenly opened out onto wild bleak moorland, they would find themselves at the foot of Bearnshaw Tower, a last stronghold of comfort before crossing the moor. In the dark when Sibyl arrived, the windows would be glowing a welcome for them, as fires were usually lit year-round to drive away damp from the thick stone walls and lack of sunshine in the deep valley.

Sure enough when they did stagger up the last stretch of the hill path Sibyl swept aside the curtain to see the familiar sight she craved - the tower was just as she'd left it and she could see the signs of life within that signalled her father had received her messages and had laid on a welcome. Immediately, Sibyl felt happier and addressed her weary travelling party:

"I am grateful for your efforts to get me here as quickly as possible - report to the kitchen and claim your rewards!" She said, peeling away from the group and dismissing her two girls when they attempted to follow. "I'll be fine." She assured them as she disappeared through the main door with a little bow to the man holding it open for her. She knew her way to the solar where her father would doubtless be waiting for her, probably sat in his favourite chair with the intricate carvings all over it and his cushion stuffed with horsehair to ease his old back.

She peered around the door to see the familiar scene, and saw her father look up and his face break into a smile. Her grief forgotten, she smiled back and trotted across the flagged floor, fell to her knees and threw her arms around his ample waist. Pierre as usual had followed at her heels and now jumped up and down around the two, licking hands and letting out the odd excited yap. Lord Bearnshaw laughed, which transformed into a cough before he'd finished.

"You haven't changed have you, my girl?" He wheezed.

"No father..." She replied, looking up with concern.

"That cough is worse though I see." She laid a hand tenderly on his arm.

"Yes," he nodded with resignation. "It is." He would have continued to say he could almost hear the clicking of the grim reaper's bony feet behind him, but in the circumstances it was probably insensitive; the last thing his daughter needed to hear. She looked exhausted. "I was proud of you you know girl. It wasn't part of the plan, but a Viscountess? You did as I asked. You did your best for the Bearnshaw name. I'm sorry how things have turned out for you now." He said.

"Thank you." Sibyl bowed her head.

"You look tired now Sibyl, you must have travelled hard to get here so fast, sleep now and talk to me tomorrow." He added after a short silence. Sibyl frowned up at him in mock suspicion.

"Are you saying that because you are in fact the tired one, father?" She asked.

"...Yes!" He said after a comedic pause to think. "Now go!" He said, waving her away as he struggled to his feet.

Sibyl watched him go and then found her way up to her old chamber. Her girls were obviously still down in the kitchens, but their pallet beds were laid out ready and her own had been made and the blankets opened out invitingly. Gratefully she flopped onto the bed and undressed herself. Without bothering to brush out her hair she threw her dress lazily onto the chair as she used to as a child and pulled up the covers. She patted the coverlet and whistled and Pierre hopped up in a flash and curled up into a ball by her side. She gazed at the ceiling and wound his wiry hair through her fingers.

It was late when Sibyl awoke. For a long time she lay simply listening to the birdsong and sounds of activity outside - dogs barking, male and female voices, pans clattering and perhaps a pony neighing. Her girls were still asleep after their hard journey so Sibyl coughed loudly to politely signal to them that she was ready to rise. They all dressed together and made their way down to the main chamber, Sibyl wondering what would be available for her to eat at the moment, having skipped any food the previous evening.

In the hall her father was again sat in his chair, but he was evidently anxious and had been awaiting her arrival.

"Sibyl," he said urgently, "Lord William is here." His voice heavy with implication.

"Already?!" Sibyl's fingers flew to pinch the bridge of her nose. "You would think he could give me a few days at least?" She said angrily.

"He's waiting outside." He said as he left, motioning for the boy hovering at the door to show William in.

Sibyl sank angrily into her father's chair, not intending to bow or be polite to William. Soon she could hear footsteps and the boy re-entered, followed by the looming figure of Lord William.

"Lord Hapton, Lady Bearnshaw." The boy said with a bow before backing out of the room, evidently wishing to remove himself from the charged atmosphere as quickly as possible. Lord William was the first to speak; Sibyl's lips were stubbornly pursed and she refused to acknowledge him.

"It's good to see you Sibyl." He said with a bow, unable to keep the triumphant note out of his voice, perhaps not wishing to.

"I wish I could say the same." Sibyl snapped.

"Now now, that's rude." William tutted.

"What's rude is interrupting a woman's grief to gloat, or make threats, or whatever it is you have come here for." She growled, looking him in the eye to drive home the point, hoping he would wither under her angry stare. She was not a slip of a girl now, she had been through things that would terrify a man, she guessed, and was now a mature widow and able to defend herself. She remembered John's flashing sword that day on the road up to Durham, his fierce anger at William's drunken threats. She felt his spirit with her then.

"I just came to say what a terrible pity it was...that you've had to come home, with your tail between your legs, and nothing to show from your marriage. An ignominious death for him and a barren womb for you!" He said.

Sibyl was shocked at his brazen words, evidently intended to stab as deeply as possible at her without remorse. She was about to scream that she was not barren, but guessed that William must not have heard about her son and if he did know he would only go on to mock John's infertility, which remained unspoken of in his life and would in his death too if she had anything to do with it. She felt as though he watched her moves and heard her words and she would protect his honour just as he would undoubtedly have done for her. She bit back the words.

"You have some nerve, Hapton." She said in her best Lady Breckley tone, pulling herself up to her full height. "Do you know what is worse?" She added as the idea formed in her mind. He cocked an eyebrow without reply, waiting to hear what she had to say. "Spending years waiting for another man's woman...pathetic!"

It was a gamble, because she didn't truly know that William wasn't married by now and it was possible she had just made herself look extremely stupid. She could see by the silent, seething reaction however that she'd hit home. Her fists unclenched with satisfaction.

"You are not another man's woman Sibyl." He said eventually, keeping his voice low. Sibyl scoffed, but he cut off any further words from her. "You just don't seem to understand; there isn't anyone else for me - can you think of any? Maybe old Lady Copthorne perhaps, who is long past child-bearing age? Or I could be betrothed to sweet little Joanna Farlington and wait another decade for my children?" He had crept closer as he spoke. "No - you were promised to me, and if you had any sense you would see that what's happened is God's punishment for breaking your promise!"

"I never promised a thing!" Sibyl cried, "Everyone promised for me!"

"Exactly," he snapped back, "when 'everyone' around you agrees, what does it mean? It must be the right thing."

"Nonsense!" Sibyl was hating this childish back and forth but didn't know how to extricate herself from it in a dignified manner.

"I'm going to ask your father again, you know..." he said, triumph in his voice and glittering, dangerous eyes.

"Well you'd better make it quick, he's clearly dying!" Sibyl snarled, "And when he is gone, I shall be the King's ward and you won't get past *him!*"

"Enough!" Lord Bearnshaw's voice rang out, startling them both into shocked silence. "William, I am appalled, leave my home immediately please." He said coldly.

Shamed, William waited a few seconds as though he was going to say something but thought better of it and stormed from the room. Her father hobbled quickly over to take Sibyl's hand. She helped him into his chair, both shaking terribly.

"I heard every word Sibyl. I never realised William was such a sly brute. Rest assured, he will not gain my approval for marriage to you. He may be short of brides but I am sure we are not short of potential husbands for you." He kissed her forehead.

Sibyl merely nodded obediently. She had hoped that, for at least a while, she could grieve in peace and enjoy being the Lady of Bearnshaw without thinking about good or bad matches. It was not to be, not while she still bled anyway.

~

Sibyl threw herself back into life at Bearnshaw. It was clear her father was a weak presence and it seemed the people who made their living in the tower and on the estate were pleased to have a stronger, decisive Lady at the helm and her father seemed not to mind relinquishing his role to his daughter.

Each morning she treated herself to ride in the cool of the summer dawns before settling down to correspondence. Belaud was getting on in years now but he knew the territory from foaldom and seemed to enjoy being back himself.

She was fine as long as she kept herself busy. She had asked for the papers she'd periodically sent back over the years and found that very few had been lost. She could now organise them into the order she wanted and saw that she had quite a volume of plants profiled. "This will make a fine addition to the library!" She thought happily. Once the day's activity was over however she would climb into bed, draw the covers around her and stare at the fire, hugging her knees.

In the flames she would eventually see moving figures, and her memories would come to life. They would trigger thoughts of the things that never would now be and inevitably the tears would start to run hotly down her cheeks. When she eventually lay down to sleep she would try to remember the sound of John saying goodnight, worrying she had forgotten his voice and knowing she would never be able to check if she was wrong or right in her memory.

Her father suggested they have Thomas home for Christmas that year and Sibyl was overjoyed at the thought of seeing him again. He would be so grown now, unrecognisable! She was desperate to see what kind of man he was maturing into. He was always so solemn as a child, had he retained that or become a loud, rough young soldier?

Unfortunately before Christmas arrived their father had to take to his bed at almost all times and Sibyl became extremely worried, wondering if she should call Thomas home early? She followed the advice of the physicians to the letter, but nothing could seem to stop the inexorable progress of the disease. Eventually her nerve broke and on a particularly bad day in November, she sent for Thomas.

Sibyl anxiously checked the view down the track on the expected day of arrival but it finally got so late she had to admit defeat and go to bed, having checked for torchlight down the valley but knowing that with no real rush the travelling party would have deemed it madness to travel after dark. They turned up the day after, her brother seated on a smart black pony that jarringly reminded her of a slightly smaller version of John's favourite Irish hobby. He was surrounded by a modest team of men to guard and aid him and they had with them a single pack mule to carry gifts and food for the journey. This small band of men could travel fast and light and Thomas knew he had all the comforts of Bearnshaw at his disposal on arrival, so he had no need to take much.

Sibyl waited patiently out on the side of the road, still as a statue and wrapped in her grey cloak as she scrutinised the party climbing the path. She made out two smaller figures amongst the clearly mature men - presumably this was Thomas and perhaps a friend he had brought along for the adventure? They had a small pack of dogs playing around them and before long she heard Thomas' laugh ring out and gave a small smile. Soon she could make out facial features and yes, he was so changed! He was thirteen now, on the cusp of becoming a man and from his proud bearing she could see that their friends in Cheshire had done a good job of training him for manhood and the day he would inherit Bearnshaw. Which may not be so very far away, Sibyl thought darkly.

She remembered how very tiny he had been when their mother died and she had been allowed into the nursery to see him, herself only eight years old. At that moment she had felt the weight of responsibility settle on her shoulders and vowed to do all she could to replace their mother. She had watched and learnt from the serving women and wet-nurse on how to look after a baby and she had been there for him as he grew. It was she who supervised his first steps, rocked him when he cried and kept him away from the fire. Would he remember?

As the horses, ponies, men and dogs filtered off the road and into their tiny courtyard Sibyl watched her brother's face anxiously. She so *needed* him to recognise her and feel perhaps admiration, gratitude or love for what she had been through for him. She needed him to seem like he was ready for both their futures to be in his hands. His eyes met hers and to her relief they twinkled with recognition and he smiled. She felt proud that she did not disappoint him. She smiled back with genuine happiness for the first time since she was told of John's death.

"Sibyl!" Thomas breathed with wonder.

"Yes Tom!" Sibyl laughed back, running towards him and giving him a huge undignified hug in front of his men which he stiffly accepted with an embarrassed half smile.

"You look...good, sister." He said, and she released him.

"Thank you Tom, I am pleased with your apparent progress too!"

"Ah, I look taller on my horse..." He said good naturedly and hopped down. It was true; he was still short and slight whereas Sibyl was quite tall for a woman. It meant he still seemed strangely childlike to her, but she reminded herself to treat him like a man. She curtsied.

"I expect you make up for it. Come, we must see father!" She said with a smile, holding her hand out to invite him to offer his arm.

"Yes, is he very bad Sibyl?" Tom's face twisted with concern. Sibyl's smile disappeared as she led him indoors.

"Some days are better than others." She said flatly. They both fell silent.

In their father's chamber they found him propped up in bed on his pillows, listening to some poetry recited by one of his attendants. The young man respectfully excused himself upon a nod from Lord Bearnshaw and Sibyl and Thomas settled themselves on either side of the bed, just as they used to before Tom was sent away.

"Father!" Tom said with a grin.

"Tom, my boy, you are almost a man!"

Sibyl saw that he looked delighted; his sallow face more animated than it had been for a while. He broke off to cough a little, struggling to contain it in order to avoid their concern. "Tell me, are you ready for a wife yet?!" He said with a wink. Tom looked away shyly.

"Not yet father.....I need an income first..." He mumbled.

"Ah, yes." Lord Bearnshaw nodded, stroking his greyed chestnut beard briefly and shooting a meaningful glance at Sibyl. She returned his gaze. She wondered how long Tom would have to wait for his inheritance. He hadn't meant that he was waiting for their father to die of course, he meant to earn himself an income through fighting perhaps, but the other two knew he wouldn't have to.

"I've seen Matilda Shawbury at court Tom, a few months ago. She's a lovely young woman." Sibyl broke in.

"Good." Tom replied noncommittally.

"Shall we eat?" Sibyl said brightly, sensing Tom wasn't quite old enough to appreciate the fairer sex yet.

~

They had a wonderful Christmas, the best Sibyl had ever experienced. They were visited by many friends despite not being able to leave Bearnshaw very much as it would mean leaving father behind. They did leave together to go to church though and Sibyl enjoyed the admiring glances of the village folk as she rode along resplendent in her furs with her handsome young brother by her side and a respectable consort of men.

It felt right somehow - for so long the people had not seen their Lord and it gave the place an air of abandonment. Now the Bearnshaws were back out in the sunlight, providing an anchor for the people. They stopped to talk whenever they could and found the people friendly and eager to pass on their good wishes to their father. Sibyl also urged Tom to hand out coins wherever he felt they may be appreciated, as she told him he could count on the loyalty of his people if he was a good and generous Lord.

As the New Year arrived Sibyl became even more anxious about their father - he was pale and struggled to breathe now; he never left his bed.

"I was wondering....when should I leave for Cheshire Sibyl?" Tom asked. "I was going to leave in the next few days, but perhaps I should stay?" He chewed his lip.

"Yes. I think it a good idea you stay for now." She nodded, then added gravely, "Maybe for good?"

Tom nodded.

Days later, Sibyl was awoken in the early hours of the morning.

"Come quick Lady Sibyl, it's your father; the physician says he's not long for this world!" Cried the cook, almost in tears.

Sibyl leapt from the bed in a trice and grabbed a blanket to wrap around herself. She was already fighting tears herself by the time she swept around the door, Thomas close behind. She clutched his shoulders as they reverently approached the bed and peered at their father's face. At first glance he appeared to be asleep, but as they looked closer they saw his eyes swivel groggily in their direction through the slit of his sagging eyelids.

"Tom..." He wheezed, a hand grabbing for Tom's.

"Yes father?" Tom's voice broke and he dropped to his knees.

Sibyl stood respectfully behind, trying to stifle her sniffing. She was still raw from John's death and now she would finally lose her father too. Having lost their mother she supposed they both felt an extra level of despair at losing their father...before either had had a family of their own, she reflected sadly. Of course, he had been ill for years but they had become accustomed to that and had always written off his inevitable early death as 'in the future', but now here it was, right in front of them. The young pair were about to be turned out into the forest alone. Her mind had wandered away from things just then and she had not caught what Tom had been told. Now her father broke her thoughts by asking for her. She replaced Tom at the side of the bed and took his cool hand in her own and sobbed aloud.

"Keep Bearnshaw safe, make it strong. I know you

can..." He whispered. She planted a kiss on the papery skin of his hand and held it to her cheek.

~

Before they knew it the siblings found themselves following their father's funeral procession in the snow down the Tower Causeway into the valley to the local church traditionally used by their family. Here many traces of Sibyl's Bearnshaw ancestors could be found - carvings, engravings, slabs, stones and vaults. Her family's money had provided this solid reminder of God's power, this meeting place for the rich and poor in this windswept, rocky corner of the realm that the King never thought about, Sibyl thought as she looked around at the features inside the little stone building.

She and Thomas took up a space at the front as their father's body, shrouded and wrapped in lead, was placed into its hole. By now Sibyl had run out of tears. She was exhausted by the vigil, the procession and the sheer amount of organisation the funeral had taken. Back at the tower there was a feast ready for all their guests and Sibyl had had to arrange everything. Tom had done his part by riding out to break the news to everyone they knew, writing letters to those further afield and dealing with the replies, but Sibyl was left to make a funeral fit for a Lord.

The incense was thick in the chill air, the priest's voice clear and authoritative as he recited the Latin, with Latin being chanted behind him also. It was a mesmerising, dizzying experience for Sibyl. The spell was broken however by a clatter of hooves outside. All heads in the church turned, and the door was gingerly opened by a boy in a livery Sibyl immediately recognised. He announced Lord William of Hapton. Then the man himself entered the room, unselfconsciously smiling and waving to people he recognised as he began his progress to the front of the church.

"Why is he here?" Tom nudged her and whispered.

"Didn't you invite him?" Sibyl bent her head to reply without taking her eyes off William.

"No. I've heard all about him, I wouldn't." Tom returned.

"I think it's a message for me. Now father's dead." Sibyl just had time to whisper before William had arrived at her side, plucking up one of her hands for a kiss before she had time to react. She snatched it away and turned back to the front, a look of pure distaste on her face. William then stood quietly and respectfully during the service. When it was finally over, just when Sibyl thought her legs would give way, she turned to him and, not wishing to make a scene, growled quietly at him:

"What are you doing here William?"

"I came to pay my respects to my friend!" He laughed, knowing all eyes in the crowd were on him.

"Friend?!" She hissed. "You greatly upset him!"

"Yes, I know. And I am deeply sorry for that. I've known your father since I was a boy; he was like a father to me. I looked forward to becoming part of his family." He said with genuine remorse, looking at her accusingly with the last. Sibyl did not know what to say and looked to the floor. This gave him his chance and he gathered up her arm in his own and steered her past the solemn crowds knowing that she wouldn't fight in public. Outside he gallantly offered her his horse. Sibyl was on the point of refusing but Thomas intervened.

"Take the horse sister, your shoes are soaked through as it is" He urged.

"You should listen to the new Lord Bearnshaw, Sibyl." William interrupted mockingly. "Good lad Tom!" He said, clapping Thomas on the back far too hard so that he staggered forwards.

Tom scowled and shot Sibyl a look. She shrugged and allowed herself to be helped onto Lord William's huge horse's back. He took the reins and they led the guests back up Tower Causeway in the grey snow slush. It was too public to talk while they were walking; their voices travelled far in the still, cold night air, but once the guests were settled, dried and enjoying their first cup Sibyl could apprehend William under the noise of the chatter around.

"Is this some kind of message from you William?" she said as guests bustled around them in the hall.

"Message?" He queried, taking a sip of wine with a flourish.

"Ruining my father's funeral." She explained with a sigh.

"Look Sibyl, you're the only one who thinks it was ruined, as is usual you only think the worst of me-" He prepared for a speech, but Sibyl cut him off.

"I'm not stupid William! You're here to let me know that you haven't forgotten about our betrothal, that now my father is dead your way into my bed is that bit clearer. Well you must surely realise that you face a far larger obstacle than my father in the King and he-" Now William cut her off.

"Oh yes, I know all about your little secret...you and the King." He said in a suddenly low voice. Sibyl was mortified; she blushed deeply and choked on her words, gripping her wine harder. William was evidently delighted with the reaction. "Yes, not barren after all are you Sibyl?"

"How?" She croaked.

"Never you mind darling," he lifted a finger to trace the hem of her headdress, then slipped the finger underneath to touch the hair before she ducked away. "I know many things you don't...or your King. While you spend your days holed up at Bearnshaw, painting your flowers, I am active. I know things. I do things...I am promised things...."

"My King? Don't you mean *the* King? That's dangerous talk William." She tried to regain her footing and worry him.

"Is it?" He said, then abruptly turned and left her, feeling worried, foolish and out of her depth. She swigged her wine and tried to think of a further step.

He seemed far too sure of himself and confident in his dismissal of Edward's power. It could only really mean one thing, she thought; that he was a fully-fledged Lancastrian rebel, and something was about to happen. Something that would make him unafraid of Edward. For her sake, for Bearnshaw's sake, for Edward's sake and possibly her son's sake, she had to act. She realised she was in a unique position to gain information.

She hurried to the wine servers and took a couple of fresh cups. Then she turned and surveyed the crowd, looking for William's hat over the heads of the others. She soon spotted him, laughing with some local women. She plunged into the crowd and picked her way towards him as the music struck up.

"William. I brought you a fresh cup." She said, thrusting it towards him. He looked at her with astonishment, which gave way to a cautious smile.

"Why thank you, Sibyl." He took the cup and waited for what would come next. Sibyl wasn't sure how to proceed. She couldn't be too obvious - William was a primitive type of man but it would be idiocy to underestimate him.

"I'm tired of fighting, truth be known. I'm a mature widow now, not a flighty young girl." She said confessionally. William merely cocked an eyebrow at her. "Please, come, sit with me." She held out her hand to him and he took it very gently and allowed himself to be led to the window seat.

For the next hour or so Sibyl was utterly charming - asking questions about William and listening intently to the replies, laughing and frowning where appropriate. She turned her body in to him and touched his arm or knee whenever she could. Whenever a pitcher of wine went past, she urged the boy to refill William's cup, and if they weren't around when it ran low she deftly tipped some of her own into it. Soon William's words began to slur and he repeated himself. She gave it a little longer and he was struggling to focus on her.

"I...I think I'm having the best night of my life Sibyl!" He confided.

"We haven't even danced or eaten yet William!" She replied.

"Ohh, dancing..." he frowned, "I think I may have forgotten about that....not sure I could now?" He looked at her quizzically.

"Would you like to go somewhere quieter? You could come to my quarters; I can have some food sent up. I'm terribly tired myself." She asked.

"People will talk Sibyl..." He mumbled, already rising to his feet.

"Yes yes, I know." She patiently patted his arm and looked for Tom.

She spotted him and luckily he felt his eyes on her and turned in their direction to see her trying to prop up the swaying bulk of Lord William. He raised an eyebrow and strode purposefully over.

"What are you doing sister?" He asked low enough for William not to hear.

"Getting information - very important - don't question me now Tom, help me get him to my quarters!" She whispered urgently.

"Are you sure?" Tom nearly choked.

"What are you two talking about?" William butted in.

"Just arranging the food!" She beamed at him then lowered her voice for Tom and hissed, "Yes of course, if he falls asleep in there I'll come into your bed." Sibyl snapped. "I need to talk to him privately first though; I need him at his most....indiscreet." Thomas gave her a quizzical look but nodded and helped push William out of the room, loudly proclaiming that he just needed to 'sleep it off' to any nearby guests.

They managed to steer the swaying William up the stone steps to Sibyl's chamber where they dumped him unceremoniously onto the bed and Sibyl gave Thomas a nod which sent him trotting off to fetch some food. Sibyl turned back to William and smiled.

"Well well well, I am finally in Sibyl Bearnshaw's bedchamber after all." He mused to himself, flopping back onto the bed, quite at home.

"Yes..." Sibyl said, rolling her eyes internally. "You can rest here; we'll eat when Thomas comes back with something." She added to remind him that Tom would be coming back at some point.

"Can we do our own dancing?" He said hopefully,

holding his arms up in a dancing pose. Sibyl frowned.

"Why don't you tell me what you've been doing recently?" She asked, changing the subject.

"Why don't you come here?" He asked, patting the bed.

"No William, I won't do that." She replied firmly.

"Oh well, I won't tell you anything if you won't come closer." He crossed his arms theatrically.

"Right." Sibyl chewed her lip - this was not going well. How could she broach the subject of a potential rebellion from here? At that moment Tom knocked on the door. Sibyl ran to it and flung it open, grabbing the food and demanding more wine before shutting it again almost in Tom's face. She handed it to William and sat on the edge of the bed, taking up a fingerful of soft bread in silence. She listened to William chewing.

"See?" He said at last, "Nothing bad happens when you come close. Christ's toes, it's like taming a moor pony..." He fed himself another mouthful.

"Please don't blaspheme William." She said quietly, cursing herself inwardly as the words came out. She was supposed to be winning him over, but it was so hard to change the habit of a lifetime, her immediate impulse being to insult and injure him.

"William, what you said before, about you....knowing things. Do you think they could be beneficial to me?" She asked innocently, keeping her eyes on her fingers tearing her bread to dip it into the sauce.

"What do y'mean?" He slurred.

"Well. Just that I'm always looking for ways to further Bearnshaw. Gain more land perhaps. Raise Tom's ranking and such..." She trailed off.

"Ah yes!" William nodded heartily as he dipped his own bread into the sauce and scooped it into his mouth, sucking his fingers noisily. "Bagging yourself a Viscount and such." He snorted. Sibyl stiffened and focussed on the wall for a moment. She doubted she could cope with any mockery of John from him. Luckily he veered off into a little rant about how Viscount was a new rank, a French thing, and didn't really mean anything. That it was probably better to be an English Baron anyway.

Tom relieved her by bringing more wine and a jug in case it was needed.

"Now, I leave our good friend William in your good hands sister," he said with great maturity, "for I must entertain our guests." He bowed graciously and ducked out of the room, closing the door behind him.

"Yes, well, we all do what we can to advance our causes, don't we?" Sibyl continued the conversation.

"Yes, like bearing the King a bastard."

"I don't even know his name to be perfectly honest with you William. I don't know where he's been sent." She sniffed casually.

"Boy then." William nodded to himself at the new information.

"Do you...think there are alternative opportunities available for anyone who has...exhausted their contacts at court?" She turned to face him and blinked as she sipped her wine, passing him a cup. William thoughtfully took a sip.

"You mean...exhausted their Yorkist contacts?" He murmured. Sibyl shrugged.

"Is that what I mean?" She replaced her wine cup and put down her bowl. William did the same.

"Are you asking me if there are opportunities in the Lancastrian camp?" He snorted.

"Come now," Sibyl said, sidling closer to him and placing a hand on his outstretched legs, "it's no secret that you haven't lifted a finger in support of Edward so far." She rubbed the leg slowly, she hoped in a seductive, promising way, hating that she was here again after her experience with Edward and sensing it was a dangerous tactic.

"I suppose not." William conceded with another swig of wine.

"What sort of...reward would you want?" He asked.

"I'd want a role for Thomas. A beneficial marriage for

him." This much was true at least.

"Matilda not good enough? You are fussy, Sibyl." William reached for her hand on his leg and studied her face.

"I'd want a marriage that was a step up William." She replied coolly, allowing him to hold her hand.

"And what would you be prepared to give, in return?" He asked in a sinister tone. Sibyl narrowed her eyes briefly and considered. What exactly were they talking about here? She didn't quite know and had to be careful.

"Support. Money. Men." She replied. Suddenly William yanked her hand which pulled her forwards before she could react so that she flew onto his chest. He grinned and pinched her wrist tightly. She yelped, "William!" in shock.

"Nothing else, Sibyl?" He held her tight against him and she began to struggle.

"No!" She cried. "Let me go or I bring my men in here in an instant with my screaming!"

He let her go with a rough push and she recoiled back to the end of the bed, cradling her wrist. He rose from the bed and stood to his full height, seeming to loom over her. With relief though she saw he was coming no closer and seemed to have no intention to. He was straightening his clothes with no trace of drunken swaying.

"You didn't seriously believe that would work, did you Sibyl?" He sneered as he straightened his hat, without slurring his words. Sibyl was dumbstruck. "I can drink a lot more wine than you and not feel it." He said before striding from the room, evidently pleased with his victory. Sibyl felt ridiculous, furious and shocked. She vowed this would be the last time she attempted to get by with 'feminine ways'. This probably served her right. She crawled into bed, miserable and shaking, and longed to be back at Waberthwaite in John's arms.

~

The next morning she was up bright and early to attend to the guests who had stayed overnight. She had to be bright and polite over the morning meal and spend a long time saying goodbye to each as they left. Finally, past noon, they were all gone and Sibyl felt like going back to bed. It was cold and she was tired and miserable and not in the mood for any sewing or the suchlike, so she did.

Just as she had gratefully clambered in, drawn up the covers around her and closed her eyes with a sigh there was a polite knock at the door.

"Sibyl it's me." Said Tom, muffled by the heavy door.

"Come in!" Sibyl said; it would be nice to have Tom's company even if she was tired.

Tom came in dressed in dark furs and settled himself on the end of the bed. He seemed just as glum as she did.

"I take it you didn't get what you wanted last night?" He asked.

"No." Sibyl said simply, picking at the embroidery on her bedding. "He was only pretending to be drunk." She sighed.

"You think he's involved in a rebellion?" Tom squinted at her.

"Yes. It makes sense. He's always been Lancastrian, as we all have, but most of us know how to adapt also. He was turned against Edward by my betrothal to John though and I think the two issues have become one for him. In the past he's been as afraid as anyone about being accused of treachery, but last night he wasn't." She explained her reasoning. Tom looked unconvinced. "I haven't seen him since I married John, Tom. He went to ground, wasn't seen at court or even heard of. Why has he suddenly decided to come out of his hole now, brazenly turning up to father's funeral and happy to be seen with me?"

"Well, I suppose he still wants to marry you and thinks the way is clear?" Tom frowned.

"It isn't though is it? He would have to gain the King's approval now, and when I threw that at him last night, he all but laughed in my face. He must see the King's power as diminished, and what would diminish it? A successful rebellion. Henry is still at large, remember?"

"The King wouldn't approve his marriage to you now?" Tom seemed to be getting at something. Sibyl answered carefully.

"No, I know for a fact he would not." This was not strictly true, she knew. Kings changed their minds, but after John's loyalty and good service and there being no bad blood between her and Edward she could see no reason that he would.

"How do you know that?" Tom seemed uncomfortable.

"Has he told you things?" Sibyl asked with a sigh.

"He....said you were the King's whore, and that was how you'd got yourself a marriage to a Viscount." Tom clearly hated repeating these words to his sister, but he had to clear the matter up in his own mind.

"Well....I suppose that is true. The thing is, we don't live in that perfect world of childhood anymore Tom. I had to do something to get out of my marriage to William and the only person who was likely to do anything about it was the King, and he wanted something in exchange. What else could I offer a King? What else would make him take time out of his busy day to talk to someone as low ranking as myself, Tom?" Sibyl hoped he would see.

"I suppose so..." Tom replied in a low voice. He was plainly suffering from seeing who his infallible older sister, someone he saw as perfect, virginal and moral, for who she really was: someone willing to trade her body in order to climb up another branch of the tree. Sibyl became a little impatient as, after all, she had done it for both their benefit - Tom enjoyed the protection of the King as much as she.

"I did it for both of us Tom! If William had married me a few years ago, before you were ready to take over the reins, what do you think he would have done? Respected our land and built on our wealth for you to take over, or sucked it dry for his own ends? You've known him since childhood too - he's a selfish, arrogant and stupid man!" She warmed to her theme, "It's only because of *me* that Bearnshaw is in such good shape for you now that father is dead! And, God forbid, anything happened to you, as things stand everything would go to him!"

"Right, right." Tom nodded, swallowing the unpalatable truth. He was silent for a few moments. "He also said you had a child by the King. Is that true too? A boy?"

"Yes." Sibyl said.

"Where does that leave me? I'm a small Lord, unmarried and without heirs or great wealth and he is the King's bastard."

"No Tom, he's gone, I don't even know his name - that child is nothing to do with us."

They both sat quietly for a moment, then Sibyl brightened.

"Tom, if we were instrumental in alerting the King to this rebellion, we would be well rewarded I'm sure and William would be ruined. What we need to do now is find out what is happening and let Edward know in good time. I'm not sure how to proceed though - my plan failed and William doesn't trust me." Tom remained silent in thought for a while. Sibyl grew impatient. She wanted her brother to assume responsibility now but he seemed not to have a tactical mind. As good at fighting and hunting as he was, he was still too immature to be trusted to look after Bearnshaw entirely, she saw.

"I think," she said diplomatically, "that perhaps now is an ideal time for you to go out into society and be our eyes and ears? You are the new Lord of Bearnshaw and the old Lord was quiet for so long - you are putting that right. You should tour our local friends and allies, make new ones, and keep your ear to the ground for us."

"Yes, I like that idea!" Tom was delighted, perhaps thinking of all the parties and sport he would have touring the locality in his new role.

"I will stay here," Sibyl continued, "and wait for information. We must think of a way to get any messages back to the King also. William and anyone else involved in the plot is sure to be watching my movements from now on, but we could not possibly trust a messenger to take written evidence across country either and it is better for fewer people to know so I would be loathe to give him anything to relate verbally....who knows who else he could tell?" She mused, Tom allowing her to plan freely. "We need someone who we know we can trust for sure..." Her mind span through all her contacts for someone suitable. Eventually she hit upon a solution. "Edmund!" She exclaimed - John's right hand man. She had no idea where he was these days, but she could send out enquiries under the pretext of unfinished Waberthwaite business.

Tom was eager to get started so brother and sister spent the rest of the day organising the staff into putting together a travelling party to take John around in befitting style. Soon the frozen courtyard was filled with horses, ponies, men and dogs, steam rising from their mouths and nostrils. A messenger had been sent ahead to John and Isabel Towneley as the intended first stay. The Towneleys were the most powerful family in the area and Sibyl felt confident their resources would not be overstretched by an impromptu visit from her brother, giving her time to make arrangements for other places.

"Tom, be discreet...and don't get too drunk!" Sibyl gave Thomas a playful slap on the arm, but it would have been disastrous for the young lad to get blind drunk and give away secrets. Tom tutted in response and off he went on his father's old horse. The horse was maybe a bit greying around his eyes now, but he was safe and an impressive size for a Lord. His smaller hunting horse was tethered to the pack train if he needed a turn of speed.

"Look after the tower for me until I get back sister!" He waved cheerfully and they were off, carefully picking their way over the icy ground and slithering down the hill in single file. Sibyl shivered and strode back into the doorway through the thick, sheltering walls to compose her letter to Edmund and consider which of the messenger lads would be up to the job of finding him.

5

Mother Helston

Lord Towneley had welcomed Thomas with open arms.

"Young Thomas, look at you now! A Lord already!" He had boomed, attempting to put a positive spin on the recent death of the boy's father.

Tom was only too pleased to soak up the hospitality - back in Cheshire he had been an anonymous boy with all the others, expected to be obedient and spoken down to by adults. Since coming home however his sister had treated him as an equal and now here he was, guest of honour at Lord Towneley himself's place and on a spying mission, effectively for the King no less! He had sent his friends home when his father's illness had worsened, but he wished they could see him now in his finery, sipping brandy with the men.

At the Towneley's he learnt the extent of the gossip about his family. The Towneleys were related to Lord William but evidently did not know the extent of what had gone on between he and Sibyl. They also seemed to know nothing of Sibyl's dalliance with the King, much to Tom's relief. It seemed that locally everyone had been pleased that Lord

William was to marry Sibyl and they had been confused by the sudden change of plan but as far as they were concerned, that was the work of a new and fickle King and now that John was dead, things would revert.

Tom made the judicious decision to play along with this. He hoped he had judged it correctly as he desperately did not want to let Sibyl down. He considered that it would be no bad thing for word to get around that he was for a marriage between Sibyl and William - with any luck, word would get back to William and he would perhaps begin to trust the Bearnshaws more, if not Sibyl, then perhaps Thomas if he could make a good enough pretence of being an ally, without incriminating himself in the plot of course.

Thomas may have been young but he was a calm and collected boy and knew that it would be extremely difficult to prove his case as a spy if the King already had knowledge of the rebellion and swooped in to kill it off before Tom could relate any information back to prove which side he was really on. Wherever possible, he quizzed the Towneleys on the action in the ongoing battle against the Lancastrians.

"Eager to get involved are you Thomas?" John Towneley had asked, "Don't be lad, give yourself time. I know all youngsters are eager to prove themselves but many can needlessly lose their lives that way. You need to gain life experience." Tom shrugged noncommitally; he wouldn't say he was desperate to get into battle, in truth he felt a little out of his depth already.

At that moment a messenger was shown into the chamber, the February snow on his shoulders quickly melting into his cloak upon hitting the heat from the roaring fire in the room. The men Tom had been sat with all looked around with interest, not expecting any messages.

"I have an invitation for Lord Bearnshaw; Lord William would like his company at Hapton Tower as soon as Lord Towneley is willing to let him go." The man smiled and bowed.

"Ah! Thomas, he must be wanting to sort out this Sibyl

thing at last, you must leave first thing tomorrow, but I shall personally escort you as I have been meaning to speak with my cousin for a while." Lord Towneley was beaming; delighted at the sociable turn the winter had taken.

Thomas on the other hand was a little stunned. The others took it that he was shocked by the 'honour' of receiving a personal invite, but in reality Tom was wondering what William could possibly want with him at this stage. Was he truly going to trust Tom, or was it some kind of hostile act? What would he be walking into? He acknowledged the invite with good grace and agreed to leave the next day.

~

Sibyl had received the urgent news from Tom stating that he had been invited to William's with mixed feelings. Just like Tom she had wondered what was behind it. Tom had said he was going to discuss the marriage plans and she had to guess that this was a front for the benefit of anyone who may have read the note who was not supposed to. Now she could only sit and wait for further news.

The wait was over one evening when she was sat by the fire with Pierre.

"Please Lady Bearnshaw, there's someone here to see you - he says he's here on behalf of Lord William, so I made him wait in the courtyard."

"Thank you Susannah, I shall go out myself!" Sibyl swept from the room with Susannah scuttling after, partly in case she was needed and partly to garner gossip.

Outside were three men, two still mounted but one holding his horse's reins. They all bowed their heads in acknowledgement when she came out to talk to them alone.

"You are from Lord Hapton?" She said, remembering not to use the more informal 'William' and suggest any kind of familiarity.

"Indeed my Lady. He and your brother wish for you to join them, Lord Hapton is eager to see you." The man on the ground said. "We are to travel with you as Lord Hapton is aware you may be short staffed here and he wants you to be well protected on the road." The man continued.

Sibyl nodded and invited the men in for the night and ensured they would be fed. She then hurriedly took herself to bed so that she would be well rested, although she spent most of the night with her mind spinning over what was happening. In the morning she was up with first light and impatiently waited for her escort to rise, eat and get ready.

The stable hands brought out her obedient little grey palfrey once again and she happily climbed into the saddle, eager for some break to the monotony of the previous months. She meant to impress the men with her riding skills and set Belaud into a pace along the stony moorland track, gravel and pebbles flying from his hooves. The men wordlessly fell in and they rode hard for a while.

The horses grew tired in the rising summer heat and needed to walk a little so the party of four slowed. It was then that Sibyl noted a dark figure on the side of the road far ahead. The figure came into view slowly as they walked towards each other and Sibyl began to pick out detail. Lone walkers this far out on the moors were quite unusual and she was interested to see who this was. It appeared to be an old woman clothed in near rags; grey and dirty. Her hair matched her clothes and as they drew up alongside her Sibyl saw the deeply wrinkled face and the tiny, twinkling eyes nestling in the crags.

Sibyl was intending to ride past, politely averting her gaze from this wandering pauper, but as she passed, she felt something grip her leg tightly. She jumped and her grey almost reared. She let out a yelp and suddenly the men around her had jumped into action and pushed the old woman away by riding their horses at her.

"Piss off Helston!" The leader shouted. "Touch anyone under my care again and you'll be flayed alive."

The old woman didn't react at all and never took her eyes from Sibyl's. Sibyl had no idea how to react. Her instinct was to protect an old woman from these brutes but she was grateful for their interference; the grip on her leg had left her feeling chilled and her heart hammered uncontrollably. The whole thing was disconcerting.

"Lady Sibyl is it?" The woman said, her voice creaking like an old door.

"I said leave off Helston..." The man growled

"Leave her!" Sibyl held up a hand as the man took his boot out of his stirrup, presumably to kick the old lady. "Do I know you?" She asked.

"No my Lady, but I know you. Are ye off to marry my Lord William?" The old woman gave her a virtually toothless grin and gave a little wheeze that could have been laughter or a cough.

"Ignore her Lady Bearnshaw; it's just Mother Helston, she lives on William's land and likes to make trouble." Robert, the leader of the little troop explained. "She's mad; a rustic shouldn't be talking to the likes of you." He spat at Mother Helston's feet to make his point.

"Why do you ask about my marriage?" Sibyl pressed on, ignoring Robert.

"No reason, just idle chatter my Lady. The whole county seems to be eager to get it over and done with." She shrugged.

"Over and done with?" Sibyl bristled. "This is my life we're talking about-" Robert quickly cut her off.

"My Lady don't let her bother you, she does this to everyone...just likes to meddle."

"I'm not the only one who likes to meddle am I?" Mother Helston said to Robert.

"I don't know what you mean Helston but you are getting on my nerves now..." He snarled back.

"Toying with Kings never did anyone any good - you just come to me if you're ever in a spot of bother Sibyl Bearnshaw, Mother Helston will help you, Mother Helston knows things, even though they say she's mad, she just knows the truth!"

Mother Helston bustled on as she said this, calling the words over her shoulder. Sibyl watched her go with a frown fixed on her face, the grey bundle of rags disappearing into the heat haze rising 'from the moor.

"Really, don't pay any heed to her nonsense my Lady." Robert ushered her forwards and they resumed their pace all the way over the stretch of moorland between Bearnshaw and Hapton.

Sibyl still felt a little shaken and confused by the time they reached Hapton Tower. She had even forgotten to think about William's reasoning for sending for her. Now there he was, standing at the front door with Tom by his side, beaming at her. Sibyl's face was expressionless as he moved towards her and offered his hand to help her dismount and then when she was stood before him, he dropped to one knee graciously and tenderly kissed her hand before bowing his head.

Sibyl cast a look at Tom and saw his anxious face reading her reaction. She showed no emotion. It was evident William had fallen for the act.

"It has been wonderful having Thomas here Sibyl; it's been as it should be, with us all friends. I'm so glad you've come round." He said, clutching both her hands in his rather intimately. Robert and the others had dismissed themselves and it was just the party of three 'friends'. Sibyl took a deep breath and plastered a smile onto her face, wondering what to say next. Tom stepped in.

"Yes, I have explained to William that we want to put the past behind us and that you are willing to accept my will." He said importantly. Sibyl caught his tone - she had to pretend to be obedient.

"Of course. Whatever my brother the Lord Bearnshaw wants I must respect." Sibyl said truthfully, knowing that her brother did not truly wish her married to William. "Could we please have some time together? I have not seen my brother for so long and need to refresh after my journey." Sibyl asked. William quickly nodded.

"Of course - I shall see you both for a meal this evening."

Tom led Sibyl through the doors of Hapton Tower. Sibyl had not been inside Hapton Tower since they were children when their family used to visit so that their fathers could talk.

Since she was old enough to understand the implications of a betrothal however she had stopped joining for the visits, which had been tough when she was younger as visiting and returned visits were the very best form of entertainment. Those were the times when she would have someone else to talk to, when she could dance in company. She had swapped all that to ride amongst the crags alone and document flowers instead.

"So Tom, you had better fill me in quickly!" Sibyl said briskly as they reached her quarters for the duration of her stay.

"Well I haven't found out much except that William is rabidly anti-Edward, which naturally means he is pro-Henry." Tom began.

"Which we knew already..." Sibyl interrupted impatiently.

"Yes, and I have been going along with that-" Again he was cut off.

"That's a dangerous game Tom, what if the king-" This time Tom cut her off.

"What was I supposed to do?! Let me speak!" He hissed. "I have also gone along with the marriage thing...said I condone it. I didn't have a choice Sibyl, if I had said I didn't I would have been turned out wouldn't I? I thought you'd value information more."

"But you don't have any?"

"Something's definitely going on Sibyl, but I don't know precisely what...I'm still being left out of that." Tom looked sorry that he'd failed her.

"So why am I here?"

"I...got nervous. I hadn't spoken to you for so long and needed further guidance."

"Right, yes, I was also wondering what was going on. I had a very peculiar thing happen to me on the way here," Sibyl changed the subject. "I met a 'Mother Helston', apparently the local madwoman."

"Oh yes I've heard of her." Tom nodded.

"She did seem mad, but also had moments of lucidity with me Tom - she knew who I was even though I'm certain I've never laid eyes on the woman, I would remember that face!"

"She could have found out you were travelling today?" Tom said.

"Maybe. She said that meddling with Kings did nobody any good and that I should go to her if I ever needed help. Don't you think that's relevant? Why say that about kings? To me, now?" Sibyl spoke the words in a rush, hoping Tom's curiosity would win through.

"She's a mad old woman, she could say anything?" He replied.

"You think it was sheer coincidence she was travelling over the moor alone at the same time as I was, apprehending me to talk about kings? Don't you want to find out what she meant?" Sibyl was mystified at how uninterested her brother was about this strange incident. He was a poor spy, she concluded. She supposed he was only interested in what men had to say, thinking it impossible a woman could play a part in plots. Sibyl felt she needed to educate him.

"Don't dismiss her as a mad old woman Tom, we need to follow up all leads and leave no stone unturned. It won't hurt us to go and see her will it?"

"No. I suppose not." Tom agreed.

"That is what we shall do then." Sibyl decided, sending him away so that she could freshen up.

~

That evening Lord William threw something of a little party for his guests, inviting his more senior men and their families to dine with them in his great hall, enjoy some music and so on. Sibyl was grateful the setting wasn't too much more intimate; she had been dreading an intense meal with only Tom and William present, with William no doubt feeling he could say or do anything in front of her younger brother, who could only go so far in protecting her.

In this setting Sibyl could even quite enjoy herself, flitting from guest to guest, sipping her sweet hypocras wine and nibbling the delicate wafers the cooks had supplied. Hapton Tower was a little more grand and a little busier than Bearnshaw, being sited closer to the activity of Burnley and the larger Towneley estate, it gave a jovial atmosphere.

Most of the guests did ask her about her marriage to Lord William to which Sibyl merely shrugged her shoulders and said she was the King's ward and he would decide. The others then tended to nod sympathetically, understanding the implication that a Yorkist King would not prioritise marrying off his Lancastrian subjects, having already tried to place Sibyl in the Yorkist Waberthwaite family once!

William was well liked among this crowd too and he was being a perfect gentleman; polite, amusing and generous. After charming everyone else he finally made his way to her side, feeling as though he had earnt the right to spend the rest of the evening with her exclusively. Sibyl politely accepted his company and sat with him on two fine chairs.

"This has been a good evening Sibyl." William said with genuine feeling.

"Agreed." Sibyl said, feeling generous, like a truce of some kind had been called.

"I've been meaning to ask you something though...please don't think I'm doing it to provoke you." He looked at her pleadingly.

"Go on...." Sibyl said suspiciously.

"Have you heard the latest from court?"

"No?" Sibyl had been alone at Bearnshaw for a long time: no travellers with news from court had any reason to call and nobody had thought to write to her. Her letters to Edmund had drawn a blank.

"Edward's married." William said. Sibyl blinked with shock and William allowed her to process the information in her own time, carefully watching the reaction. He saw the various thoughts flitting through her mind etched on her face though she tried to hide them. She finally settled on nonchalance.

"Who is his bride?" She asked. She knew she had no

claim to Edward; it was unthinkable someone of her rank could actually marry a King and, if she was honest, she found him a little loud and brash compared to her beloved John, but of course, a tiny part of her still flared with jealousy at the thought that another woman had finally claimed the prize.

"Elizabeth Wydville." William replied with a slight smile. "Remember her?"

Sibyl racked her brains, but couldn't. She shook her head with an enquiring frown.

"Of course not: she's a nobody. Daughter of Jacquetta Rivers, but this is the daughter by her second husband, the knight." He related. Sibyl's eyes were as wide as saucers - she remembered the story, the scandal! "He was married in May, but kept it secret until September!"

Sibyl's mind flew back to May the previous year, around the time of the Battle of Hexham, the death of her John, and Edward telling her about it. Of course, he had not made any mention of it then, why would he? It felt peculiar to know that she was around him at that pivotal time and had been none the wiser...just like everyone else, apparently. Sibyl felt that little stab of jealousy once again - she was of a similar status to Elizabeth. She could have had a shot at being Queen....

"I just wondered if you'd had the news." William snapped her out of her thoughts.

"No, I hadn't, thank you." She murmured absent mindedly.

"It won't affect you will it?" He asked.

"I doubt it." Sibyl said, before changing the subject onto her plans to ride with Tom tomorrow, on their own so they could catch up. Lord William's mood darkened visibly as he wondered if there was anything behind her emphasis on them riding alone, but he nodded anyway.

~

Tom had a vague idea of where Mother Helston lived and when they drew near they were able to ask where exactly, as everyone knew where Mother Helston lived on the outskirts of Burnley where Lord William's land met the Towneley's. The house was sited very close to an enormous oak tree which had grown peculiarly around it, so that the house was in gloom even on a sunny day such as this. Tom was unwilling to go in; he couldn't really see the point in disturbing a creepy old woman on the off chance she had information. He would rather be back at Hapton Tower, perhaps practising archery with William and showing Sibyl how good his aim was these days.

Sibyl was eager to go in though and was happy to leave Tom 'on guard' outside holding her horse's reins. As Sibyl walked up to the door she was suddenly aware she was completely clueless about the etiquette of entering a rustic's home. She supposed she would just knock on the door? She wouldn't be welcomed or introduced by any servers that much was certain. Her knock triggered the barking of a dog inside and the door creaked open with a noise much like Mother Helston's voice.

Just as Sibyl had thought the door had opened itself, Mother Helston suddenly appeared from behind it, the tiny glittering eyes like a pig's looking Sibyl up and down. Sibyl forgot what she was supposed to say but was saved by the old woman saying she should come in.

"Oh, thank you." Sibyl stepped into the hovel, ducking to avoid the low door frame.

"Please, seat yourself dear." Mother Helston ushered her into a chair and returned to her pot on the stove as though nothing unusual had happened, that she was expecting Sibyl's arrival.

Sibyl stared around in shock - the home was quite well furnished and remarkably clean. Given the old woman's appearance on the road she had expected her home to match - grubby and tattered.

"Those were merely my road-clothes dear..." Mother Helston said, taking a sip of what she was making. Sibyl realised the old woman knew what she was thinking and quickly gathered her wits.

"Thank you...for your offer of help." She began.

"Oh you're welcome my Lady!" Mother Helston beamed at her, stirring away merrily.

"I wondered, what kind of help is it you are offering?" Sibyl queried.

If Mother Helston was indeed just mad she had no intention of compromising herself by mentioning rebellions to her. Word could quickly spread around the hills and become distorted as it passed from community to community.

Mother Helston stopped stirring, wiped her hands and sat down opposite Sibyl in a dark wooden chair with a sigh.

"People come to Mother Helston with all kinds of problems, Lady Sibyl. I like to think I can help them all in some way. I have two things for you." She replied.

Sibyl was surprised by this, that the old lady would be so specific. Two things? She was about to answer that she didn't have any problems, but that would have been a lie. Her mind struggled with the idea that Mother Helston could possibly know her problems, which were private...or so she thought. As she tried to find words, Mother Helston helped her.

"Would you like them?" She asked patiently.

"Yes...I suppose so?" Sibyl replied, bewilderment etched on her face.

"Very good. Good choice..." Mother Helston seemed pleased and steepled her fingers while Sibyl waited intently in the gloom inside the cottage, unable to see Mother Helston's face clearly as she was silhouetted against the one small window.

"The first thing I have for you is information. I thought you would be very interested to know that the old King is in this very area." She spoke calmly even though her words were outlandish.

"H-How do you know?!" Sibyl gasped, eyes wide with shock.

"I told you dear, people come to Mother Helston with all kinds of problems...I get to knowing things."

"Where?" Sibyl demanded, hoping to catch the old woman out.

"All over - they move him around. He is currently at Waddington Hall though." Mother Helston explained. Sibyl could not think of a word to say in response. "I'm sure you're canny enough to think of a way to test what I'm saying Sibyl, but if I were you I'd act on it before it's too late...."

"And the second thing?" Sibyl blinked and shook her head before looking back at the silhouette of Mother Helston's head, seeing only the glint of her little eyes.

"Ah," the crone said, "that is something else entirely. That is for you, yourself."

She heaved herself out of the chair and walked over to a dresser laden with bottles and pots of all shapes and sizes and selected a squat jar. Sibyl watched as she carefully removed the stopper and deftly pulled a square of red silk out of a drawer, laid it flat and poured a measure of a grey-brown powder into a pile in the middle of the silk. The old woman hummed to herself as she worked, rifling through the same drawer for a tiny cord.

She pulled the silk up around the powder and tied the cord tightly around it to form a little pouch. This she held out in front of Sibyl's face for her to take. Sibyl's hand automatically reached out and gently took it, feeling how light the little packet was.

"If you're ever beyond hope Sibyl, make a tea with this and drink it. Remember though, it is only for you - don't speak of it to anyone and if you need any more I am always here."

Sibyl obediently secreted the little bag in the folds of her gown and nodded dumbly. This was all incredibly strange and she was preoccupied with the thought of verifying the tale of the old King and warning Edward. She thought she would come back to the powder and why Mother Helston would give it to her, with her disturbing talk of being beyond hope, when she had the time to think of it.

Sibyl rose to her full height and looked down on Mother Helston, still without a notion of what to say. Thank you seemed inappropriate; she may have been lying, and who knew what the powder was?

"I may see you again." She nodded, turning and sweeping out of the door without waiting for a reply.

She hurried over to the two horses and took her grey's reins from Tom's hand.

"What happened? What did she say?" He asked, bursting with curiosity now. Sibyl looked around at the trees and bushes lining the lane for anyone in the immediate vicinity. All was quiet, but she spoke in a low voice anyway.

"She said the old King is nearby, being hidden at Waddington Hall currently."

"Waddington!" Exclaimed Tom.

"Shhh Tom!" Sibyl clapped a hand onto his forearm. Tom looked ashamed of his outburst. "We must confirm this for ourselves - she could be lying, for whatever reason. We must make our excuses and leave William, go and stay somewhere from where we can place Waddington Hall under surveillance. As soon as we have confirmation, we must get word to Edward."

Tom held Sibyl's stirrup and elbow in order to help her mount and the pair then sped off back to Hapton Tower as fast as they dared travel.

6

Capturing a King

"I'm afraid we have to leave William." Sibyl said firmly.

"Oh!" William exclaimed. "So soon?"

"Soon?" Sibyl queried. "Tom has been your guest for months!" She laughed lightly.

"Yes but *you* have only just arrived, we have much to discuss don't we? We were going to put on a hawking and archery display for you in the gardens tomorrow?" William seemed genuinely aggrieved.

"That would have been lovely, I love to see how Tom's skills are developing, but our friends the Harringtons are expecting us - we received word from them today that they are waiting." Sibyl explained.

"The Harringtons?" William seemed thoughtful as he looked at Sibyl. She silently registered his suspicious reaction but saw that he transferred his gaze, narrowing his eyes, to Tom stood nearby. Tom was frustratingly poor at hiding his feelings so far and Sibyl inwardly winced.

"Well, if you have to go, I suppose I shall have to let you."

William said after a lengthy, awkward silence. "You are welcome to come back to Hapton as soon as you've made your rounds, Thomas." He said formally and nodded their leave. Sibyl grabbed the chance and all but fled from the room with Tom.

Within hours they were on the paths towards Pendle Hill, the huge, long bulk of it languishing over the landscape ahead. The day was bright but with a cool wind and afforded good travel on dry lanes. They would soon skirt around the hill and be at the home of James Harrington, a knight known to be loyal to the Yorkist cause.

For that reason, Sibyl did not know the Harringtons well as in the past the Bearnshaws had been Lancastrians, but she felt confident of her ability to bluff a more intimate relationship. If they turned up on the doorstep with Tom as the new Lord Bearnshaw expecting a warm welcome, if there was no specific reason not to give one Harrington would simply have to comply out of sheer good manners.

"Have you got a plan, Sibyl?" Tom broke away from the small group of men travelling with them and spoke to her, slightly breathless from the quick pace.

"Not as such. Not yet." Sibyl panted back. "I think we shall have to act fast however - did you see William's reaction to the news we were going to the Harringtons'?"

"Yes!" Tom replied excitedly. "He must know!"

"It's not a cause for glee Tom. It means he may well monitor us, or send word to Waddington and the King will move if he is indeed there." She said in a low voice in case any of their travelling party was listening. They couldn't risk telling their men just yet. "Our head start is really our only hope in this."

"So.....how can we find out?" Tom asked. Sibyl sighed - must she think of everything?

"I'm thinking Tom!" She snapped.
They lapsed into a tense silence while both tried to think of a plan.

"What if we split up?" Sibyl said at last. "You go on to

the Harringtons and formally introduce yourself and explain to Sir James. I will feign lameness in my horse and detour to Waddington Hall - that is a legitimate route, as it is on our way. No one need suspect a thing. Of course their stablemen will find my horse sound and I will be on my way in no time to tell you the result. If it's true the old King is there, be ready to ride with your most trusted man as fast as you can to the King in London."

"Alone?" Tom replied with a note of excitement in his voice.

"It's not a game. Yes alone. It will be very dangerous." Sibyl said grimly. "But I want Edward and his forces here as soon as possible; Harrington is likely to want to handle things himself but he may not realise that Henry has support from Lord William and the like and the fight could be bigger than expected."

Sometime later they came to the turning for Waddington Hall. Sibyl made a show of pulling up her horse and ignored the puzzled looks from the men. She asked Tom what she should do and he authoritatively told her to lead the animal to Waddington Hall and come along to meet them when she had a replacement or it was better.

"Sir!" One of their men spoke up. "Shall I accompany the Lady?"

"I can take care of myself thank you Hugh." Sibyl glared at Hugh, a man in his forties who had served their father.

"But...it is unthinkable for a woman to travel alone, sir? Hugh ignored Sibyl and spoke directly to Thomas, who looked uncomfortable as he wrestled with the dilemma of approving his sister's wishes or appearing strong to his men. Eventually he spoke, his mouth contorted with embarrassment at having to override Sibyl.

"You're right Hugh." Tom looked at Sibyl pleadingly, hoping she understood. "It would be...not the done thing to let my sister travel alone."

Sibyl nodded once and turned to leave, forgetting her mount was supposed to be lame. Hugh called out to her.

"Lady Sibyl, ride with me." He offered. Sibyl stopped dead, inwardly chiding herself for forgetting these important details. Silently she accepted the helping hands of the other men to dismount and then they hoisted her onto the back of Hugh's large black horse from their own stable and the reins of her grey were handed to him.

Tom's party disappeared around a bend in the path through the trees and suddenly Sibyl was alone in the quiet of the woods, forced to cling intimately to Hugh's waist as they plodded through the dappled shade.

"Can we go faster please Hugh?" Sibyl said at last, a tense shrill to her voice.

"I doubt it my lady, you would be jounced off!" He laughed.

"This horse has a good ambling pace has it not? I shall not fall off!" She snapped.

"Very well." Hugh complied and pushed the horse into its faster ambling pace.

After a little while Hugh spoke again.

"You need not fear me my Lady."

"What! I do not, Hugh." Sibyl scoffed. But it was not true, she was concerned about being out of sight and earshot of others and was suspicious about Hugh's motives for wanting to accompany her and how intent he had seemed on having her ride with him. She didn't know whether she was just being paranoid or whether this was actually a golden opportunity for a man to perform deeds he perhaps should not.

It was not something she had considered before and it struck her that she felt safer travelling alone than she now did with someone she knew. Instinctively she suddenly felt that whilst everyone was quick to expound upon the dangers of bandits, robbers and rapists ready to leap out on unsuspecting travellers they rarely mentioned harm coming from parties known to the travellers. Which was more likely? She calculated probably the known source - they were there, after all.

Sibyl considered uncomfortably that she had plunged herself into the world of men again and although she had not courted any kind of amorous activity with them this time, somehow she had ended up with the threat of it whether she liked it or not. She raged inside and cursed herself for not carrying some kind of weapon - a dagger secreted on her person would have made her feel much better.

"You are not afraid, to be alone with a man in the woods?" Hugh asked.

"No, Hugh. I'm not." Sibyl said in a tired way. "For if any man touched me the King himself would bring the wrath of Hell down on his head. Kings are very protective of their concubines." She added casually and smiled to herself with satisfaction as Hugh stiffened and spluttered in the saddle. "I...I was only trying to urge you to be cautious Lady Sibyl. I've known you since you were a girl, and you are taking great risks." He hurriedly explained, genuinely, Sibyl thought. She patted his arm.

"I know Hugh, but sometimes I have no choice."

Sibyl was shocked to see the state of Waddington Hall. It looked shabby and ill-maintained. A single man hobbled out to greet them at the stables and expertly took the reins of Belaud, smoothing his nose with a gnarled hand. All seemed quiet otherwise. Without help Sibyl slid down and regained her footing on the ground. Hugh remained mounted.

"What can we help you with, travellers?" The man asked pleasantly with a toothless smile and twinkling pale blue eyes flicking from Hugh to Sibyl, evidently not sure who was who in this instance. Sibyl took the lead.

"I am Lady Sibyl Bearnshaw." She began and the man looked startled and hurriedly bowed. "Don't worry yourself about all that," she brushed off his attempt at proper manners, "I was travelling with my brother the new Lord Bearnshaw to the Harringtons' place when my horse went lame. I came here as the nearest place to get help." She explained.

"Ah yes, we heard about old Lord Bearnshaw, our condolences to you..." The man shook his head sadly as he bent to examine her horse's legs. She and Hugh stood in awkward silence as the man carried out his work. Upon finding nothing visible he led the horse around a little with a frown.

"I can't find anything wrong with him my Lady?" The man shrugged.

"Oh!" Sibyl feigned surprise. "My mistake....may we have something to drink before we leave?" She asked brightly. Hugh shot her a look of confusion and suspicion which she ignored.

"Oh er, yes of course, I'll show you to the kitchens." The man nodded and tied up the horse.

"I'll stay here." Hugh said grumpily. Sibyl cursed to herself. He was obviously expecting them to be off quickly - how much could she possibly find out in such a short time? She worried she was going to ruin everything by not being able to think of better plans in a timely fashion.

She followed the old man, who introduced himself as Gilbert, into the kitchens where they met 'Bessie', a woman not quite so old as Gilbert who evidently ran the kitchens with the aid of just one small boy, Richard.

"Are things...well, here at Waddington?" Sibyl said over a cup of brewed garden herbs. Bessie and Gilbert shot each other a glance. Gilbert spoke, evidently trying to be tactful.

"Our resources are stretched...but we're getting by." He took a sip of his own drink. "We were on the wrong side of the conflict." He added quietly. Sibyl nodded sympathetically. She liked Gilbert. He'd been very good with her horse and she had a feeling she could trust him. She hoped it would pay off.

"How far on the wrong side?" She asked, hoping he understood what she asked. Gilbert's blue eyes were suddenly boring into her own. His gaze was intense, but assessing rather than unfriendly. Sibyl held it confidently.

"Very far." Gilbert replied. "So far we cannot get back."

He said ruefully.

"Edward's a fair man. Perhaps a financial incentive could persuade your master back into the fold?" She said boldly and directly.

"So that's why you're here." Gilbert nodded.

"What's going on here?" Bessie sounded cross.

"I'm just letting you know that the good times can return. Come back to the King. Let your master know that Edward extends the hand of friendship to those who help him." Sibyl began to sweat and stood up to leave, knowing that she was speaking out of turn, with no real way of making good on her promises.

"What King sends a woman to do his work?" Bessie's voice rose. "This King seems awfully susceptible to women's witchcraft!"

"Bessie, Bessie, calm yourself, remember our guest is a *Lady*." Gilbert said firmly, holding his hands out placatingly. "I'll see her out."

Bessie turned back to her work at the oven furiously, obviously not fearing the reaction of Sibyl being spoken to that way by a person of inferior rank.

"Gilbert, try your best if you think you can. Good times *can* return to Waddington." Sibyl said urgently to the old man as he led her out. Sibyl resolved to find some sort of compensation from the Bearnshaw coffers for Gilbert at least if what she promised from Edward did not come to pass.

"I will talk to Lord Tempest." Gilbert nodded and helped her mount, all thoughts of lameness forgotten by all parties. Hugh glowered when Sibyl gave him a fierce look as she took up her reins, wheeled around and cantered off. He hurriedly followed, without bothering to say goodbye to Gilbert.

They flew down the paths to the Harrington's place, Sibyl aware she was pushing her horse too much but wanting to show Hugh exactly what she could do and that she had never been helpless. They swept into the courtyard of the property unchallenged and the grateful horses ground to a halt, steaming and blowing. Sibyl threw the reins to a flustered stable boy and jumped to the ground, gathered her skirts and marched inside.

Once in she collared the nearest person wandering past and demanded to be taken to wherever her brother was now. The woman knelt mutely and hurried off, Sibyl following closely, her shoes clacking on the paved floor. The woman gestured to a doorway and Sibyl thanked her quickly, pushing on the door herself.

Inside Sibyl checked herself as she was surprised to come upon quite a gathering. She swept the faces for Tom's, and found him stood with the most lavishly clothed men in the room. She vaguely recognised Harrington, who was peering at her with an arrogant expression, wine cup poised half way to his mouth. Tom looked too worried to smile.

Sibyl walked forwards towards the group of men before executing a quick kneel, walking forwards again and kneeling once more before joining them. Once she was alongside and manners had been served, her deference evaporated and she looked around the circle with confidence. Tom remembered his manners and blurted out an introduction, and the men all dipped their heads to her.

"Sibyl this is of course Sir James Harrington, Thomas and John Talbot, and John Tempest, brother of Richard at Waddington Hall...." Tom gestured around the group at each man as he spoke and Sibyl nodded and smiled to each one in turn, ignoring their polite but obviously cool reception.

"What news sister?" Tom asked, and Sibyl assumed Tom had explained all to them and she may speak freely.

"I didn't get any solid evidence of Henry being there, but I spoke to the serving people and I believe he is indeed there." She replied.

"He is there." James Harrington said quickly.

"He was recognised by a monk who reported it to me," John Tempest added in a friendlier manner. "I am embarrassed by how far my brother has gone in this." He said with a rueful shake of the head.

"We're preparing to ride over there and capture him now." Harrington finished his wine and slammed the cup down on his server's tray with finality.

"Is that...wise?" Sibyl said, treading carefully as she sensed that Harrington had little patience for her.

"What do you mean?" Harrington smiled, astonished Sibyl was questioning his plan, what on earth did it have to do with her?

"Do you know how deep this runs, Sir James? Thomas and I know for a fact that Lord William is involved but there could be others also. I would hate to see our forces overwhelmed and Henry to escape - would it not be better to think of an alternate plan?" She tried.

"What alternative do we have?" Harrington snorted, gesturing with a bejewelled hand.

"I have seen Waddington Hall and, with all due respect to our friend John Tempest's family, the place has seen better days. John - think you not that your brother would be open to the idea of giving up the King voluntarily and secretly in exchange for financial recompense from the King? We could then keep Henry in Waddington Hall and his followers would be none the wiser until reinforcements arrive from the King!" She said, trying to hide the note of excitement in her voice. The men were silent for a moment.

"I think our forces can manage, thank you Sibyl." Harrington said with a tight smile. "And if you think you can wander in here at the last moment and claim any of our glory for yourselves you are sorely mistaken!" He gave a little bow before striding off without a second glance.

The other men remained, stunned at their friend and ally's rudeness. The two Talbots hurriedly bowed to Sibyl and followed Harrington but John Tempest stayed to answer her direct question.

"I hope that my brother would be open to such an offer Sibyl, he has been a fool but I think the chance to come back into the King's fold would be attractive to him now." John nodded. "I did not recognise Henry and he has lied to me for a year about his true identity! They have been living like commoners in that sorry hole all this time and I think my brother is ready to end it!" He said with a wink before hurrying after the others.

Sibyl took a deep breath and looked to Tom. He looked mortified.

"Harrington's not an easy man Sibyl." He said at last.

"Yes..." Sibyl nodded, releasing her breath and shaking her head a little. "We can't waste time though Tom." She said suddenly, regaining her wits.

"What do you mean?" Tom frowned at his sister - had Harrington not just clearly stated what was to happen now? The men were saddling up and arming outside, they could both clearly hear the noise of it.

"You must ride to Edward, immediately. You must let him know we were instrumental in this. You heard Harrington, he has no intention of sharing the rewards for this - our names will be left out of his account of whatever happens today even though we did figure it out for ourselves and have lent our men...small though our forces may be. Even if he is correct that his forces can overcome the rebels, which I am not sure of at all, we will gain nothing if he is left to recount events. For the sake of the future of Bearnshaw, you must reach Edward!" Sibyl told him urgently.

"Right. I will do it!" Thomas said, thrilled with the adventure and responsibility.

"Take my horse, he is a lady's horse but you are light and he is younger and faster than father's. You shall have to live with the shame - needs must and the rewards for your success will outshine your transport, Tom!" Sibyl held his hand.

Tom nodded and stood on tiptoes to kiss his sister's cheek before freeing his hand from hers and taking his most trusted man with him out of the hall and into the noise of the preparing men outside. Sibyl herself didn't know what to do. She took up a cup of wine and helped herself to some of the food that had been left on a table. Looking around she saw that a lot of women had been left in the hall like her, but they were eyeing her suspiciously. She didn't recognise any.

She took great mouthfuls of wine and stabbed pieces of meat for herself, eating as quickly as she could under the eyes of the women, contemplating how effective her eating knife would be as a weapon after her experience with Hugh earlier when she had wished for a dagger. With that thought she wiped and sheathed it, picked up two pieces of bread and left the hall, hearing the buzz of talk strike up as she walked away.

In the stables just one horse was left; her father's heavy old chestnut that Tom had left behind. Sibyl stroked his greying muzzle and fed him a piece of the bread, eating the second herself. The horse was still wearing his tack and as Tom had gone and Sibyl felt distinctly unwelcome around the other women she supposed she should really go home. Be quiet. Wait to see what happened. Sibyl was too curious though. She could see no real harm in following the men at a discreet distance and watching what unfolded?

~

Lord William had not sat idle. Later that day he was sat in a copse of trees overlooking Waddington Hall with his best man Robert and a small, discreet band of others.

"I don't want to march straight in." William had explained to his gang. "As you know I have to be careful lest the King finds out I have any involvement...I don't think he'd need much excuse to chop my head off!" He laughed.

"What are we watching for then sir?" Robert asked after chuckling indulgently.

"I'm not sure myself really Rob, I just damn well know that Sibyl and the whelp had very good reason to leave for the Harringtons in such a hurry and I have doubts as to whether it's just a friendly visit by old chums, shall we say." William scanned the approach to the hall as he spoke.

He had been suspicious of Sibyl ever since the funeral of her father. He knew that she was firmly a Yorkist thesedays, devoted to their handsome King. He felt Tom was more impressionable and had been pleased to host the boy and see that he at least seemed to consent to a marriage to his sister. That had given William hope. Of course however, the one problem as was usual, was Sibyl herself. He had thought it too good to be true that she had acquiesced to her brother's rule so readily and as soon as he heard the word 'Harrington' he had known it was all a lie.

"What if we do see them?" Robert pressed.

"We shall have to see what happens...we have no idea what they are doing or how many they have on their side and we are few. I didn't think it a wise move to bring all the lads out for a march, that would look mightily suspicious." William replied.

"Indeed sir." Robert nodded once in agreement and fell to silently watching with his master.

"I think for now it's best we keep an eye on King Henry and stay abreast of any developments." William concluded.

They did not have long to wait until they spotted movement on the path to the hall. All the men immediately perked up as they saw Hugh's black horse emerge from the trees and made out the shape of the smaller grey being led. Then they noticed that the rider on the black's back was impossibly large, but that as they passed by closer on their way to the hall's entrance they could all see it was a woman perched behind the man.

"That's Sibyl - it's her grey being led." William muttered.

"There's none with them...she must have had problems with her horse." Robert whispered.

"Hmm yes, I think I recognise the man she's with as one of their own, but I find it hard to believe Sibyl would choose not to ride her own horse?" William agreed.

"Are we going to capture them sir?" Robert asked hopefully, his hand travelling to the hilt of his sword.

"What for Robert? I would greatly love to bring her to heel, but what if Harrington's behind her? What if the King himself got to find out that I had taken her prisoner without good reason? We must tread carefully here, this isn't some local dispute." William said firmly. Robert nodded thoughtfully and both men watched as the pair of riders disappeared into the complex of the hall.

The small group of men were surprised when such a short time later Sibyl was leaving the hall on her own horse again, riding like the wind without a hint of a problem in her mount, trailed by the heavier black and the familiar man. William was completely confused by this turn of events, but it was clear Sibyl was going somewhere in a hurry and there had to be a reason for that.

"Robert send someone you think suitable after her, make sure he stays hidden and reports back to us if he learns anything - we shall introduce ourselves at Waddington and see if we can't learn anything ourselves." William ordered Robert. Robert turned and thought for a moment as he looked at the group of faces hanging on his words.

"You, Simon, trail the maid secretly; report back to Waddington if you discover anything." He pointed to a tall, redheaded lad who nodded obediently and vaulted into his saddle with a creak of leather, before cantering off into the trees.

The rest of the group led their horses around the back of the hall and tied them up in the trees lest any other eyes were watching and Lord William sneaked into the stables where he found Gilbert and asked to be taken to Richard Tempest.

William strode into the room after being introduced by the old man to find the entire Tempest family, King Henry himself and his man John Tunstall all sat together. The atmosphere seemed tense. He smiled at all and knelt to the King who merely smiled beautifully back at him.

"William! Surprised I am to see you!" Richard Tempest leapt up from his chair and heartily shook William's hand, clapping him on the shoulder. "Gilbert, fetch us some food fit for our guest!"

William thought that was odd terminology to use - implying that what they usually ate here at Waddington would not have been suitable for guests in some way. William was shocked at how things had deteriorated here, he hadn't been to visit in person for months. It was clear that the cost of maintaining a King in secret, alone, was dragging Tempest down.

"What news William, are things...moving?" Richard Tempest asked with a note of desperation.

"Well Richard, I am not sure myself. There have been some happenings and I have reason to suspect that Harrington may be making a move."

Tempest's wife and older daughter gasped and Tempest himself looked stricken.

"We should fly!" He cried. William hurried to calm him.

"There are few places to go - fear not Richard, nothing is certain yet, I have a spy abroad right now who will report back to us if we are in any immediate danger."

William used the terms 'us' and 'we', though he had every intention of extricating himself as quickly as possible if things seemed to be going wrong. King Henry had said nothing, as was usual. A leader like that was hard to lay down one's life for; he merely offered William somewhere other than Edward's court to lay his hat.

"May I speak to you alone William?" Richard asked, already steering William from the room.

"Of course!" William replied, allowing himself to be gently pushed into another small, dark chamber.

"William, I had a visitor earlier," Richard wasted no time, "it was Sibyl Bearnshaw - is she not your betrothed?" William stiffened, unsure of how to respond but luckily Richard didn't give him time but continued his worried chattering. "She saw my man, Gilbert, who is extremely trustworthy. Gilbert says he thinks she knew we have Henry! She did also say however that Edward would merciful, even rewarding, if we handed him in-"

"Richard you can't trust her." William cut him off.

"What?" Richard looked genuinely confused.

"She is an untrustworthy creature, Richard."

"Isn't she...your future wife?" Richard queried.

"Probably not, no. The new King married her off to Viscount Waberthwaite. He died at Hexham - crushed by his horse - but she is firmly in the pocket of the King and he won't marry her to me...not that I now want to be responsible for such a wild woman. Rest assured, she works on behalf of Edward and is not on our side." William said grimly. Richard visibly slumped.

"I'm done, William. My coffers are empty. Perhaps if I had my brother's backing, the entire Tempest wealth at my disposal, I could continue to maintain the King indefinitely, but not as things stand. You have to help me - his horses and men, small in number though they are, eat an astonishing amount! I am constantly having to pay for clothing, pay wages, pay for straw and corn, and divert hay from my own herds and stables for his. He has nothing." Richard wrung his hands. "This will be the ruin of my family!"

"Relax, friend." William placed a hand on Richard's shoulder. "You have me behind you: I only brought a handful of men today because it might have attracted attention, but there are plenty more back at Hapton and my swift riders could have them here in a trice. What of the others?" He spoke of their allies.

"They have been remarkably quiet of late..." Richard shook his head woefully.

"We will deal with this." William assured him.

"Have you got any gold for me William, or spare crops perhaps? To ease the burden?" Richard asked plaintively. William froze and his open mouth wavered for a moment. Just then, Gilbert popped his head around the door.

"Food, sirs." He said simply.

"Let us eat. Everything is better on a full stomach, brother!" William beamed and led Richard back into the main room.

All seating in the room was taken so William took his plate over to the window seat and watched with morbid curiosity as the man Tunstall silently helped Henry eat.

Although Henry was looking around and smiling, he was incapable of looking after himself. It was very curious, but Tunstall had to poke titbits of food into Henry's mouth with his knife. Once the food was in, Henry happily chewed; he just couldn't seem to make the decision to feed himself. Everyone was aware of the uncomfortable, bizarre situation and all ate in silence, unable to speak directly for fear of breaching the thin veneer of propriety around the King.

Suddenly a noise was heard outside. All in the room but Henry stopped their eating. William turned to look out of the window and Richard and Tunstall leapt to join him. Their worst fears were realised as they saw the scene of a small army approaching the hall at speed. All three men cursed fiercely despite the presence of women and children.

"That's Harrington's livery!" Richard shrieked. "What happened to your spy?"

"...They must have been ahead of him!" William replied.

"We must fly, we must fly!" Richard was clearly panicking, his wife fled from the room.

"They've stopped." Tunstall growled. The three men peered back down to the yard between the two gables of the hall, where men filled the area and backed up right down the path.

"Looks like Talbot livery too." William winced, sweating. He saw James Harrington and the two Talbots and John Tempest break from the main group and run into the building.

"They're already on their way in!" Tunstall jumped to Henry's side and began dragging him to his feet, caught between urgency and the instinct not to manhandle the King. Henry, still smiling, complied but slowly. William saw that Tunstall and now Tempest were shoving the King towards a small door at the back of the room. William saw his chance and opened the door, running in first himself and then making a show of 'leading the way' for Henry, tugging on his sleeve as he was pushed through the doorway.

Henry seemed scared however which delayed them long enough to hear the main door to the room swing open.

William heard Harrington's voice in the room.

"Everybody stay where they are!" He bellowed. For a moment, everyone complied like rabbits in the grass, knowing the dog is upon them. John Tempest stepped forward and took Richard by the shoulders.

"Brother, I know who that truly is and this is your last chance - hand him over and come to us, we will be rewarded! It is the best thing for the Tempests now." He urged him.

Before Richard had a chance to reply, William saw Tunstall spring from his place at the King's side with a roar and his sword drawn. Luckily for John, he fumbled and his sword smacked down with the flat on John's arm, raised in defence. Nevertheless it was sickening blow and John screamed and fell back, as Harrington and the Talbots lunged forwards in retalliation.

Tunstall shoved Henry firmly through the door where he fell into William, who steadied him. Tunstall was by now slamming the door shut and bolting it, then desperately putting an arm around Henry and dragging him down the tight, spiral staircase. William said nothing but ran ahead, the sound of hammering on the door receding as they descended.

They emerged at the rear of the hall behind a strategically placed bush. William had drawn his sword but was relieved to see that the hall was not surrounded. He could see the way clear to where Robert would be waiting with his men and horses but was undecided as to what to do with Henry and Tunstall. If he took them with him two of their party would be on foot. They would be doomed.

Tunstall, his arms still around the old King, and William looked at each other for a moment, breathing heavily. Tunstall sensed what William's plan was and that he had no intention of taking them with him. A practical man, he realised he had no time to lose, spat at William's feet and pulled the King off to the right, heading for the river.

"We'll defend you!" William cried after him apologetically, hating the shame of Tunstall's dismissal.

Tunstall paid no heed, merely ran with Henry into the

trees. William pelted as fast as he could to where Robert was waiting. Breathlessly he mounted and Robert did not need to be told that things had taken a turn so he and the men followed suit.

"King Henry...we must protect him!" William said and wheeled his horse around to gallop after Tunstall. Robert drew alongside.

"Robert if it looks at all bad, cut and run - we save ourselves first!" William ordered.

"Aye sir." Robert agreed.

Once in the trees to his astonishment William saw that Tunstall had already been prepared anyway - a pair of ponies were tethered in the trees. William's party ground to a halt, dead leaves scattering from their hooves as Tunstall turned and threw an accusing look at William, helping Henry to scramble onto a horse's back. With no tack Tunstall shoved the tethering rope between his animal's teeth and ran the rope of Henry's under his thigh, thwacking the loose end onto his own's rump, sending both animals into a quick pace through the woods.

Henry clung to his animal's mane, doing fairly well but constantly swaying and at any moment William expected him to tumble off. He mused on the idea that if Henry were to topple and break his neck now, things would get a lot easier for all concerned. They were evidently making for Clitheroe, perhaps Tunstall's plan was to 'disappear' the King amongst the people of the town, William considered. That would also give William the chance to slip away down a side street and get back to Hapton as quickly as possible, scrambling across country in the hope that Harrington couldn't follow.

The Harrington force was already struggling to follow at speed through the trees and they were able to maintain a distance between them all the way down to the Brungerly stepping stones over the river Ribble. Here though they knew that the horses would have to be led, picking their way over the river bed while their riders hopped from stone to stone. It would be a difficult and slow manoeuvre. William's jaw worked as he tried to think of a better plan, or a way to buy time, or something - anything!

Suddenly a bright colour against the verdant green of the hills around Clitheroe ahead caught William's eye. With horror he looked up and saw men wearing a livery he was unfamiliar with. They were clearly a mounted force however, and what else could they possibly be doing hanging about on the path to the river, but waiting for them? He turned in the saddle and looked behind. Harrington's forces were now broaching the tree line above and beginning the plunge over the grassed area between them and the riverbank.

"We're done, Robert!" William shouted, swerving to the right and leading his men on a charge down their side of the riverbank, away from both armed forces and leaving Tunstall to take his chances.

They galloped for as long as they could on tired horses and saw that none had followed. Gratefully they rode to the top of a ridge and sheltered amongst the brush, allowing the horses to rest.

"Oh this is a nightmare!" William railed. "We are stuck out here, no fresh horses and a long ride ahead of us back to the safety of Hapton!" He paced up and down, kicking at tussocks of grass. "I didn't even care about Henry!" He bawled. "We are now going to have to pay for Tunstall and Tempest's bungling!"

"We can do it sir!" Robert had faith.

"No. They will come for us anyway. Harrington, the Talbots, John Tempest, and whoever that was on the other side of the river. Then if we survive all that, Edward's going to be on us, we are confirmed traitors now!" He thundered, and then all went quiet as he thought. "No, we are lost." He concluded. "We shall have to abandon Hapton; we'll go and clean the place out of anything valuable, take our horses and money and ride to Wales. We can stay there until things change." He nodded to himself. Then a thought occurred to him.

"Robert." He placed a hand on Robert's shoulder, his

friend's long dark hair curled and damp with sweat, his blue eyes looking up at him expectantly from the grimy face.

"Sir?" Robert's head tipped to one side curiously.

"I want the Bearnshaws to pay for this. Sibyl was at Waddington...she knew. She and that whelp schemed this all upon us. What is the most important thing to Sibyl, Robert?" William asked, his face sinisterly happy despite his life being in grave danger.

"I...don't know?" Robert shook his head. He barely knew the girl and didn't really understand William's obsession with her. She was pretty, but there were plenty of pretty girls out there and pretty wasn't everything. A horse could be the most elegant creature, but useless if it reared every time a saddle was placed on its back.

"She and Thomas are the last Bearnshaws. All her hopes rest on that brother. Get rid of him. Teach her lesson about meddling in the affairs of men through a puppet boy-Lord." William sneered, Robert taken aback at the feeling in his words. "You are a clever man Robert, I trust you to deal with things in an appropriate manner, and upon your success, come find me in Wales and I will find you a good bride and buy you a new horse."

"Aye sir!" Robert nodded fervently at the promise of such great promotion and mounted his horse. "I will take care of things - make sure she's a blonde!" He said with a grin, and disappeared over the nearest rise in the ground.

~

Sybil had followed Harrington's forces, out of sight and earshot but finding the trail of hundreds of men and horses easy to follow. When she arrived at Waddington she ducked into the undergrowth, seeing that the force was parked in the yard. Luckily her father's horse was long past his excitable days and was happy to stand and rest a leg while she waited. As she had watched she saw clearly how something disturbed the men and they began to swarm around the back of the building.

Then she heard the crashing, snapping and thundering as they gave chase into the woods. Heart pounding she hurriedly picked up the reins and streaked across the open ground around Waddington, paying no heed to the thought of arrows. Once in the woods she slowed and urged her father's horse to trot steadily along the trail of destruction. Suddenly the trees broke and the ground sloped away below her down to the riverbank. She urgently scanned what was happening down there and saw that there was no fighting. All seemed calm, the chase must have finished.

She was unsure whether to go down herself given Harrington's frosty reception of her earlier; she did need to get across the river in order to lodge in Clitheroe on her way home however and she raised her eyes to scan the surrounding area for inspiration. Then she openly gaped as with a jolt, she saw another force making its way down to the river. Although they were a long way off, she recognised the colours as Waberthwaite's and one of the banners was simple enough to see from a distance - a clear sunne, flapping in the breeze; the badge of Edward.

Uncertainty gone, she kicked her hefty chestnut into a lumbering canter and rolled precariously down the slope, grateful to reach the flatter ground and stop the feeling of uncontrolled tumbling when going downhill at speed on the old animal. The men below formed up defensively but fell back when they saw it was a lone female rider. Sibyl cantered easily through their ranks to the stepping stones, where she found the leaders surrounding Tunstall.

She recognised Henry who was peculiarly smiling despite having just been captured. He was clearly bound to the saddle by the stirrups however and his man who Sibyl did not recognise was bound in the dirt at their feet. Harrington looked up with shock.

"Sibyl?!" He said with disbelief.

"Yes James." She replied haughtily, not stopping to talk as she walked to the river's edge. There she swung down from the saddle, gathered up her skirts and picked her way over the stones, her horse following slowly but without hesitation, his thick ginger legs cleaving through the flow of the water.

"Do you know them?" A Talbot had called after her, but she ignored him too.

Once on the other side she saw that a lone rider had broken from the group and was cantering towards her - it was Edmund and she was overjoyed to be back amongst friendly company.

"Edmund!" She cried with delight, waiting for him on the riverbank.

"Lady Sibyl!" He said, beaming as he jumped from his horse and bowed before her. She hoped Harrington was watching. "What on earth is going on here?"

"I'm not quite sure myself, but I do know that Henry is captured!" Sibyl said excitedly. Edmund gawped.

"Well done!" He shook his head in awe. "Edward will be well pleased with you."

"James Harrington, the Talbots and a Tempest have provided the might really." Sibyl conceded. "But you must make sure the King knows which side we were on!" Sibyl urged, taking hold of Edmund's forearm pleadingly. Edmund placed his hand on her's firmly.

"I'll be sure to tell him." Edmund nodded.

"Is he here with you?" Sibyl asked eagerly. Edmund laughed.

"No! I haven't foggiest where he is right now; I've been busy in the North for months and tramping after you for days!" He said with a tone of mock reproachment.

"You mean he's not behind this?"

"...No, I came because of your letter in January. I'm sorry I didn't respond earlier but it took a long time for the message to find me and I couldn't justify leaving any earlier without knowing what the issue was...I'm sorry about that Sibyl, I must confess I knew it was important to you but had no idea of the magnitude-"

"No matter now, it's just wonderful to have you here on

my side.   Harrington is a little frosty."   She cut off his apologetic talk.

"Is he indeed?"   Edmund looked amused and took Sibyl by the hand to help her back across the river to meet the men assembled on the other side, his armour glinting in the sun.

~

Tom had followed Harrington's forces until they turned off to Waddington, where he had carried on to Clitheroe and crossed the Brungerly stepping stones shortly before Tunstall, William and Henry had attempted.   Here he was perplexed to encounter Edmund's small army.   He wasn't familiar with the Waberthwaite livery or badges and recognised only the sunne of the King.   His heart leapt at such good fortune, but he knew he had to tread carefully, desperately not wanting to let Sibyl down.

The men were interested in his approach as Tom was obviously a highborn man judging by his clothes, but none had seen him before.   They took him to Edmund, where Tom asked if they were moving on behalf of the King.

"Well, we are Yorkists but no, not currently under orders from him.   I'm responding to a request I can't really talk about freely."   Edmund replied.   "And yourself?"

"I have a message for the King, but again, am not at liberty to divulge to anyone else.   Know you where I may find him?"

"It's possible he is at London currently."

London!   Tom thought, swallowing hard despite himself. He had wanted to visit London for a long time.

"Can I help you further?"   Edmund said patiently as Tom hadn't spoken for a moment or two.

"Er, no, that's very helpful, thank you.   I must really get this message to the King.   Thanks again."   Tom hurriedly bowed and was allowed on his way, Edmund greatly intrigued at what all that could possibly be about.

Tom stopped with his man Adam once they were safely

out of view of Edmund's men.

"Adam I thought we'd be going to York or somewhere, but it appears we have to go to London after all...do you know how far it is?" Tom tried to appear confident but his inexperience showed. Adam was twenty-four however and had travelled a little more in his time.

"It's about two hundred miles from here Tom, I'd probably recommend going via Salford, Derby and Northampton." Adam understood he would have to guide Tom completely. Tom had paid attention to maps in the past though and vaguely knew the route.

"Well, I think we should probably press on to Accryngton for today, it feels wrong to stop so soon in Clitheroe." Tom said at last. Adam agreed and the pair rode in to Clitheroe.

~

That night Robert was in Clitheroe having shed his livery. He was now in anonymous clothing and essentially, a free man. It was exhilarating for him to have this task, as he had been languishing around Hapton taking William's orders for so long. Now he was making his own decisions and free to partake of the local ales and women, eat what he wanted where he wanted, set his own pace and answer to nobody - his master would be in Wales.

Now he was in the busiest Inn in town, hoping to pick up any gossip on the whereabouts of Lord Bearnshaw. He knew the town would be abuzz with talk of the day's happenings, and he knew that the incoming force was staying here. He had immediately learnt that Henry himself was being held in the castle high up on the hill overnight and that he would be transported South the next day.

He was undecided as to whether to ask around for Lord Bearnshaw's whereabouts. On the one hand he may progress quicker by asking outright, but on the other it would draw attention to himself and what he was doing. He came to the conclusion it was better to wait and listen, so he sat in the shadows and kept himself to himself while those around chatted and ate and drank, sang and danced, and he listened to every conversation he could.

Late into the night, a man stumbled into the inn evidently well into his cups. Things had quietened down now with the advance of the night and everyone starting to consider turning in for the night. The man who stumbled in obviously recognised a friend and they sat down for a last drink before bed.

"What a day!" The first exclaimed as he supped his ale.

"Yeah!" His mate agreed. "One minute we're on our way to someplace no one's ever 'eard of called Bearnshaw or somesuch, the next we're escortin' the old King down to London!" He shook his head in disbelief. Robert's ears pricked up at hearing the word Bearnshaw, but he let nothing show.

"It was good you turned up, we'd all got ready to march on Waddington but they got away into the woods." The first replied.

"Yeah I know..." Said the second, having heard the story many times already today. His friend ploughed on regardless.

"Apparently you lot showing up made 'em think the King was 'ere, and they gave him up without a fight!" He chuckled.

"Yeah." The friend replied.

"Our Lord Tempest got a nasty wound though; fella of Henry's broke his arm. Nasty business." The man pulled a disapproving face. "But you ain't even here for the King after all?!" He brightened again, reliving the coincidences of the day once more.

"Yeah that's right, Sibyl Bearnshaw called us. We didn't know what for so didn't respond that early, but she musta known Henry was here all along!" He took another swig. "Hey, do you want to know something really strange though?" He said conspiratorially.

"Yeah?" His friend leaned in close to hear and Robert strained to catch the words.

"We met that Lady Bearnshaw's brother today, only, we

didn't know it was him. Edmund stopped him and asked what he was doing but he said he had a message for the King and couldn't say what. Ed didn't know he was Lord Bearnshaw and of course the lad didn't know Ed at all so he let him pass, it was only when Sibyl turned up later that it all came out!" He whispered, but poorly, so that Robert heard almost every word.

"These are strange days alright friend!" His pal concluded. "Even the nobles don't seem to know what's going on."

~

Tom had reached Accryngton in good time, Sibyl's grey was a fast ambler and the ride was smooth and steady. He and Adam had rested and eaten and agreed to press on as fast as they could while they were still fresh, aiming to cross the Irwell at Salford and next take a rest when they were across. For now they were travelling through the oak Forest of Blackburnshire, their horses dodging the foot travellers and pack trains heading back and forth from Salford.

Behind them Robert had wasted no time. He knew the most direct and likely route to London and took a gamble that Tom had taken it. Having established that Tom was with only one man, Robert began to ask along the way if any had seen his young master, a thirteen year old lad in fine clothes; they had become separated on their journey and he was eager to be reunited with him so as not to leave his young Lord unprotected. Most were only too happy to help and yes, they had seen him, riding a little grey ladies' horse.

Soon he was being told he was not far behind and as evening fell he finally caught sight of the little figure on the grey, riding beside a taller figure on a taller horse. Robert suddenly felt quite guilty about what he was planning. This 'Lord' was just a mere boy really. Technically a man, but no match for Robert. Robert had also gotten to know Tom well during his stay at Hapton and knew that he was a good natured, harmless boy. Any trouble caused had really come through the woman and she should be the one to pay.

He wondered if there was a way to satisfy William and keep the boy alive but came to the conclusion there was not. While the boy lived he would gravitate back to Bearnshaw, right next door to Hapton, and it could not be denied that here he was carrying messages for the King, starting his career of court politics no doubt fuelled by and emulating his troublesome sister. Give him a few more years and this cub would grow into a dog fox like the rest and the hens would all be dead.

Tom heard a throat-clearing male cough behind him and he and Adam swivelled in their saddles to look behind.

"I have a message for you, Thomas Bearnshaw." Robert called out. Adam and Tom reined in and turned to face him. Robert continued walking towards them.

"Robert?" Tom squinted in the twilight under the oak trees. Adam remained stonily silent - wasn't this man from the Hapton camp they had just discovered sheltering the old King? His hand moved to his sword, but Robert was still smiling and advancing to them as if they were old friends.

"Yes, me, Robert." He said as he came towards them, ignoring Adam completely.

"Can I, help you?" Tom said after waiting for Robert to get his breath back.

"I have a message for you." Robert repeated. "From Lord William." He finished and in a deft, well-practised movement, jerked his arm which freed a small knife to slip down his sleeve and into his hand, which he then flicked into Adam's neck before Adam could draw his sword.

Tom looked on in horror, not quite understanding what had happened as Adam clutched his neck, toppling backwards from his horse which reared and danced away, leaving Adam to thud sickeningly onto the packed earth of the road. Tom shuddered and felt a wave of nausea pass over him, he blindly kicked his sister's horse in the ribs and with a grunt the grey rushed away from Adam's twitching form, only too glad to escape the smell of blood.

He ran on to Irwell, knowing that his only hope would be to reach it and gain safety amongst witnesses, hoping there were plenty of people still trying to cross the river at this hour. He became aware however that his horse was tired - it had been used near constantly since Sibyl had left Bearnshaw a couple of days ago and soon it dropped the pace.

"No, no no!" Tom cried, ruthlessly spurring the animal. It complied with a short burst of speed but soon struggled to maintain it and slowed again. This time when Tom dug in his spur the animal stopped with a breathy scream of pain and reared. Tom sprang clear, knowing it was about to wheel right over and sure enough moments later it lay in a heap. Tom did not stay to watch; he took off into the trees, not knowing his way but hoping to find a hiding place of some kind.

Robert was an experienced hunter though; he knew how to track and had keen hearing. When Tom went quiet as he went to ground, Robert simply took out a lantern from his saddlebags. Peering at the ground he could see the disturbed rocks and leaves from Tom's scrambling rush and followed the trail to a thick thorny bush.

Tom had forced himself inside the enormous thicket, ignoring the stinging scratches of the thorns tearing at his clothes and biting into his skin. He held his breath as Robert's light drew closer and soon he could see him walking right up to the bush and holding up his sword to stab into it. Tom jumped up, ripping himself free of the bush, knocking Robert's sword to one side with his own as he dived clear.

"Robert! I thought we were friends!" He gasped.

"So did I, Tom. So did William. Then we find out that you and your lying sister have reported us? You can't do these things without consequences, lad." Robert replied.

"Fine, if that's how you feel, so be it. Maybe you're right? Face me like a man though, come down off your horse and let's go!" Tom held up his sword and challenged Robert.

"Very well!" Robert seemed cheered by this, which made Tom quaver a little more. He knew he couldn't truly best Robert, but if he was going to die he wanted to make sure he died in a way that would make Sibyl and his father proud, not cowering in a bush.

The two faced each other and each waited for the other to make the first move. Eventually Robert pushed the issue with a basic chop from right to left which Tom quickly guarded, Robert's blade scraping harmlessly off his own. Without giving Tom time to react, Robert threw in a few more thrusts and chops which Tom expertly deflected. Robert spat in annoyance.

Tom gained confidence from being able to hold off the older man but Robert was merely testing him, seeing how good he really was. He carried on thrusting and chopping at the same regular speed for some time, then when he saw that Tom had settled into the rhythm he had set, he broke out of it with a blistering sequence of cuts and stabs delivered with all his force. He literally beat Tom back for a few steps, not stopping when he hit flesh but merely going for it again and again.

Tom crumpled under the onslaught, falling first to his knees, then rocking back and being knocked to the side by a final blow. Robert could hear his rattling, gurgling breaths in the darkness, and sensed that Tom would not wield his sword again. He allowed his own breathing to settle, then wiped his blade clean and sheathed it. Then, workmanlike, he patted Tom's body down and found his purse. He pulled off any rings and jerked the necklace from around his throat, to the sound of indignant wheezing, roughly letting him fall back into the leaf litter.

Without another word he left, travelling back to tempt Tom's horse back onto its feet. He calmed it and took off its fine tack, placing it in a sack. He replaced the bridle with his own horse's simple rope halter and led both back to the path, the sack over his shoulder. Adam's horse had gone, so Robert dragged the looted corpse into the woods, mounted up and set off to Irwell. There he sold Sibyl's grey to a horse dealer, saving his having to pay for its river crossing, who promptly sold it as a cart horse in Salford the next day. The saddle and bridle were sold in separate locations along Robert's route to

Wales, financing the journey.

7

The Whyte Doe

1470

Sibyl sat in her personal chamber in a chair in the square of golden light on the floor formed by the unshuttered window in the thick stone walls of Bearnshaw Tower. All was quiet and peaceful; just birdsong outside and the occasional crow of a cockerel in the distance. She sat amongst her clutter - bones, teeth, antlers, feathers, dried and pressed leaves, flowers, mushrooms and berries in an assortment of bunches, bundles and jars.

She had started her documentation project again only this time, with no one to tell her it was silly, she had begun bringing it all back to Bearnshaw itself and filling her chambers with the specimens. It had all been shelved now though as truth be known it wasn't filling the hole inside her. It had seemed pointless if there were to be no future generations of Bearnshaws to admire it. That was set to change however.

She was sewing a decorative flourish onto the dress she was making specifically for her wedding that evening. She was aware these were her last moments of peace before she would have to begin supervising, checking and organising for the evening and then getting herself ready - washing, dressing, plucking and applying make-up.

In the years following Tom's disappearance a gloom had settled over the Bearnshaw lands. After a brief, dazzling spring in which Sibyl and Tom had ridden amongst their people, giving hope of activity, investment and prosperity, the promised summer had been snatched away again by the mysterious disappearance of their bright young Lord. Nobody knew what had become of him or who was now at the helm, officially? Sibyl fulfilled the role of course, but there was a chance Thomas would return so the matter could not be fully closed and the lands remained in a state of limbo.

Sibyl herself had been exhilarated to have played a part in capturing Henry and the admiration it brought her from Edmund. In the excitement she had agreed to accompany Edmund South in the party escorting Henry and she had expected to arrive in London shortly after Tom had. Immediately upon arrival however she had asked for him, but no one had the faintest idea who she was talking about as few had ever seen him and none had been expecting him.

She began to worry at this news of course, but as is natural in these circumstances she convinced herself there was a harmless explanation. She had probably been too hasty to trust him on such a mission alone and he had been held up in an ale house, suffering from the effects of drink too much to move on. Perhaps he had been swayed by a pretty maiden and opted to spend a day or two in bed, she had thought with a flare of irritation if that were the truth.

Days passed and still no word came. Sibyl found it hard to enjoy the jubilant atmosphere of court and prepared to leave, intending to search Tom's likely route for him, or talk of him at least. Before she left she asked Edmund to arrange a meeting with Edward himself, so that she knew the King's eye would be on the lookout for Tom. This time she met with Edward in public, he seated at the top table of a banquet on his magnificent thronelike chair, with Elizabeth Woodville beside him, a hand possessively on his as Sibyl was led forward, kneeling and averting her gaze.

Sibyl remained kneeling, hands in her lap and eyes on the floor until Edward invited her to speak. She could feel the critical eyes of Elizabeth assessing her and was glad she had thoroughly prepared and was presentable; it made her feel able to meet this formidable queen with confidence. Sibyl knew she could never match Elizabeth's golden hair, languid eyes and high hairline but equally she knew she was not a pig in comparison. She also knew they were both of a similar rank, and only a quirk of fate had placed one above the other; Sibyl had been close.

"Widow Waberthwaite!" Edward said warmly. "I understand you have another problem?" Managing to expertly mix concern with a subtle knowing smile she caught as she raised her head. She flicked a quick, wary glance at Elizabeth before replying.

"Yes, my King. My brother, he is missing. I sent him ahead of us to urgently carry the news of Henry's whereabouts to you, as I thought Henry's reinforcements would be a larger force than it was and we would need your help. He has not been seen since." Sibyl heard the words as she said them aloud and suddenly the reality hit her. It was unlikely he would ever be seen again. Tears welled in her eyes which she stifled with a subtle sniff.

"That is terrible, I cannot think of an explanation Sibyl!" Edward said with pity. "I will send out a party of men to hunt for information for you. I hear you are leaving us for Lancashire? I assume you will look for him on your route - my men will scour the alternatives." He gave her a smile which entreated her to cheer up.

Edward hated to see a woman upset, and was genuinely interested in why Sibyl Bearnshaw's brother should have gone missing. It smacked of assassination, but with Henry safely in Harrington's hands at that point what possible benefit would it have been to prevent news of Henry's discovery getting to London? It seemed like something he should take an interest in, so he was happy to send the men. Elizabeth however was quick to interject.

"Husband, can you spare the men? Sibyl can surely organise her own search party?" She said carefully. Edward looked from one woman to the other and the note of jealousy in Elizabeth's voice did not go undetected. Inwardly he was amused, if a little irritated that Elizabeth would let her feelings get the better of her at the expense of Sibyl's feelings when her own brother was very likely freshly dead.

"I know what men I can spare wife, worry you not. Think you not that it is important for me to follow up the disappearance of a man charged with carrying news to me?" Edward asked. Elizabeth said nothing and Sibyl remained silently rooted to the spot, mortified that Edward would admonish Elizabeth in front of her, certain that Elizabeth was not the forgiving type and this would be held against her in future, as though it were her fault. She would have to tread very carefully.

"Sibyl, you and your brother have been good allies to me, I hope you find him." Edward dismissed her with a raised goblet and a nod. Hurriedly she thanked him and backed away.

On her way back to Bearnshaw Sibyl took her time and asked almost everyone she came across for information. Nobody had seen or heard of Thomas Bearnshaw, a well-dressed lad on a small grey and Sibyl's party trudged into the small courtyard outside the squat tower with heavy hearts. They clung to the hope that the King's men would find something on alternative routes but deep down, they knew that the only reason Tom could realistically have for not at least getting in touch himself by now was that he was dead.

Sibyl was numb. She felt she couldn't go forwards under these circumstances. Apparently Tom was dead. Everything she'd worked for was gone. Bearnshaw's future now rested firmly on her shoulders alone. Or did it? Maybe not. There was a chance. She had no choice but to carry on. She would have to be a strong Lady, for the sake of the people that now relied solely on her.

She wasn't lonely as such; she had her maids who ate with her and slept in her chambers for company and Bearnshaw Tower was alive with a host of people who lived within its walls and maintained it, and her. The stables, the kennels, the dovecote and so on. But she found herself hankering for like-minded company; someone to chatter with who was not separated from her by a barrier of rank or manners. Someone who would stay with her for good, build a life with her and not move on, or go to their own family in the evenings.

She had been on the verge of going back to court with the seed of an idea of trying to arrange a second marriage for herself but things had taken a peculiar twist - news came that Edward's own brother George had resurrected the rumour that Edward was the product of his mother's liaison with an archer, and with Warwick's help had tried to overthrow the King, executing Elizabeth Woodville's kin in the process.

All knew that Warwick had been unhappy ever since the Woodville marriage and Edward's terrible behaviour towards the French with whom Warwick had hoped to forge bonds had publically embarrassed him. In the full knowledge that Warwick had spent months negotiating with the French and had been given many lavish gifts, Edward had given the French insultingly poor gifts and declared them his 'ancient enemy' in response.

Warwick had left court in a rage and little had been seen of him since. Anyone who knew him would know however that he was not the type to be undermined so easily. Now he retaliated with this plot and the Duke of Clarence. They had managed to take Edward prisoner, to the astonishment of all, but thankfully had been forced to release him, presumably unwilling to murder a King in cold blood?

Sibyl had no stomach for wading into court in the midst of the Neville-Woodville-Clarence-Edward maelstrom and trying to arrange a marriage for herself; she would merely have been a nuisance and with Elizabeth at the King's side thesedays, how likely was she to succeed? If only Edmund were not already married. He was kind, capable, the right age and all. It was hard to read his letters about the steady stream of children he was producing while she sat in her cluttered chambers alone in her damp tower, taking the occasional walk to Eagle Crag to gaze at the view and break the monotony.

One September evening as summer drew to a close she leant on the thick stone sill of a high window of the tower, looking out at the view and letting the chill breeze play about her cheeks. The wide sky was blushed pink and orange, Todmorden moor ablaze with colour. It occurred to Sibyl at that moment that she'd been greedy and letting her heart rule her head. She did need a husband, but he did not need to be like Edmund. He did not need to be her age - he needed to be wealthy, dependable and to find her physical form enough of a jewel to overlook her modest land and wealth.

There was an obvious candidate. Sir John Towneley was the wealthiest landowner in the locality. He was well-groomed, polite, kind, a Yorkist and in his fifties having just lost his second wife. The thought of approaching a man who had been her father's friend for marriage was a little awkward to say the least, but Sibyl decided that would merely have to be swallowed. The very next day she donned her favourite dove grey outfit and rode to the Towneley's place.

She was shown to the room in which John was pouring over his paperwork. He looked up and his eyebrows shot skywards as he recognised Sibyl. She knelt politely and heard his familiar loud voice boom with a slight chuckle.

"Sibyl! To what do I owe this pleasure?!" And he moved over to her, kissing her hand and showing her a chair which she gratefully took as she was shaking a little with nerves at what she was about to do. She steeled herself as he offered her a drink - she had to remember she was a grown woman now, a responsible widow. She shouldn't feel nervous or intimidated in making business arrangements like this.

"Well, Sir John. I come to you with a request." She began after clearing her throat following a sip of the wine.

"I'm glad you did, I'd be only too happy to help my old friend Bearnshaw's girl!" He said cheerfully, knotting his fingers after stroking his manicured greying beard once. Sibyl gave a tight smile in response and continued.

"It is a large request I'm afraid, but I have to do something to rectify the position I find myself in." She said with a grimace. Sir John nodded sympathetically - he knew all about the loss of Sibyl's parents, husband and brother. It must have been hellish difficult for a young woman to handle things all alone, no wonder she needed his help!

"I'll help if I can." He said gently.

"Well. I....need a husband, Sir John." The words tumbled out of her mouth in a rush once she had committed to them. "And I considered you."

Sir John reeled back in his chair, his left hand involuntarily slapping down on his table, rattling the wine cup. He was stunned into silence for a few moments, his mouth slightly open as he struggled to articulate a response. He was usually so composed and Sibyl would have enjoyed having had the ability to produce this reaction, had she not been so tense about the outcome.

"But....why girl, why me?" He managed at last with a deep frown. "Surely a woman as pretty and accomplished as yourself can easily find a strapping young buck?" Sibyl had begun shaking her head before he had even finished speaking.

"No Sir John no, I am past all that. I have not been at court for a long time, my land and wealth is pitiful. I have very little to offer and you know yourself how tempestuous court is currently, with Edward at war with Warwick of all people! I have no wish to be caught up in it all, I must concentrate on saving my family now." She said with finality.

Sir John was silent for a moment, looking into her eyes with pity, turning it over in his mind. Obviously, any sane gentleman would jump at the chance to have this graceful, slender, smooth, bright young wife on his arm. However, it felt uncomfortable to be contemplating producing the heirs of his own late friend. He wiped his forehead absent mindedly, looked to the floor.

"I...I see." He mumbled.

"John I am not a young girl anymore, I am a responsible woman and I would promise to uphold your good name. In the past I have acted...in an unladylike manner. Getting involved in things I should not perhaps. But I have learnt my lesson, I have been punished; it brought me only loss! Now I intend to be a respectable wife and a good mother." She rested her hands in her lap and waited for him to give her an answer.

"My dear girl! You don't have to try to impress me, of course I know you would be responsible and a respectable wife! That is not my concern. My concern is....well, you must surely know? What passes between man and wife...with my friend's daughter?" He shifted uncomfortably. Sibyl smiled and waved her hand dismissively.

"My father is gone; surely I may decide what I do with whom? I am a practical woman Sir John; I know what needs to be done." She assured him.

He shook his head slightly with disbelief, unsure as to whether this was a positive thing or not. The whole thing sounded like a horse deal or somesuch. He too was a practical man, but not devoid of heart. He worried about the girl. He considered that she must know he already had heirs from his second marriage; even if he died shortly she would inherit little of any consequence, so this must be a genuine plea.

"I suppose, if you are sure, I can commit to looking after you Sibyl." He said, emphasising his reasons for accepting. He looked at her with no smile, only concerned assessment. Sibyl was similarly restrained in her reaction, merely nodding once with a slow blink.

"Thank you, my Lord." She said simply, then added: "May I request one thing...I do vow not to make a habit of asking too much of you though!"

"Of course." Sir John nodded.

"May we have a lavish ceremony? Last time I was married it was small and hurried. This time I want to look magnificent and have lots of witnesses." She was aware it sounded shallow, but it was true - she wanted to look pretty and for everyone to know she was married to a powerful man.

She didn't want gossip about desperation and a rush to get married, she wanted everyone to know that she was a desirable prize for a higher ranking man and a capable businesswoman - a wonderful, well-executed ceremony would prove all this, and if she was going to make this sacrifice, she may as well make sure she got her worth out it.

"Come Pierre, time for you to go to the kennels, you'll only be under my feet if you stay and I have much to do!" She said brightly after sewing the last bead and laying the finished kirtle onto her bed. It was time to begin her preparations for the ceremony that evening, so she called her girls to begin work.

Some hours later Sibyl arrived in the great hall of Bearnshaw in her gown sewn with an acorn and oak leaf design, her long caramel hair once again brushed out, laying sleek down her back. The hum of talk died down and every head turned to look as she entered and she smiled shyly at their approving faces in return. She scanned for her husband-to-be and saw his face and the long swallow he gave at the thought that he was marrying this beautiful creature. He hurried over and reverently bowed to her, kissing her hand. She found it remarkably easy to play this role, Sir John was so gallant.

The hall had been lavishly decorated with greenery and candles, the tapestries had been spruced up to bring out the colours, the stone floor swept and scrubbed, incense was burning and all the guests were in their finery. The priest was ready at the head of the hall now so Sir John took Sibyl's hand in the crook of his arm and turned her to walk the length of the hall as the crowd of their friends and family parted to let them through, clapping as they passed.

"You all know Sir John Towneley and Sibyl very well no doubt and will wish them well." The priest began. "I am here to lend formality to their intended union, and-"

Suddenly he was cut off. With a crash the heavy wooden door met the stone wall behind and all the ironwork rattled. Sibyl heard some of the female guests yelp with shock, and turned like everyone else had to see what had caused the noise. Before her head had even fully turned however she heard the voice and an icy hand began to grip and twist her stomach.

"Stop everything!" Lord William bawled, striding through the shocked guests, out of breath as though he had been riding hard and trailed by a group of men with swords unashamedly drawn. "By order of the King!" He added as he drew close to Sibyl and Sir John.

"William!" Sibyl cried angrily, not believing what she was seeing or hearing.

"Oh I love hearing you speak my name!" He said with a grin.

"What is the meaning of this sir?" Sir John boomed, placing his hand on Sibyl's, which gripped his arm tightly.

William brandished a piece of rolled parchment in front of John's nose. John snatched it away angrily and unrolled it, his eyes almost popping out of his head when he saw Henry VIs mark.

"Edward...is in exile!" William said loudly so that all around could hear, unable to mask the triumph in his voice. Sibyl's hand flew to her mouth and all the guests gasped, equally as shocked. "Yes," he continued, "I have just come from London, where I have been helping my Lord Warwick liberate our rightful King Henry VI! He was most grateful for my support, and gave me a great gift in return. Yes that's right Sibyl, he approved my marriage to you in writing and bade Henry sign it..." He waited for Sibyl's response. Sibyl stayed perfectly still for a second, thinking like lightning. Then she turned to Sir John.

"Speak the words John, quickly, then we will be married and it will be too late! Speak!" She urged him, "Do you consent to being my husband?!" She was almost shrieking now, the tears beginning already and choking off her words. Sir John looked down at her, stricken, and opened his mouth.

"Speak Sir John and it will be treason." William said hurriedly. Sir John merely shook his head, dumbfounded. "Everybody out!" William cried. "Yorkists, go home and hope that good King Harry is merciful to you!"

His men began herding the guests out like cattle, the noise of the shocked crowd receding into the night as they left, Sibyl unable to look up to see if they were looking back at her or just hurrying away more concerned with the news of Edward's exile than who she was getting married to.

"William this is madness!" Sir John shouted angrily.

"It is the King's word, you can see that yourself. I'm taking her to London tomorrow where we shall be married before the King and all the nobles...so there will be no disputing the validity." William said with satisfaction. "I think you should leave me and my betrothed alone now Towneley." He gestured to the door.

"No!" Sibyl cried. "Please, please Sir John, don't leave me alone with him!" She was sobbing openly now and found herself clinging to his arm. "Stay tonight, please!" She begged. Sir John looked down at her with pity and worry in his eyes, and then pulled her into his arms. She gratefully hugged him tightly and he spoke to William.

"How can you do this?" He growled to William, then reassured Sibyl. "Hush dear, I will stay."

"I really think you should leave..." William began, motioning to his men who began to advance menacingly on them, respectfully giving time for Sir John to make good his escape as they expected him to do. Sir John was brave and battle hardened however and did not move a muscle, but instead stared them down.

"You would harm an unarmed man?" He asked them with incredulity. "There is nothing in your master's paperwork about my being barred from Bearnshaw Tower. I swore to look after Sibyl, and I intend to honour that!" They looked to Lord William for guidance. He nodded for them to step down and they sheathed their swords. "Sibyl, go to your chamber. I will sit here all night." Sir John touched her cheek and sent her out of the room.

Sibyl stumbled past the armed men and made her way along in the darkness by herself - everyone must have fled. In her chamber where they had intended to come after the wedding a small fire was still burning and she absent mindedly threw some logs on it to get it going again. She was deathly cold and shivering violently. She got into bed, drew the covers up to her chin and sniffed and sobbed and choked as she had done after her first John's death. How had this happened? How had Edward - so powerful, charismatic, clever and sure been bested by that treacherous goat Warwick? Why had God deserted her? She had avoided that assumption so far - blamed luck - but this was so cruel and bizarre, it could not be pure coincidence.

She became searingly angry with whatever stupid animal John had been riding in Hexham. How could her brave and quick witted husband have met his end in such a stupid manner? If he had only been a few feet to either side, things would be fine now. She screwed her eyes shut, at a loss as to what to do. She could not now think of a way out of this - the King's orders were clear, and she had no one left to fight her corner. It seemed there was no hope.

No hope.

A memory fluttered through her brain, floating through the burning black chaos like a chink of white light that attracted her eye, distracted her and calmed her. Once everything else had melted away and it had her full focus it changed from bright white to blood red and gradually formed into the little silk pouch that Mother Helston had given her years ago and she had completely forgotten about.

It hung there for a moment in her mind's eye. Then the physical thing began calling her and, grateful for something proactive to do, she threw the bedcovers clear and began rooting through her cluttered specimens, heedlessly throwing rejected items left and right, opening and closing cupboard doors with urgency. Eventually she uncovered a splash of red, and there it was in her hand, glowing slightly in the light from the fire. She clenched her fist around it, lit a candle to light her way and ran to the kitchens.

There the kitchen workers jumped to attention as she came in. She vaguely thought she'd heard them talking about Edward's exile, but that was of no matter now. All the food for her wedding was laden on every surface, the heat from the fires used to cook such a feast was still lingering.

"Some boiling water, now!" She snapped, and the shocked staff leapt into action, scooping some out of a pot hung over a fire and hurriedly thrusting the cup into her hands, fear in their eyes at the fierceness they saw in Sibyl. Sibyl snatched it and left without another word - manners mattered naught to her now. She hurried back through the quiet chambers to her own room and placed the candle, cup and pouch on the small table by her bed and sat down.

After a moment's hesitation, she carefully undid the thin golden cord and let the square of silk fall open, revealing the little pile of grey-brown powder, unchanged after all these years. It didn't look very appetising at all but she carefully tipped it into the cup regardless and stirred it with her finger, ignoring the pain of the hot water. She took a tentative sniff as the cup brewed; it smelt earthy but perfectly inoffensive.

The next step was taking a sip and it tasted like a cup of brewed soil. She smacked her lips for more flavours but none came. She was surprised; she had expected it to be sweet, interesting and comforting. Had the old woman just given her a pile of dust as a joke of some kind? She concluded the power must be in the effects, so downed the whole thing in a few big, unpleasant gulps, swallowing away the gritty residue.

She lay back on the bed and folded her hands over her stomach, looking at the ceiling and waiting to feel better, marvelling at how Mother Helston's package had taken her mind off William already. At first nothing felt different, but after some time in which she couldn't really remember if she had been dozing or not she realised she did feel different. She no longer felt any anxiety, she felt reassured in some way, like she now had the ability to deal with her problems.

She sat up on the bed and gazed around, seeing how her

very eyesight had changed - she seemed to be able to see more at once, almost all the way around her was in her vision at any one time, and the fire's crackling had become louder and more defined. Then she noticed that the smells of her room had become more vivid - she could smell the dust on the floor, and all the smells of the twigs and feathers she had collected in a cacophony flooding up her nostrils.

She stood up and felt amazed at her body. Her mind did not question how, but she felt instinctively stronger, faster and more agile. She tested the theory with a bound from the bed and felt herself soar for a few seconds before landing softly a few feet away. Pleased with herself, she tried the reverse; leaping back onto the bed in a neat arc. She stopped and grinned to herself - this was wonderful! She had been given powers; she was so much more aware and physically able.

Suddenly this state felt familiar. It was one she hadn't experienced since she was a child and of course it was slightly different then. Her mind raced back to her fawn dreams, of lying in the waving summer grass, and being discovered by a young William out hunting. Now things slotted into place and she knew what to do. She had to run, she had to break out of this captivity and escape to the wild. In her new adult form she could run and escape. Run and escape.

She had started moving about the room on her long white legs, seeking a way out. She could no longer remember where the doors were or how to operate them so she blindly scrambled around the edges, sniffing high and low for anything that might indicate an escape route, jumping onto tables and pawing things down from shelves, going round and round the room this way, merely jumping straight over the bed when she encountered it, rucking up the covers.

Downstairs in the great hall William and Sir John were arguing furiously. Sir John attempting to remain civil as he sensed William was never far from violence. He had not known the full details of William's betrothal and listened to his tirade about how Edward had robbed him of his bride, his heirs and his happiness in life. It occurred to him that William never mentioned Sibyl's desires once in all this.

"She is clearly dead against it William, have you ever considered the girl's feelings?" He asked, appealing to William's conscience. William scoffed.

"Have *you?*" He snorted. "Or were you too eager to get her into your bed?"

"Sir!" Sir John cried. "Think you that that is what all this is about? I have had two wives, have a grown heir and a comely mistress in Burnley - this plan does not come from me, Sibyl requested it!" He said forcefully.

"I cannot believe that! What does Sibyl have to gain from marriage to you? If you die, she would get virtually nothing, so what advantage could marrying an old man hold for her?" He sneered.

"Protection." Sir John said simply. "And I did not understand before why she needed it so." He added with intense disapproval. William shrugged it off.

"I was appalled when I found out your plan John. Sibyl will be better off with me, my principle wife - not in the shadow of two others and their offspring." William shook his head as he took a swig of beer, pacing back and forth as he spoke. Sir John seated himself.

"Sibyl made her choice William, she chose that." He said quietly, seeing that William was not going to be reasonable on the matter. He was a crazed man. John pitied Sibyl and wished more than ever there was something he could do, but he could not commit treason for her - he would always place his family, lands and name first.

Then they heard the thuds and crashings coming from upstairs through the heavy wooden ceiling.

"What the devil?" Sir John muttered, looking up with confusion.

"Is that Sibyl?" William asked. The two men looked at each other for a second and heard more banging. With mutual agreement they abandoned their argument and ran from the room, a handful of William's men following with interest.

William led the way, bounding up the stairs in easy leaps.

He arrived at Sibyl's door and wasted no time in throwing it open. He stood in shock for a moment at what he saw inside. There was Sibyl, silently pawing and scrabbling her way around the room which looked as though it had been looted by an invading force! He looked on with bewilderment at the floor littered with all manner of strange items - twigs, bundles of leaves and skulls, papers and pots and jars. The firewood had been scattered, bedclothes were strewn across the room and a candle had been tipped over, the flames beginning to lick up the side of the bed as he watched.

"What have you done, William?!" Sir John bawled.

William could not articulate an answer, but immediately entered the room and grabbed the nearest blanket, smothering the flames. Then he looked across to Sibyl, aghast as he saw her face, eerily unresponsive to him in the light of the fire in the grate. She stood stock still, staring at him with eyes wide and alarmed, her chest heaved. For a second they looked at each other and then Sir John was entering the room, moving towards her.

"Sibyl? Sibyl dear are you all right?" He asked tenderly, fear in his voice.

This broke the spell, but Sibyl did not respond to him: she had spotted the open door and bolted for it, moving with long bounding strides on tiptoe. Just past the door she encountered William's men who realised she was trying to escape and threw down their swords, all trying to grab her as she passed. In a state of panic Sibyl scrabbled her way through them, kicking and leaping, boxing at their faces with her fists and finally pulling free of the group and fleeing down the passageway.

She did not stop for anything and flew through the main door of the tower, which was ajar as more of William's men hung around waiting for further orders. The ones clustered around the door watched with amazement as Lady Sibyl streaked past, the skirts of her special wedding gown and her hair flying behind her out into the darkness. After a moment some had the sense to realise they should chase their master's fleeing bride and started after her, the rest following when

William himself burst through the door yelling,
"Get her!"

As soon as Sibyl's feet touched grass she felt at ease. She still ran, but the running came easily to her and she knew for certain the men could not keep up with her. She knew where to aim for - Eagle Crag. Here she could lose them, using her agility to bound down the steep valley side and hide among the rocks. If they did manage to follow, she could use her speed to leap back up the valley side and streak across the moors at the top, leaving them far behind, blundering up the slope after her.

It was a dark and cold October night, but Sibyl felt perfectly warm and her new eyes picked up every scrap of light so that she could easily find her way among the naked trees. As she neared Eagle Crag she could hear that no men were following and with great satisfaction she slowed and picked her way to the crag itself, smiling as she looked at the familiar jutting rocks which famously looked like a giant eagle about to launch itself from the hilltops.

Revelling in her new abilities, Sibyl raced along the ridge at the top of the valley, the moonlight making her pale grey gown almost glow as it fluttered in her wake. She bounded from rock to rock when she hit the area around the crag, climbing higher and higher until she reached the rock eagle itself where she tiptoed up to stand on its very shoulders. Below she had a magnificent moonlit view of the surrounding landscape, jagged and quiet. Immediately below was the darkness of the tight, shadowy valley. It was steep, but not a sheer drop and Sibyl knew she could make it.

A sound reached her ears, echoing sharply in her mind as she sniffed the wind. Turning to her right from the direction she had come she could clearly hear the hoofbeats and rasping breaths of a horse, labouring along the valley side with a heavy rider spurring it on. She then saw the torches burning through the trees and heard a sound which chilled her soul - the bark of a dog.

Suddenly her confidence turned into fear. Dogs were another matter. Horses, weighed down by riders, she could best, but dogs were as fleet as she, with scenting powers as keen and tireless endurance. She could almost feel their ripping teeth at her throat and she panted and tensed as they broke from the trees beside her.

William looked ahead at where the dogs were headed and immediately saw Eagle Crag silhouetted against the moonlit sky. Its shape was obviously altered, the pale ghostly form of a slender woman stood on its shoulders. Instantly he recognised what was about to happen and tried in vain to call the dogs back, screaming until his throat burned. His scream turned to a howl of horror as he saw Sibyl look his way and tense to spring.

The pale form elegantly disappeared into the shadows under the rocks and William heedlessly drove his horse headlong towards the crag, not particularly caring for his own safety at this point, wondering how his plan had gone so terribly wrong. He knew Sibyl was a passionate woman, but had no idea she would self-destruct in the face of marriage to him!

Sibyl felt herself falling and prepared to land. At the point of impact however she felt things go wrong. Instead of landing easily and springing off into another leap, she crashed clumsily into the ground and found herself assaulted by sharp pains. She knew she was hurt, but the bigger concern was removing herself from those hunters so she jumped up and carried on. Her running was now impeded and each step shot through her body in a flash of pain. Her progress was too slow and now she felt the hot breath of the dogs on her back as she tumbled down the valley side.

Suddenly one of her limbs was yanked back, sharply crushed in the jaws of a great black hound. Sibyl's progress was halted completely and she knew this was it, she was caught after all. She went limp and submissive, falling and not heeding the bash of her hip against the hard ground, aware only of the excited barks of the dogs all merging into one pounding, echoing bray all around her. She panted through gritted teeth faster and faster, her heart feeling like it would fail at any moment from the exertion, and then all faded to black.

William was stunned into silence as he urgently jumped off his horse and began to clamber as fast as he could down the hillside towards the grey bundle ahead. He knew the dogs were not harming Sibyl; they were her own hunting hounds and would never harm a human. They had merely been excited and, as he knew they would, followed their mistress. As he drew nearer he saw that she was very still and the excited hounds had calmed themselves and were lying all around her, some licking her with hopefully wagging tails.

They looked guilty and cowered as William arrived, looming over them, now unable to contain his shock, guilt and distress anymore, gasping and coughing as he cuffed them out of the way and laid his hands on Sibyl's cool body, looking her up and down, at a loss as to what to do.

"Sibyl! Sibyl what have you done?!" He wailed at her unresponsive, slack face.

Her graceful, pale legs were exposed as her skirt had ridden up, clearly showing horrendous bruises beginning to form and William saw how a clutching dead branch had snagged on her arm and dress, drawing blood. He sat in silence, watching the wound slowly seeping blood into the fabric of her gown. Then he realised that flowing blood meant life and quickly began gathering her up into his arms.

Once he had staggered to his feet he hugged her head into his chest and kissed the damp hair. He staggered back up to where his horse had waited, eagerly cropping the grass while its master was distracted. He carefully caught the reins with one hand and swiftly tied them around a branch. He laid Sibyl as tenderly as he could across the animal's rump, desperately calming it when it skittered at the unknown sensation.

"Calm yourself Duke; you have to do this for me!" He choked, smoothing the sleek neck hairs. Then he swiftly mounted and twisted to drag Sibyl around so that she sat in his lap, gathered against his chest once more. With his free hand

153

he reached for the reins and grunted as he tried to untie them and keep himself from dropping Sibyl, her form weighty and uncooperative.

With a rumbling whicker Duke began his progress back along the ridge, Lord William's hand light on the reins, resisting the temptation to pick up the pace as he knew for a fact he would drop Sibyl and the fall from that height would surely finish her off. The dogs trotted along at his heels and the only sound was the jangle of the bit as Duke's teeth worked on it through concentration.

8

Loss of All

Sibyl awoke the next morning without opening her eyes. For a long time she kept them shut, aiming to let things come to light slowly. The first thing was to untangle the pains. She knew without having to move that her ankle was on fire and her hip ached. The skin of her legs and arms was torn and bruised and she felt a sore patch on the back of her head. Immediately after that she felt a presence - there was a warm mass to her right and the slow, even breathing of a sleeping man.

She opened her eyes at last to confirm her suspicions and twisted her head with some difficulty to find William tucked up against her in her bed, an arm over her torso. He looked haggard and grey and it was obvious he had shed tears - for a moment, Sibyl actually felt some sympathy for him. Her eye was caught by the state of the room, her things were scattered everywhere and slowly the memory of the night before trickled in.

She shook her head with confusion, wondering whether she should be angry with Mother Helston or not? Yes, she had ended up hurt, but the memory of her state beforehand with her heightened senses and abilities was intoxicating and she clearly remembered that moment as she stood upon the shoulders of the stone eagle before the dogs had come...

"Sibyl?!" William groaned, looking blearily into her eyes. Sibyl said nothing. "Be you well?"

"No, William." She croaked.

"You are yourself again though." He said with relief, seeing that her eyes were comprehending his presence now, that she was lucid. He placed a hand gently on her stomach as though he were her husband already and he was tenderly comforting her after an event that was nothing to do with him, she thought angrily.

"What happened Sibyl? The Devil got into you last night! I....I thought you were dead!" He said. Sibyl looked away, resolving to speak to him as little as possible. William began to sit up and looked around for inspiration on what to do next. He was hungry and thirsty and Sibyl probably was too. He also needed to get someone to attend to her wounds.

As he looked around his eye alighted on a scrap of scarlet on the floor next to a cup on its side. Closer inspection revealed it to be a perfect square of silk. He had seen these before. Realisation dawned as he remembered the times he'd had dealings with Mother Helston's customers. The poor creatures ended up dependent on the substances that came in these pouches and he was the one who had to maintain order when they began thieving to pay for the things they were so drawn to, at the expense of even feed for their families! He could not believe that this had happened to Sibyl.

"Oh, Sibyl." He said sadly. She frowned at the new tone he had taken. "I'm going to stop this," he continued, "you will not suffer that fate! As soon as you are cleaned I will convey you to court and we will get away from this festering tower, this place where evil stalks..." He looked around at the scattered clutter as he stood up. "You need to spend some time in the light - talk with other women, dance and enjoy life. Not just sit in this tower in the dark on your own, allowing the devil to seep into your soul!"

He left the room.

~

Later that day Sibyl's wounds had been carefully cleaned while she sat silently watching the window, her face expressionless. The girls had worked equally silently, aware that this situation was awful for Sibyl but completely powerless to do anything about it. Her ruined wedding outfit had been taken away to be cleaned and taken apart to be made into something else entirely, the hours spent sewing that acorn pattern and all her future plans with it.

She had been helped into her usual grey kirtle, Sibyl gingerly easing her bruised legs and swollen ankle into the fabric before her hair was neatly arranged into a modest headdress for travel. Her girls then helped her downstairs, she leaning heavily on them and wincing as she took small steps, then out through the wide, low doorway of Bearnshaw Tower into the yard where her litter and the travelling party awaited.

Once out of the door her back straightened and she hid her pain as she leant on a girl either side. She held her head high as she walked across, knowing that in complete contrast to the looks she received from her crowd of guests last night these people were now looking on her with horror and pity. They took in her pale face, marked with scrapes, and the stiffness as she walked. Few had been told what exactly had happened and they were very disturbed by the sight of their beautiful, intelligent, vibrant mistress reduced to a ghostly shell that morning.

Hugh, now in Lord William's pay, and the rest of Lord William's men were loitering around the litter, keen to get a glimpse of the crazed creature Lord William was inexplicably intent on. They openly gawped at her. Sibyl looked into their eyes directly in turn as she approached the litter, willing her stare to burn their very faces as retribution for helping Lord William in his horrible scheme. Most looked away with shame when challenged and Sibyl felt a grim satisfaction as she gratefully settled herself in the litter and took the weight off her excruciating ankle.

Sibyl had the curtains drawn and laid her head against the padded side of the litter. She was exhausted and had no wish to see Lord William emerge approvedly from the front doors of her tower, now master of her fate. She did hear the thud of his boots on the yard however, and the creak of leather as he mounted and murmur of talk from his men. Then the litter lurched into motion and she tried to sleep.

She was left to her own devices all the way to the crossing of the river Irwell, where they found accommodation in Salford. This was a hastily arranged journey, so there would be no visits to noble friends on the way, with drinking and chat, nice beds and so on. They planned to simply stay in inns and keep Sibyl under the close eye of Lord William and his men. They suspected her of trying an escape, but in all honesty Sibyl was well past such thoughts. If she did escape, where would she go? If she went anywhere familiar Lord William would simply track her down and force this marriage again. She had no comprehension of what she would do if she did not return to court or Bearnshaw. There was no getting around this paperwork from the King.

Sibyl spent the journey in almost complete silence. Nobody wanted to talk to her and she didn't want to talk to anybody either. She allowed herself to be dressed and undressed, directed into and out of bed and the litter, and picked at her food. Pierre took in the sombre mood and behaved himself impeccably, snuggling up in her lap whenever he could for comfort. It was cold and she drew her cloak tightly around herself and shivered most of the way.

Lord William was less attentive with her than usual. In the past whenever they had met he had been intent on talking to her, hovering over her unpleasantly. Now they both knew he had her where he wanted her and he became strangely distant, taking her compliance for granted and merely expecting that his people saw to her needs rather than getting involved himself. Sibyl watched him discreetly, striding around, confidently giving orders and arranging things.

Right now he was organising her being removed from the litter and shuttled into her bedchamber where she could await the evening when they would be married over the evening meal. Of course, Sibyl thought, they would arrive and be married in the same day in a huge rush, regardless of how tired she might be or how much her ankle hurt. This wasn't about her. In the past, Sibyl would have interrupted the conversation he was having, questioned the need for such speed, suggested they rest a while. But not anymore.

She was shown into a fairly small room with a decent bed. Of course, when at court and not their own towers, both Sibyl and William were only minor nobility and all the really grand chambers would be taken. Sibyl was left with her maids and stood looking at the bed, not heeding the girls' activity as they unpacked the things and began arranging the room for their purposes. Sibyl's eyes were on the bed, wondering if they would come back to this room after the wedding or Lord William's. Would this bed be the one where William would finally have his way with her?

Her eyes welled with tears and her stomach flipped over at the thought. There was no time to dwell though, already the girls were preparing to wash her, wash her hair, pluck her eyebrows and hairline and get her into her wedding outfit. They had done all this only days ago, but it needed doing again after the journey and events of that notorious night at Bearnshaw. As she sat mutely in the chair while her hair was brushed Sibyl reflected bitterly on this being her second wedding day in as many weeks. How many other girls went through this? She wondered.

"I want my hair covered." Sibyl stated with finality when the brushing had ceased. They were the first words she had spoken for a long time and the girls were surprised to hear her voice, stopping to stare mid-task. After a split second they acknowledged her request and began to move again, the ones working on her hair obediently began tying it up and trying to find a suitable headdress.

Sibyl did not want her hair brushed out and on display as though this were some happy, carefree occasion. She wanted to look like the prisoner she was. If she had had her way she would have worn her plain grey kirtle, but Lord William had commissioned a magnificent gown in his own blood red and gold colours. It was spectacular, but not her. Sibyl preferred cool, pale tones to this lusty red.

All too soon the October sun had set, Sibyl watching it go and feeling like her soul was disappearing over the horizon with it and that a kind of dark night was coming for her. She turned her face back to the floor and waited, the girls enjoying a quick drink after their hard work in front of the fire, leaving her out of their conversation. There was a knock on the door and Sibyl rose without prompting and waited to hear the announcement. Sure enough the messenger related that they were now expected in the main hall to dine with the King and be married. Sibyl followed without reaction at the head of the party of girls, aware of their whispering but not really hearing the words.

The noise of the great hall hit her like an ocean wave as the door opened, sending her brain reeling for a moment. She struggled to regain clarity and tried sweeping the room for familiar faces out of habit. She could immediately see that there were few recognisable faces here - here were all the rebels that had lain hidden while Edward was on the throne: there was King Henry at the top table, his characteristic mild smile on his lips while Lord Warwick talked animatedly next to him.

As the guests turned to look at her a hush descended. They had been awaiting the bride - a public wedding like this lent an extra frisson to the evening's festivities, especially on a dull October evening such as this. Upon turning to catch a glimpse of a lovely young bride however, they caught sight of Sibyl, pale and drawn with dark rings around her eyes, her face scratched and her hair kept tightly out of sight under a sober headdress. She could see concern and confusion in their eyes - evidently they had not known this marriage was against her will and their minds were now churning on why Lord William would be publically marrying such a sorry looking woman at such speed.

The crowd parted as it had done in the smaller ceremony at Bearnshaw, only this time it did not reveal the jovial face of John Towneley, welcoming her down the hall to security and happiness. No, this time it revealed William, looking at her in the way a hawk watched a mouse. She took a deep breath and started towards him, one slow step in front of another. Some lively music started, but the perceptive crowd recognised that it did not match the mood of the scratched and bruised bride who stiffly padded down the hall, her jaw clamped tightly shut. Soon the only smiling face was Henry's.

When Sibyl drew level with William she noticed his hand outstretched, ready to take hers. She looked up at his watchful face with a sneer and took it as lightly as possible, her body stiff and leaning away from him. He completely ignored her quiet protest, took her cool, dry fingers firmly in his larger, warmer hand and turned with satisfaction to wait for the ceremony to be complete.

Henry was famously pious and there was no shortage of holymen to lead things along. Sibyl did not hear the words; they were echoing in the distance in her mind as she concentrated on her burning hatred. Lord Warwick was sat opposite them next to Henry and she focussed on him, knowing that he was behind this deal with William far more than Henry was. Henry was obviously merely a puppet for this man and Warwick had used her as a pawn. It stung far more than her deal with Edward; she had chosen that, made the deal herself. Here she was merely being used by all around for their own ends and receiving nothing into the bargain.

Warwick was actually fairly uninterested in this wedding. He was as bemused as anyone about why Lord William was so dead set on marrying Sibyl Bearnshaw but it was a handy thing to be able to promise her to him and join their resources which William promised to use in Warwick's favour should the need arise. Warwick was aware he had done an ambitious thing; to send a king into exile and resurrect one that he had helped depose...he would need allies to see this through for sure.

He was a little surprised at the speed and gusto with which William had acted, racing off to Lancashire before the ink was even dry and insisting on dragging the poor girl all the way to London and having the ceremony in front of everyone as soon as possible. Now he saw Sibyl, much changed from the dim memory he had of her in those heady post-Towton days. She was aged now, looked exhausted, was covered in cuts and bruises and had an air of angry resignation about her rather than the sparky intelligence of old.

She looked up at him as he casually sipped his wine, patiently waiting for the ceremony to be finished before carrying on his rather important conversation. He was slightly disconcerted by her appearance and intense, accusatory staring. He wondered if he had done the right thing, if William had maybe beaten the girl? There was something not quite right about the fellow and at every turn things seemed to get more distasteful. He raised his glass to Sibyl and prepared to turn away under the pretext of whispering to his companion, noticing the disgusted look of dismissal she gave him as if to say 'that's right, run like a coward from my gaze!'.

Sibyl blinked slowly as she returned her gaze to the flapping of the priest's mouth. Then she became aware of a popping sound and realised it was the hesitant applause from the crowd, unsure of what they had just taken part in, and that she must now be married to William. She looked slowly around at him and he was holding his hand up in a wave to the crowd, smiling at the King, and Warwick, and all his rebel friends around. She remained mute, with a look on her face that made some watching think she may vomit at any second.

William steered her off into the crowd to chat with his friends. Sibyl used the time to think about Bearnshaw now. There it would be: bleak, dark and empty with only a skeleton staff to keep it from falling down completely. Eagle Crag would be looking out over the valley and the wind would likely be whipping over the moors on the tops and blasting into those thick stone walls. She imagined herself up there now, hearing only the howling wind.

"Sibyl? Sibyl I asked if you'd like something to eat now?" William's voice drifted in over the wind and soon drowned it out completely. Sibyl shook her head in reply. William looked concerned and stroked her face. "You look tired; I've told everyone of your illness, so you can go rest now. I shall just spend a little more time talking and then follow."

Without waiting for her answer, he motioned for her to be led to her room. *'So it will be that bed.'* Sibyl thought to herself.

By the time they got to the bedchamber, Sibyl's anger had completely vanished and was replaced by a helpless desperation, an impotent fear. Her girls looked equally stricken, knowing full well what was about to happen and not wishing this fate on their worst enemies. One of them burst into tears as they slipped her into her nightshirt.

"Sibyl, oh Sibyl!" She wept. Sibyl's eyes focussed on her, having been staring into nothing while she was undressed.

"Don't worry Agnes." She croaked. "Far worse has happened than this. I....I have been through worse myself." She fought to stop her voice from cracking as her thoughts flew back to those dark days of suffering on the Westcote estate, the difficult purging of her and Johns' little problem. She had never been forced by a man, but she wondered how bad it could really be? William was odd, uncaring and repulsive to her but she did not think he was brutal, as some men could be.

They laid her down in the bed and sat huddled in a group, staring at her with wide, worried eyes, Agnes occasionally sniffing. There was no knock on the door when he arrived, laughing heartily to the men he'd arrived with.

"And now gentlemen, I am finally, *married!*" He bellowed and threw open the door. The men outside roared and cheered but when William looked inside to see a roomful of morose, red-eyed women, he quickly dismissed his men and Sibyl motioned for her girls to leave too.

"Sibyl?" He asked softly, taking off his boots. She didn't answer. He stretched out beside her, shaking out his dark, smooth hair and tossing his hat to the floor. She could smell the sourness of wine on his breath and his hand had crept onto her stomach as John's had done during their intimate moments alone, the touch giving her a chill even through the blankets.

"Sibyl." He repeated, looking intently at her face. She sighed heavily in reply.

"Let's just get this done, William." She said tiredly, looking at the ceiling. "We've known each other long enough not to bother with any fakery, I think. You win."

Her words died away and the only sound in the chamber was the crackling of the fire. After a time she grew curious about why he wasn't replying, opened her eyes and turned to face him. He was still just watching her, a curious mixture of emotions she had never seen before in him flitting across his face as he struggled to articulate his feelings.

"Sibyl...I don't want to force you..." He began.

"It's a little late for that isn't it William?" She snapped, hardly believing what she was hearing from him after the events of the last few days - since when had he ever cared about whether she was compliant or not?

"Sibyl," he continued exasperatedly, "I do...love you."

Sibyl was struck dumb. He'd never said that, and to her mind his actions had never given this impression. He acted like he wanted to own her at any cost, like a precious jewel mounted on a chain around his neck to display as a reflection of his greatness, not like he loved her.

"Well!" She snorted. "You know the old saying...if you love someone; force them to marry you against their will!"

"It's not against your will, not truly! We've known each other for years Sibyl!"

"Yes and in all that time you have hounded me and I have tried to evade marriage with you - why on earth would you think this is not against my will?!" Her voice rose and she hurriedly closed her mouth to avoid losing her composure.

"Well you were very young before, didn't know what was

best for you." He said quietly.

"Let us be honest with each other, if this is how things have to be then you at least owe me no pretense!" He frustrated her, always. Even now, when she had expected him to reel in drunk and make a quick job of serving her so she could hurry off to blissful sleep, he was here whining about love and telling her she didn't know what she wanted!

"Sibyl I've never pretended - I have always wanted you." He said earnestly, leaning over and loosening her headdress. Sibyl's stomach twisted itself into a knot as she realised that it was beginning and she kept her mouth shut, debate evidently meaningless with this relentless man.

He spent some time combing out her hair with his fingers while she stared at the ceiling and then suddenly lunged forwards and placed his lips on hers, giving her a kiss that wasn't returned, Sibyl doing everything she could to stifle her instinct to shake her head free. Then he disappeared and she could hear him removing clothing, though she had no wish to look and confirm that.

The bed dipped when he settled himself back into it under the sheets and wriggled up to her, his skin burningly hot against hers which felt cold. Then suddenly his weight was settling onto her and she found her breathing quickening. He propped himself up on his hands and used his knees to press her legs apart and then Sibyl tensed bodily as she felt an insistent pressure between them.

'John, Oh John! Where are you now?' she thought despairingly as William poked and prodded and gradually eased his way into her. She imagined John leaping up behind William at this moment and running him through with a sword. In reality though William merely lowered himself onto her and settled into his thrusting, his shoulder pressed painfully into her cheek, him looking the other way, obviously lost in his own world while Sibyl was all too present in this one, feeling every thrust chafing her raw as her body tried in vain to reject him.

Eventually she grew so sore she couldn't help but whimper with each jerk of his body, but just when she thought she could stand the pain no longer and she would have to begin fighting back, he was done and catching his breath before rolling off and onto his back next to her. They both lay side by side, looking at the ceiling, Sibyl's arms reaching around to clutch at herself and his happily behind his head as exhaled deeply.

"It's done." He said, sounding as though he himself didn't quite believe it.

"Yes." Sibyl agreed.

A few days later and Sibyl was back in Salford in her litter as the travelling party made its way to the Irwell crossing. Robert was seated on his fine bay horse, feeling the chill of October more than usual. He was impatient to be home to Generys, his Welsh wife, and was mightily fed up with this whole trip South. At least now William had what he wanted, however nonsensical it was, and the rightful King was back in his place so presumably they could all settle down to a kind of normality rather than chasing about the Welsh hills in hiding, or trying to capture Lady Sibyl.

His thoughts were interrupted by a sharp cry from the litter. Instantly he was on the alert, preparing to draw his sword, his eyes casting left to right for whatever danger was abroad. He saw only the busy street however, full of traders and their customers haggling over goods, struggling up and down with heavy burdens. He frowned. Then Sibyl burst into view, stumbling from the litter before it had properly stopped.

"Belaud!" She cried, running across the muddy street, rapidly ruining a good pair of shoes. Robert simply could not fathom what was going on. Lord William reacted quickest, his horse sidestepping with considerable agility to keep up with Sibyl, tail swishing.

"Sibyl? What is this, what's going on?" He called to her, which she completely ignored.

Robert rolled his eyes - was this to be his life now,

nursemaiding this insane woman? Then he froze in the saddle as he watched when Sibyl reached what she had been aiming for. She had run to the head of a grubby grey pony as it pulled a rickety wooden cart down the street. The man driving it looked utterly confused, torn between cuffing this stranger off his horse but clearly mindful of her highborn clothes and the armed men clustered around her.

"What is the meaning of this?" He finally blustered to Lord William, hands held out palms upwards in a careful gesture of bewilderment rather than anger against a Lord.

"I know not..." Lord William replied quietly, not taking his eyes from Sibyl, who was now crying into the horse's mane. The horse was thin, with a long staring coat and an unbrushed mane, clearly near its end.

"This is my Belaud!" Sibyl finally wailed, anger in her voice. "Tom was riding him when he went missing!" She barked when her statement was met with baffled silence. Frustrated, she broke away from Belaud, who whinnied after her, and ran to the owner, gripping his clothes and leaning into his face when he recoiled. "Where did you get this horse?" She demanded.

"Sibyl, this is most undigni-" Lord William started,

"Quiet! Let him speak!"

"A broker my Lady!" The man held his hands up.

"Where?!" She snapped, eyes fierce.

"Kersal Street!" The man seemed genuine, and Sibyl could not for one minute see why a poor trader such as this man would have the motive or means to kill her brother. It did not require a giant of intellect to deduce that he had innocently bought this horse from the dealer. The question was, how had the dealer come by him?

Robert's skin had started to prickle with sweat, and he fought to stay indifferent to the situation unfolding. He relaxed a little when he became sure that the man with the beast had not been the same he had sold to and therefore would not recognise him. He thanked his luck, having never considered that Sibyl passing the horse was a possibility until this moment.

"I will give you a shilling for him." Sibyl offered in a tone that suggested the man had no choice.

"A *shilling* for this nag Sibyl? You may have the use of any horse from my stables, there is no need-" Lord William once again tried to break through to her.

"I want *my* horse." She growled in reply.

All waited for the man to give his answer. They could see his thought process - tempted by the money, doubtful about how he would transport his cart from here...thinking again of the sum and finding it too great to turn down.

"Done! A pleasure doing business with you!" He grinned, holding out his hand expectantly. Sibyl merely marched off to unhitch the horse herself, motioning to William to pay. William snorted exasperatedly, shaking his head as he fished the coins from his purse and thrust them into the man's grimy palm.

Sibyl threw the poorly maintained harness onto the cart, fashioning a halter from one of the reins and smoothing Belaud's nose. She was grimly determined to get him home and give him a deep bed of straw and the best feed the marshal had and never work him for the rest of his days...short though they may be.

"We go to Kersal Street!" She said, giving the halter a slight tug and striking out in a random direction, intending to ask the way from a passer-by.

"No!" Lord William snapped, aware of the eyes of a small crowd gathering to watch the spectacle. "You have tested my patience and purse enough Sibyl!"

"I have to find out what happened to my brother!" She argued, gesturing wildly, invigorated by the thought of discovering her brother's fate.

Lord William and Robert exchanged a glance. William did not know the details of what Robert had done after getting rid of Tom but could easily decipher it for himself given the circumstances.

"A foolish errand, when our party are cold and so close to

home. Your brother is gone and you need to accept it; now get back into the litter before I order Robert to force you back in!" His voice rose throughout the last sentence until he was bawling and Sibyl knew she had no other option. She openly sneered at Robert and led Belaud back to the litter, clambering in without help and holding the string of the halter through the window.

She had time to think over the possibilities as they travelled, keeping an eye on poor Belaud and the nodding of his scabby muzzle as he struggled to keep up with the fitter horses. She didn't like to push him in this state but knew that no one would tolerate a slower pace on his behalf. She consoled herself with the knowledge that once back home he would never work again.

A few things were now clear. Whatever happened to Tom had happened fairly locally. He could have sold Belaud himself for some reason (a gambling debt perhaps? Or his money had been stolen and he needed funds?), but if he had lived to do so then why would he not contact her at all? The more likely scenario was that whoever had harmed him had sold the horse. Perhaps simply roadside robbers. Or perhaps the deed being so local was a clue...Sibyl could only think of one local who had reason to target Tom at that time, and that was her husband.

~

"Will we spend some time at Bearnshaw soon?" Sibyl asked glumly as she waited for William to finish eating as they dined privately in bed in order to stay warm. She had asked this before but he had always refused. It wouldn't stop her trying though; she had little else to do thesedays as William kept her as a kind of prisoner, only allowed out of Hapton Tower with him or a guard.

"No Sibyl." He replied tiredly. "And what's more, we're never going there again!"

Sibyl's head snapped up. This was new.

"What mean you William?" She narrowed her eyes.

"Precisely that. That place is bad for you. You surely remember what happened? Full of all that garbage...dark...old." He shuddered theatrically. "No, that is no place for us, you will be....healthier, right here." He added cheerfully.

"But...my staff, I haven't been there for weeks, there is no one to run the place; what will the townspeople think if they don't see their Lady?"

"Bearnshaw will be administrated from here." He posted a morsel into his mouth and chewed noisily. Sibyl blinked and sought the right words. He filled the pause for her. "I'm having the tower pulled down."

Sibyl jumped to her feet.

"What! You can't!" She shrieked with horror.

"Sibyl, I can do what I like!" William chuckled. "Good King Harry took a dim view of your being so instrumental in turning him in to the usurper - your lands were turned over to me. That means they are mine to do with as I wish and it's high time that mouldering old heap was replaced with something befitting my new status."

"Heap?" Sibyl said quietly, tears welling in her eyes.

"Worry you not - Hapton Tower is coming down too, and a new hall is being built. You will love it." He waved a hand dismissively and returned his focus to his food.

"You truly wish to destroy me utterly, don't you?" She sobbed.

"What?" William seemed baffled. "Destroy you? Sibyl you are my wife and you have proved yourself fanciful and treading a dangerous path for your mind and soul: I have to do what's best for you." He explained.

"Was it best for me that you kill my brother?" She said in a low, sinister voice, finally spilling the question out of the tightly locked casket she had kept it in for the last couple of months.

Time seemed to slow as she examined William's reaction and she saw clearly the moment of incomprehension, then the flash of understanding and growth of panic which evolved into exaggerated outrage as he sought to smother any slippage of emotion. It was too late: she had seen.

"Sibyl, that's...You have some *nerve!*" He slammed his dish down and paced up and down, smearing his face with his hand and smoothing back his hair agitatedly. Sibyl merely sat on the bed and watched with evident satisfaction.

"Murderer!" She spat when he seemed to be calming a little and sure enough he fired back into life, rushing over to lean into her face, a hand raised.

"Don't ever say that again!" He cried, but they both heard the quavering note of distress at the end and after a second looking into each other's eyes intensely, he turned and fled the chamber.

Sibyl took a great gasp and sobbed aloud for a moment. It was true. Tom was dead, and William had murdered him. And there was nothing she could do about it. She had the satisfaction of knowing that William knew she knew, but that was all. Everything and everyone else was gone. All her struggles over the last few years had come to nothing. All her bravery and cunning had done her no good in the end.

She stood up quickly and crossed the chamber to collect up the fine fur-lined red cloak William had commissioned for her. She didn't have a moment to lose - it was imperative she saw Bearnshaw one last time and that would only happen if she escaped Hapton and in order to do that she needed to capitalise on this chance while William was still reeling. She clutched the cloak around herself and hurried lightly from the chamber, flying down darkened staircases and along corridors which were now familiar to her.

It was late on a winter's evening and happily for Sibyl everyone was huddled around a fire so she found herself unchallenged as she trotted out of the front door. Unfortunately there was of course a porter on the gate and she screwed her eyes shut and held her breath as she made purposefully past him, hoping against hope that he would merely let her go, but knowing that he would not.

"Miss?" He challenged her and she stopped, head down, now breathing hard and with pounding heart. Behind her she heard footfalls as he clanked towards her and she could tell that he was hesitant, that he didn't know why there was a woman, probably his master's wife, stood in his gateway in the darkness not answering his question.

"Lady Hapton?" He queried, and she sensed a hand hovering near her shoulder. Indecision gone, she tensed and then flung her arm around behind her with all her might, clouting the man right around the jaw with the back of a bejewelled fist. She heard his cry but didn't stop to investigate the damage; she simply used the chance to pelt away into the darkness, hearing a clamour rise up behind her.

"Come in child!" Mother Helston seemed genuinely surprised and pleased to see Sibyl and Sibyl was relieved she had found somewhere she could hide and someone who was unlikely to be on Lord William's side. Mother Helston stepped aside and gestured into the merry room, warm from a roaring fire and twinkling with numerous lights.

"Thank you, Mother Helston. Please forgive my intrusion at this hour, but I find myself in most unhappy circumstances and have nowhere else to turn." She said unhappily, the corner of her mouth beginning to tug down as she sat in the chair and shrugged off her cloak.

"Whatever is the matter dear?"

Mother Helston did not use any of the formal greetings or rituals she should have in the presence of a highborn woman, but Sibyl did not mind. She enjoyed the lack of formality and Mother Helston's easy, maternal manner with her. It was something she had had precious little of. She dreaded to think what acid-tongued Lady Breckley would make of her current situation.

"I...don't know how much you know about me Mother Helston." Sibyl stared into the fire as she spoke.

"A little gossip about the nobles is common currency amongst the rustics, you must know that." Mother Helston steepled her fingers and settled back into her familiar chair.

"You will likely know then that I have been forced to marry Lord William."

"Yes, I did." Mother Helston nodded slowly to confirm. "We had no idea you weren't willing in the old days; we thought you and William made a fine match! It has however become clear that you were not." She paused. "I had my suspicions long ago. I know Lord William well and could not imagine a Lady as independent as you to be much enamoured with him. That's why I gave you my powder."

Sibyl turned to look at Mother Helston thoughtfully. So that was why.

"It was....good. Exciting. Took my mind off the matter..." Sibyl replied carefully. Mother Helston beamed with pleasure.

"That's what all say! I like to help."

"I have escaped from the tower tonight. He's knocking down my own tower and I must see it again before the chance is gone!" Something told Sibyl not to tell Mother Helston about William murdering Tom. That was one powerful rumour she felt it would be best to unleash at an opportune time, rather than let spread now. "I thought I would come here to hide for a little while until the search parties have gone further afield. I also wanted some more powder, if that were possible."

"I have plenty." Mother Helston assured her. "Unfortunately, it is expensive to acquire and I have to charge 1d per pouch for it." She added with surprising speed.

"Oh, oh yes of course." Sibyl responded, patting herself down and realising she had left all her money at Hapton in her hurry. "Ah, I seem to have forgotten my coin purse." She said, embarrassed.

"No matter, you may pay me later." Mother Helston was already at her dresser, taking out another of her silk squares. Sibyl watched her glumly. Although her heart beat faster at the thought of another few hours of escapism, the rush of her enhanced abilities after taking the potion, something about it nonetheless felt wrong, like she was travelling down yet another path she didn't want to go down. She held out her hand resignedly to receive the little silk pouch and clutched it tightly in her lap.

"I think William's men are probably ahead of me now. I will go, and get the money to you soon." Sibyl didn't make eye contact.

"You don't want something to eat before you go?" Mother Helston queried.

"No. No thank you - I have to reach Bearnshaw in darkness so I'm not seen." She stood and wrapped her cloak around herself, towering over the little old lady. She made to open the door for herself and stepped out into the biting cold, exceptionally unpleasant after the toasty warmth of Mother Helston's cottage.

"Very well, take care Lady Sibyl..." Mother Helston called after her with a little smile as she closed the door behind her.

Sibyl stood in the middle of the darkened lane for a moment, seeing the steam of her breath twisting skyward in the bright moonlight. All was quiet. She shivered violently and set off towards Bearnshaw. The pouch was almost weightless in her hand and she brought it up to look at it for a moment as she walked. She wanted to take it. There were a few miles to go before Bearnshaw and she needed to be fast, she knew after the powder was taken she would not feel the cold, or pain, or fatigue.

She had no hot water so could make no brew. Regardless, she untied the cord and untidily stuffed the pile of powder into her mouth, struggling to swallow it and make enough saliva to help it down. It was not a pleasant experience to eat that dust tasting of soil, but equally it was not repulsive so could be done fairly easily. She discarded the silk square and it fluttered down to rest lightly on the mud of the road. Sibyl folded her arms and hunched, upped her pace and waited for it to take effect.

Sure enough she began to forget the cold and noticed that her vision became clearer, her hearing became sharper until her own breath roared in her ears and she began to scent everything - the damp earth around, the mouldering leaves, the scent of a pig in the trees wafted to her and the smell of her own clothes, the smell of Hapton tower on them - cooking, incense...William.

Her strides became longer, her muscles taught with pent up energy ready to be released at any moment. She broke into a run. Her senses would warn her of anyone on the road and currently she wasn't picking up any fresh signs of activity, so she ran on and on and on along the lanes and when she neared the village of Cornholme she knew the country so well she was able to leave the track altogether and strike off across the fields and through the brush, scrambling up the steep valley side to where she knew her tower waited.

She knew her lungs were raw and her legs were burning by the time she reached Bearnshaw, her feet blistered and had she even lost a shoe? Or both? But she felt no discomfort, only exhilaration at having made the journey so quickly without a horse. Around the area of the Tower she began to strongly scent people and her eyes swished from side to side, taking in the strangely distorted view she now had.

She froze as she spotted the tower and gulped down a cry of anger as she saw that it had indeed begun to be torn down, the familiar outline torn like a piece of parchment into an unrecognisable shape, empty windows forming squares and arches of bright moonlit sky in the jet black silhouetted walls. Desperately she looked around the base of the tower and spotted the hovels and tents of the workers. It was now the dead of night however and although she could hear them breathing and smell their sleeping bodies, she could sense no fires, lights or activity.

Hurriedly she skipped forwards, hopping from foot to foot in great bounds, trembling as she made her way through the chaotic encampment, taking in the sad-looking piles of stones scavenged from Bearnshaw as her saucerlike eyes leaked big warm tears. Once at the tower walls, her hand reached out to touch the chilly stone and then she scuttled along the wall, feeling for what was once the doorway.

Inside the floor was thick with dust and litter from the demolition; in some places the wet had leaked in and created patches of mud bearing the footprints of the workers. Sibyl crouched as she entered the building, feeling uncomfortably enclosed. She panted, but remained resolute and travelled deeper into the building, feeling for the staircase she had used so many times. As she placed a foot on the bottom step, seeing that the work had obviously not yet reached this inner core of the building, she heard a noise.

Her head flicked to the doorway of the tower; there in the moonlight she saw the dark shape of someone watching her and near jumped out of her skin. Panic burned through her in a flash and she belted up the stairs, whimpering as she heard a cry behind her. She flew along the corridor and skidded into her room, slamming the door and sliding down behind it. Alone with her ragged breathing she could hear the sounds of camp coming alive below drifting through the open window.

Quickly she looked around and saw that although the furniture had been removed, her collections were untouched - strewn around the floor. She slithered away from the door and began scurfing things aside with great swipes, looking for her volume of documents. She now felt that it was needed after all. If her tower wasn't to survive, her work should, and could. She would be able to carry it with her, hide it. They would never take it!

Suddenly, there it was in front of her sitting in a beam of moonlight. After recognising it she snatched it up and clutched it to her. Then there was a loud noise outside the door, echoing round her brain, continuous and confusing. The door was flung open and suddenly men were tumbling in, brandishing sticks and yelling in the darkness. Sibyl struck up an unearthly scream and kicked herself along the floor away from them, sending items flying. The men fled in terror, the door slamming behind them.

Sibyl found herself unable to stop screaming though, she had ceased to be able to tell where their noise ended and hers began, so she gripped her tied stack of parchment to her chest until her joints ached and screamed, pressed into a damp cobwebbed corner.

~

Lord William listened to the men, his face grim. He had been out all night searching and was mightily displeased to have gotten word of the disturbance at Bearnshaw. He was in no mood for this, standing out in the cold as the dawn broke shell-pink around them, listening to them as they all garbled over one another, but he got the jist of what they were saying.

"It was terrible sir!"

"The noise!"

"Like the Devil himself!"

"We just locked the room up; she didn't stop, just kept screaming 'Edwaaaard'!" The man mimicked the sound, the worried look on his face staying throughout.

William's face hardened at the last. He was beginning to regret his quest to marry Sibyl thesedays, something he had never expected to happen. She used to be beautiful. He supposed she still was, but it was wrecked by her gaunt face and darkened eyes, the lack of a smile and any spirit to go to court or hunting. He had imagined dancing with her but only his express orders to dance made her do so, which somewhat took the fun out of it.

The same applied in the bedchamber and of course she was still bleeding every month so no sign of any heirs. She looked so sickly he doubted there would be, certainly had she been a broodmare he would have sold her for stew long ago, knowing another colt would not pass her hips! And now more undignified, embarrassing, downright strange behaviour from her! He knew exactly what she'd done. He didn't know whether to rage at her or mourn for her.

He nodded to the men and dismissed them, then strode

177

into the tower and sighed as he heavily climbed the stairs, looking around at the devastation. He had to admit it was a peculiar feeling to be here at Bearnshaw, one of his childhood haunts, with the roof missing and the walls jagged above his head. With slight trepidation he removed his thick winter riding gloves, pulled back the makeshift bolt and laid a hand against the damp wood of the door to Sibyl's chamber. It opened easily.

Inside he spied her, lying in the smart red cloak he'd given her like a splash of blood on the floor, amongst the dirty rubbish strewn inside. He sighed again as he walked over to her and bent to shake her shoulder. Sibyl came awake with a subtle gasp and looked up at him with heavy lidded, reddened eyes. William said nothing, and neither did she. He looked at her with open distaste and she looked back coolly without a hint of remorse.

With a matter-of-fact sniff and a slight shake of the head he turned and left the room. He emerged out of the tower and walked back over to his men, the people of the camp watching the goings on with anxious interest.

"It's her. Get her back to Hapton. I don't much care how. I have an errand to run before I return." He murmured to Robert who gave a sly smile and nod in return. "Carry on your work!" He yelled to the workers, springing into the saddle and sending his horse slithering down the steep hill away from Bearnshaw.

"Open up you daggle-tailed drassock!"

William thumped repeatedly on the door, relishing the violence. He could hear Mother Helston chuntering like a disturbed vixen on the other side. As soon as the door opened a crack he pushed it fully open, sending the crone reeling back. He knew however that this was no ordinary old spinster. He knew she would not be genuinely afeared of him, she would merely be pretending in order to play on his chivalrous instincts and weasel her way out of trouble. In truth, Helston was strangely impervious to violence and threats, perhaps due to years of practice thanks to her insistence on playing her little games.

Without waiting for any of her ranting William forced his way in and stood, the ceiling barely clearing his hat, with his sword menacingly drawn.

"I'm here to let you know this is your last warning Helston. I've put up with you for too long and now you target my own wife!" He began.

"She comes to me!" Helston hissed defiantly.

"After being sucked in the usual way I suppose?" William countered. He bent down to speak into Mother Helston's shrivelled face. "You give her any more and you'll hang." He snarled.

"What for? Ain't no rules 'gainst what I do William and well you know it!" She spat back. "Hanging a defenceless old woman!" She muttered under her breath. William cut her off.

"I've done worse..." He sneered, prodding her arm with the tip of his sword. Her eyes glittered.

"Have you?" She returned thoughtfully.

"I'd have you for disturbing the peace; using witchcraft to manipulate my wife into scaring half the district out of their wits! The workers are too carked to continue at Bearnshaw now!"

"Is that my doing or yours?" Mother Helston asked pointedly. Lord William scowled as he thought of a response.

"With my money and influence? Yours. Beyond all reasonable doubt." He said in a low, threatening voice.

"I have money too, William....why don't you try some powder for yourself? It would help you relax?" She asked casually, removing herself from his swordpoint and picking up a pouch from one of her cluttered surfaces. She threw it at him before he had chance to respond and he was forced to straighten and bring down his sword to catch it angrily in one hand before it hit his face. He looked at it with a look of disgust and threw it back at the old woman, who cackled in response as it bounced off her.

"I have no need of your potions!" He made to leave. "I mean it: any more of this and you'll be facing the noose, I promise it."

He didn't bother to close the door and could hear Mother Helston still chuckling to herself as he rode away to finally get some sleep.

9

The Curious Miller

Sibyl felt strangely elated by her small success. Bearnshaw was gone, but she had rescued her work. Robert had been extremely rough with her but she had gripped the sheaves so tightly and threatened to bite him, so in the end he was forced to allow her to keep hold of them as she rode in front of him back to Hapton. She had also begun to form a plan which would enable her to escape the tower more often, without so much strain on her fists and reliance on chance.

It was a simple plan. She spoke to her chambermaids and paid them handsomely to secretly obtain some extra of the fabric used to make their clothing, whereupon she used some of her sewing time to construct a servant's outfit to use as a disguise. She felt the pay was necessary as she knew that Lord William was a handsome man and charming when he wanted to be. Young, impressionable girls may feel more loyalty to him than their strange, ungrateful mistress.

Once in the disguise only her hands and face showed which made her fairly anonymous, especially with the brim of the cap pulled low. The girls found it highly amusing to see their Lady dressed as a servant, and Sibyl was pleased with her work. With their help she could now sneak out whenever she wished to 'run errands' as a servant girl.

Just before Christmas she received a stroke of luck. She was dining privately with William in the solar when he made an announcement.

"I intend to go to court for the festivities Sibyl." He said. Sibyl outwardly made no reaction. Inwardly she wilted. Although it would have been lovely to see some life again few of her friends would be there and of course, she would have to play the dutiful wife to William.

"I can see you're thrilled." He said sardonically, interrupting her thoughts.

She must have been silent for a while she realised. Still she said nothing; she only spoke to him when absolutely necessary. She was determined to make this marriage as miserable as possible for him.

"Well, worry you not. I'm leaving you here." He had intended his words to be cutting, to suggest she was like an old, no-longer-fashionable purse to be left behind. Sibyl however, visibly brightened and sat up in her chair, though she feigned nonchalance by reaching for another piece of cheese.

"What?" She was genuinely surprised to hear this.

"Don't excite yourself too much; my steward will be given instructions not to let you out of Hapton without specially chosen guards."

"Still. I think we shall both have a happier Christmas this way." Sibyl smiled prettily.

Lord William took a swig of wine and looked around the room, smacking his lips noisily as he thought. Then his eyes snapped to hers as he asked quickly:

"Are you still bleeding?"

Sibyl looked at him assessingly. She suddenly felt like she'd lost her footing...like she was in danger. He was staring at her so intensely, to make it plain that her answer was of dire importance. It was not lost on her why he had asked this now, just when she had made it so obvious she was pleased he was going away. They stared at each other in silence and Sibyl wondered if he actually had it in him to do away with her if she couldn't produce an heir for him. Tom loomed in her mind and she judged it best to give back the upper hand, so she bowed her head and quietly confirmed that she was indeed, not with child.

William's face didn't change for a moment. He was pleased she had received his threat and it had evidently worried her, but she was also not with child and he would really rather not have to start again with someone else now. He also struggled to envisage life without Sibyl Bearnshaw; she had been in his life since childhood and had always been pictured at his side....but not as this hateful creature seated before him now.

"That is unfortunate." Was all he said, without expression.

~

William was gone and Sibyl had one thing on her mind. Everyone else at Hapton tower was distracted by the festivities, but Sibyl had no stomach for them. The idle chit chat and over consumption held no appeal, felt pointless. All she wanted to do was experience the warmth, the vivid colours, the heightened senses and carefree sensation she got from that earthy powder. From now on she had no reason to leave her room and nobody had reason to chase or interrupt her, she would be at no risk of hurting herself or attracting attention, and could while away the hours that way.

Getting out of the tower had been easy in her disguise and she had left her girls to travel to market where she would rejoin them, basket in hand as though she too had been buying food and supplies for the community, to get back in through the gate later. Now she turned up at Mother Helston's door, almost hopping from foot to foot with excitement, which Mother Helston noted with satisfaction when she recognised those distinctive grey eyes peering at her expectantly.

"Sibyl!" She chuckled. "I didn't think I'd see you again...I see you don't think much of Lord William's threats? Neither do I." She beamed and pushed a cup of spiced wine into

Sibyl's hand. Sibyl was then halted in her tracks - Mother Helston had company, which surprised her for some reason.

"Oh, these are just my friends, we're celebrating together!" Mother Helston explained, gesturing to the small group of women gathered around her fire. They looked back at Sibyl and nodded politely, but seemed guarded.

"Oh, er, sorry for intruding then." Sibyl stammered. "I won't stay, I have to be back at Hapton shortly, I came to...settle my debts?" She wasn't sure what she should mention in front of these friends.

"Oh you may speak plainly with us Sibyl," Mother Helston reassured her, "we're all friends here - you want some powder no doubt? How many pouches?"

"Five?" Sibyl queried. Mother Helston's eyebrow momentarily raised and then she nodded and began dishing it out for her.

"I should probably introduce you to my friends - this is Alice Acker," she gestured as she worked, "this is Joan Bancroft, and this, is Avice Dexter. I particularly think you two should get acquainted."

Mother Helston finished her work with the pouches and handed them to Sibyl, taking the coins in return with thanks. Avice had meanwhile risen from her chair and advanced towards Sibyl to nod a greeting. Sibyl saw that Avice was thin, was unusually tall like Sibyl herself and had slightly sinister dark blue eyes in a pinched face. Although she smiled, it seemed tight and felt unfriendly.

"Now Sibyl I think you should get to know Avice because it's not really safe for you to come to Mother Helston's from now on." Mother Helston continued, evidently more talkative than Avice.

"It isn't?" Sibyl queried.

"No. Lord William does not like me supplying you with this powder. I gather your behaviour has...attracted attention." Mother Helston tried to be tactful. Sibyl felt a faint blush rise on her cheeks. She felt around six years old under the gaze of the four old women.

"I'm only going to use it in my private apartments from now on. I have nowhere to go and nothing to do. Before I was running from William and trying to rescue my things from my tower." She explained.

"That's fine," Helston was quick to mollify her, "we have alternatives which will allow us both to avoid William's suspicions. Avice sells the powder at Cornholme Mill, you can travel there in your wonderful disguise and no one will suspect a thing, a servant would naturally go to the mill to drop corn and collect flour!" Mother Helston beamed with apparent delight at the plan.

"Yes....that would be very helpful!" Sibyl nodded.

"See you soon, Sibyl." Avice smiled, and Sibyl felt she had been dismissed so hurriedly gathered her skirts and trotted back out into the crisp winter air, not without relief, as she was now free of the scrutiny of those women and could hurry back to the safety of her chamber.

So Sibyl spent the festive period secreted in her chambers, taking a lower dose of the powder on a regular basis and having food delivered up as required. Without William around there was no one she had to answer to, no one to rein in her anti-social behaviour and ask things of her. The steward saw to the running of the tower and that William's orders in keeping her in were adhered to, but had very little interest otherwise.

January came however and Sibyl had run out of powder. She tried a day without it, not quite believing that she now seemed to need it, but found herself mind-achingly bored, pacing around her chamber. It crossed her mind to go and find someone to talk to, do some work, but the ideas seemed tedious compared to lying in bed, relaxing, watching the flames play in the fire without having a thought about anything else for hours at a time.

That night she found she couldn't sleep either. She lay awake staring at the inside of the bed curtains for most of the night, her heart racing as she dredged up old memories and frustrations over and over. When she finally awoke in the thin dawn light she rushed straight to her chest containing the servants outfit and tugged it on as her maids brought her fire back to life and tidied the room.

When they were done, she left the room with them carrying some of their items and none gave them a second glance as they disappeared into the servant's quarters where Sibyl wordlessly handed out coins to them all and one agreed to accompany her out of the gates.

"Are you...all right Sibyl?" Emma asked once they were safely past the gates. She was concerned by the agitated manner of her Lady.

"Yes yes, fine. Just, you know, I've been indoors for so long, it's good to get out and see the sun!" Sibyl hurriedly answered.

She smiled up at the sun; it was a beautiful, crisp, clear day in truth and she did feel good to be doing something proactive. Her maid nodded, satisfied with the explanation - it stood to reason that one would feel a little odd if they were kept in a tower against their will at all times. She knew herself how much she enjoyed the freedom of a trip to the bustling market when she'd been at work in the tower for so long.

"We're not going to Burnley market today, we're going to Cornholme. You can come with me this time, it will look better for appearances if we go together." Sibyl explained.

"Cornholme? Why do we go to Cornholme?" Emma's brow furrowed as she looked up at Sibyl.

"The mill. I have to meet someone there. Don't worry, you'll get your day in Burnley and I'll pay for whatever amusements you wanted there, but today I have to go to the mill."

Emma gave her agreement despite their new destination doubling the walking she would have to do that day, based on the promise of a day in town paid for by someone else.

~

Robin Miller was also enjoying the sun that day. The interior of the mill was at least brighter if not warmer, but his shovelling kept him warm enough. It was a relatively good day for him. Soon the sacks for this small run were full though and he stopped, knowing the cold would settle in soon so he should go outside into the sun and then maybe into the kitchens for a cup of something hot.

He stepped out into the sun and swiftly removed the coif he wore for milling, shaking free his untidy black locks, watching the flour dust fly free, clearly defined in a cloud settling around him in the bright morning light. Then he patted off his clothes out of long habit and wheeled around in the direction of the kitchen where he knew his mother would be cooking and happy to serve him something.

As he walked a movement caught his eye and he swiftly looked up for a better view of the path. There he spotted two young women walking to the mill. He frowned - nobody was due to pick up the flour for a while and they appeared to have no pack pony to transport it? He decided to wait for them and see what they wanted.

When they reached him they politely greeted him but didn't seem to want anything further from him. Frustrated and confused, he pressed them for more information.

"Can I help you ladies? Is there a reason you've come to my mill?" He emphasised the last in an unfriendly way while they uncomfortably looked at their feet, seemingly at a loss for words. Emma was not capable of taking the lead and Sibyl was caught out by this intrusion. She had assumed Avice would be here, but this miller seemed to be the only one.

"Pardonne moi, I do not speak much English." Sibyl shrugged apologetically.

"You're...French?" Robin said with surprise.

"Oui!" Sibyl offered nothing further, then thought she better had, as his icy blue eyes were staring into hers with a look of confused skepticism. "I am...'ere as a servant to ze Lady Sibyl." She said, mimicking the French accents she had heard regularly at court, thinking it unlikely a miller would accurately know a French accent anyway. She guessed correctly, he seemed satisfied with this.

"Oh, right." He said, dusty hands going to his hips.

"Yes," Emma piped up, "That's right, I'm showing her around, you know."

"I see." Robin said, sensing he wasn't getting everything here. He examined Sibyl's face, noting the distinctive grey eyes; saw the milk white skin and the slender neck. She was tall, too, perhaps even a little taller than him when her head wasn't bowed?

He compared her to the shorter, rounder Emma with her skin; weatherworn despite evidently being younger than the Frenchwoman, and her hands as work-worn as her face was weathered. Then he quickly glanced at the toes of their shoes, peeping out under their skirts and saw that Emma's were scuffed but that Sibyl's looked far newer. Things were obviously different in France. It must be a sophisticated, wealthier place altogether he reflected.

"What is your name?" He asked with a slight smile - he liked the look of this one, the exoticism.

Sibyl's eyes widened for a moment but she held Robin's gaze and quickly cast around for the Frenchest name she knew.

"Isabelle." She stated firmly.

"Very nice..." Robin nodded, Emma completely forgotten, shuffling her feet as Sibyl and the miller carried on.

"Do you...know Avice Dexter?" Sibyl asked innocently, swiftly moving things on. "She is meeteeng oos 'ere."

Robin's face immediately darkened. Sibyl's stomach clenched with sudden worry, had she said the wrong thing? Spoken to the wrong person? Robin was turning away already, a hand waving dismissively.

"You'll want my father. He's inside." And he stalked off, disappearing into a darkened doorway in the side of the water mill without another word.

Sibyl and Emma looked at each other.

"Emma you wait here; whatever I've gotten myself into

you shouldn't be a part of it. I shan't be long." Sibyl said and trotted into the mill, assuming she should follow to find this father.

Inside she found herself in a kitchen dominated by a large roughly hewn table which was lined with people of all ages while a woman, probably the mother of the family, bustled over a fire nearby. Robin had already seated himself and was hunched over a cup, sipping miserably. There was only one other man, an older one, and Sibyl assumed this must be the father. They all looked to Sibyl for an explanation but she floundered under their gaze and they transferred to Robin, who looked at the older man with obvious bitterness and disapproval.

"She wanted Avice." Was all he said before looking back at the table, taking another swig of his drink and slamming the cup down when he'd finished.

Thankfully the older man seemed to be more pleased about her presence and he hauled himself out of the chair and motioned for her to follow. Sibyl smiled and nodded politely to the family on her way, squeezing past them to disappear gratefully into the little doorway.

"M'name's Walter love; I sell for Avice." He explained warmly, opening a little wooden box.

"Oh..." Sibyl said. "I am called Isabelle." She nodded, playing the ignorant foreigner and not responding to the rest.

" 'Ow many bags d'you need?" He asked, Sibyl watching the straggling, thin strands of grey hair sprouting from his glossy bald head in the sunlight streaming through the one tiny window as he peered into the box.

"Cinq!" She said for authenticity. "Er, five." She added as though she had had to think of the English translation. Walter raised his eyebrows momentarily as though he was surprised to hear that.

"That'll be 5d?" He confirmed. Sibyl nodded.

"Zis is fine, eet iz for ze Lady Sibyl." She replied, handing over the coins. Walter took the money in a gnarled hand, secreting it in his own purse at his waist.

"I see..." He nodded slowly. "You're foreign eh?"

"Oui, I am French, I am sent 'ere to be serveeng girl for ze Lady." She smiled. "Eengland iz nice."

"No finer place." Walter beamed, taking her elbow and steering her back out and past the diners. Sibyl glanced quickly at their dismissive faces and looked to Robin particularly. He was eating now and didn't even look up.

Outside she waved goodbye to Walter and hurried over to Emma who was seated on a bank nearby, anxiously looking around and hugging herself in the cold, despite the sun.

"Done. Now, let's hurry back."

~

Robin steadily made his way over the nine or so miles to Hapton Tower, the rope to the mill's trusty old grey mule's halter hanging loosely in his hand. Pilgrim needed little attention; he'd been delivering flour for more years than anyone could remember, so Robin's mind was free to wander in the peace of his solitary walk, so different to the busy comings and goings of the mill.

Unfortunately Robin had no younger brothers, only sisters, so not only did he have to do all the milling due to Walter being past it, it also fell to him to make deliveries when required too. Usually he would rail against this, pulling faces when Walter told him where he had to go, and punishing everyone around him by being surly for the rest of the day.

It did not go unnoticed therefore when he suggested making the delivery to Hapton himself. His family knew better than to question anything Robin did though, so they exchanged looks and said no more until he had gone on his cheerful way.

"It's that French one." Walter said sagely.

"Do you think anything may come of it this time?" His mother Margery asked.

Walter grimaced cynically and Margery knew he wasn't sure; their Robin didn't have a great track record with women as they grew tired of his moods and general resentment of the world. Even though they enjoyed a fairly privileged position as millers, he was constantly carping about the nobles and how society should be more 'equal'. Most peasant girls knew their place in the world however and could not give Robin the feedback he seemed to need.

Now he drew closer to Hapton Tower, looking up at the dark stone structure with contempt. Lord William was his new master now Lady Sibyl was married to him, and a bigger rutterkin you would struggle to find in Robin's opinion. In the past he'd had little cause to come to Hapton but since the merger of the two estates, Cornholme would now serve Hapton too.

Old Lord Bearnshaw had been fair enough, and Young Lord Bearnshaw wasn't around long enough to cause trouble. Lady Sibyl had barely glanced in the direction of the mill and so far neither had William, but all knew he was a more malignant Lord, always eager to extract the extra few pennies where he could, and a bit too free with the noose. Arrogant. Swaggering. Pompous. High-handed.

Robin's stream of insults was interrupted by his arrival at the gatehouse where he was waved straight through by the porter, familiar with Robin and Pilgrim. Once inside he threaded his way through the huts, workshops and pens, nodding to those who greeted him, to the bakehouse. Here he dropped Pilgrim's rope to the floor knowing that the old mule would stay put and lugged the sacks through the doorway.

"Robin!" Beatrice Baker looked up from her work, her cheeks glowing with the effort of kneading.

"Beatrice." Robin gave a smile and a nod and seated himself on the sacks, calmly helping himself to a small bread bun. Beatrice gave him a look of mock disapproval.

"I'll tell Lord William!" She chuckled.

"Ah, tell him." Robin rolled his eyes.

"To what do I owe this pleasure then young Robin?"

"Not so young anymore. Nearly thirty." He sighed.

"Ha, try being fifty!" Beatrice carried on kneading.

"I might. I might not." Robin rocked his head from side to side as though trying to decide and Beatrice laughed.

"You're in a good mood?" Beatrice shot Robin a look.

"I met a lass the other day." Robin nonchalantly took another bite of warm bread. Beatrice immediately stopped work and let her jaw drop.

"No!" She cried. "Which one?"

"That's what I'm here for." He answered, leaning forwards conspiratorially.

"Oo!" Beatrice was genuinely excited at this piece of gossip, it was too good that the object of Robin's affection resided at Hapton - this could provide much entertainment!

"She's the new girl, the French one." He told her happily. Beatrice immediately frowned.

"New girl? French?" She struggled to recall anyone that fitted that description.

"Aye, Isabelle she's called - she's come over to look after Lady Sibyl I gather?"

"Sorry Robin, I think you've been misled? We don't have any French girls here. Lady Sibyl doesn't need much looking after; she spends all day moping in her room and isn't allowed out on William's orders. He's worried she'll do her deer impression again." Beatrice snorted with amusement at the predicament Lord William found himself in - a wife who periodically imagined she was a deer. Served him right for forcing her to marry him; the Devil had gone and sabotaged the marriage anyway. Robin was quiet.

"Why would she...?" He managed eventually. Beatrice shrugged.

"Nevermind Robin, you'll find someone." She said consolingly.

"Yeah." Robin said absent mindedly.

Suddenly a crash sounded outside and the words "blasted breedbate" were roared just outside the door. Robin jumped up when he saw Pilgrim's white hide trotting merrily past the doorway and ran out to catch him. There he met the angry owner of a swinging broom.

"Damn thing stole some apples - you owe me!" The man cried as he managed to stop his broom before it clouted Robin rather than Pilgrim's rump.

"Sorry!" Robin said, fishing some coins from his purse and clamping them into the man's hand before going to retrieve Pilgrim's rope in a state of confusion, over "Isabelle's" lies as much as Pilgrim's behaviour.

~

That evening the Miller family were seated around their table by candlelight, eating supper and chatting about various matters. Robin wasn't saying much, he was simply wolfing down his food and intending to get an early night once he'd finished. Then came a familiar knock on the door and all stopped eating. Avice let herself in.

"Good evening, Avice." Margery gave a tight nod to the thin old woman. Avice nodded back unsmilingly. The children all bowed their heads respectfully. Robin did not react at all but stayed hunched over his bowl, noisily chewing, his long fringe obscuring his face.

Walter stood and led the older woman into the smaller room. Nobody spoke in the kitchen, but all looked at each other when to their surprise, Robin stood, straightened noisily and calmly wandered into the room after Avice and his father.

"Mama, Robin's acting strangely thesedays!" Matilda, the eldest and prettiest of Robin's younger sisters whispered to Margery, unable to contain herself.

"Hmm. Yes." Margery agreed but went no further, indicating they should all stay quiet.

Inside the smaller room Robin watched for a moment as Avice offloaded a bundle into Walter's hands and then held hers out expectantly for the purse in return. Walter handed it over and Avice fished in it for a few coins and handed them back with a nod.

"Business is good." Walter said in a low voice.

"Indeed, we have a wealthy new customer." Avice

replied, the tone of her voice belying the good news in her words.

"Lady Sibyl, aye." Walter said with a disbelieving chuckle. "You've done well there!"

"It was Helston's doing." Avice said, diverting Walter's praise away.

Robin's ears pricked up at the mention of Lady Sibyl and he interrupted them.

"Do you know a French girl, Avice? Named Isabelle?" He enquired. Avice turned and was visibly shocked that Robin would speak to her.

"No." She said with her usual composure.

"You sweet on that girl Robin?" Walter said, then explained to Avice. "We met her doing the buying for Sibyl a few days ago. Lovely accent, nice girl, very clean and tidy." He went on, Avice looking bored.

"You haven't met with an Isabelle in your dealings with Lady Sibyl?" Robin pressed.

"No. I deal with Sibyl herself." Avice said pompously. "I wouldn't know who she does or doesn't have working for her, but I do know I've never met a French Isabelle." Avice turned back to Walter and counting the coins with a subtle roll of her eyes to the older man. Robin had already left.

From then on Robin kept an eye on the path at all times, waiting for when Sibyl would next come for her powder. It was a strange idea, that it was Lady Sibyl herself coming to his mill, speaking to him no less, disguised as a Frenchwoman in order to buy powder without Lord William's knowledge. Although Robin despised this powder trade he had to admit it gave him a sense of satisfaction to know that Lord William's wife was no better than the rest of them and William needn't feel so high and mighty.

It had become imperative for him to prove to himself that he was right. He knew however that Lady Sibyl probably had good reason to be keeping this a secret and he had no wish to cause her further trouble so he formulated a plan to discover the truth without anybody else finding out. The day came when he recognised the tall, thin figure, hunched against the fiercely cold wind with her shorter, rounder maid beside her.

Not for the first time he marvelled at the lengths people would go to to obtain this powder. Then he waited and watched as she made her way up to the door of the mill's kitchen and knocked. He heard the muffled voice of someone welcoming her and her polite, French answer with a little smile to himself. Then he quickly sprinted out of the door and over the path into the trees on the other side. There he easily found the tree he'd climbed as a child and shinned up it to wait, blowing into his hands and regretting not coming out with a doublet at least.

In a very short time Sibyl was back out of the door and Robin watched her intently, savouring a good look at her before he threw a rock into the calm pool of the day so far, which he knew would send her scurrying for cover...

"Sibyl!" He bawled quickly, aiming his voice at the mill so that it would bounce from the walls and not give away his position.

His eyes were trained on her like a hawk's and sure enough he saw her jump and look around before she could stop herself. She looked all around but not up of course, then took Emma's hand and hurried away in a panic. Robin folded his arms and sat back against the tree trunk. His mind spun - he was pleased with himself for finding out the truth, but angry with her for lying to him. Flashing those grey eyes at him, knowing she was out of reach...he realised he was being unfair there and dropped from the tree to return to his milling.

~

Sibyl had heard the shout and chided herself for looking around. She thought she recognised Robin's voice but hadn't spotted him. It was clear it had been a trick, so that he could confirm her identity. It came as such a shock that she just ran. Emma was just as frightened by it as she was complicit in Sibyl's schemes and did not know how she would be punished for her role if found out.

"He was at Hapton the other day m'Lady!" She panted when they were safely out of sight of the mill and could slow the pace.

"What?" Sibyl looked at her aghast. "Why didn't you tell me before?" She clutched her head.

"Well....I thought it best I kept it quiet. He came looking for 'Isabelle' and Beatrice Baker's told everyone the story. None of the girls have told though Sibyl, honest!" Emma seemed genuinely remorseful. "...Is that....Is that why we come here?" Emma asked quietly at last.

"What?" Sibyl asked in disbelief.

"To see him - Robin Miller. Are you two...sweethearts?"

"What? No! That is ridiculous Emma! I don't know him!" Sibyl was irrationally angry with Emma, even though she had come to a natural conclusion. Sibyl realised she was being harsh on the girl who was good enough to accompany her for an eighteen mile walk on a grey, bitingly cold January day just to cover for her and calmed herself.

"I'm sorry Emma, we won't come again, I'll find another way to do my business." Sibyl concluded, clutching the pouches of powder in her purse tightly, desperately wanting to dip a finger in and take some to calm her pounding heart.

Once she was home she had a quick brew of it after donning her usual clothes and then folded her servant's clothes to put back in her chest. She considered that she would have to arrange for the powder to be delivered to Hapton surreptitiously - that was a far better idea than traipsing about in the snow, she didn't know why she hadn't thought of it before? She just had to get to the mill one last time to arrange it, and then these clothes could be given away. Emma would not be involved this time either.

A few days later Sibyl waited for all her maids to leave and the Tower to go quiet as all concentrated on their daily tasks.

She then slipped into her disguise and brazenly made her way out, brim pulled as low as possible. She let herself into the larder and tipped a basket of apples into another, the apples just about fitting, then placed the basket under her arm and confidently wandered down to the gatehouse.

The grounds of the tower were busy but she could see that the gates were unused at that moment and she felt sure that she would be attract attention if she tried to get out alone. If the porter stopped her he may recognise her if he took a closer look. She waited until a cart was leaving, then lightly hopped onto the back as though a passenger and rode right through without comment, assumed to be the carter's wife. Once on the other side and out of sight she slid off without the carter noticing a thing and carried on on foot.

She now felt very afraid, being alone and on foot. On fleet little Belaud she would have been capable of outrunning any thieves, but now here she was on the road as the peasants were, on a much more equal footing and a far easier target. She of course looked less wealthy now, but it wasn't always coins on the mind of the bandits, so she had been told. She put her head down and hurried, reaching the mill in just a couple of hours.

She had decided to tackle Robin head-on, let him know that she would not be bothering them again and there would be very little to gain in spreading any of this around. She hadn't heard any talk of it so far but was keenly aware that she was usually the last person to hear the rumours about herself. She bustled up to the door of his work area after making her purchases and let herself in.

His head lifted from his work at the grinding stone upon seeing the door open and she saw the jolt of shock pass through him when he recognised her. Her heart had skipped a beat at being face to face with him in an enclosed space so suddenly too. He was a formidable presence, an air of anger hung around him and she instinctively felt like she needed to be careful lest she triggered his rage and she suddenly found the reality of confronting him a little more disconcerting than she had thought.

"Hello Robin." She said in a formal tone.

"You're not French today then?" He bit back, returning to his task, absolutely no deference offered.

"No." She said, a little embarrassed. "I never was." She admitted.

Robin sniffed in the silence, unsure of what to say.

"Why are you here?" He asked at last, busying himself tidying some sacks.

"I came to ask...that you keep this to yourself, if you haven't told already." Sibyl perched on a nearby worktop and looked anywhere but at him as she spoke. He took quick glances at her and she looked so sad that he felt he wanted to reassure her.

"I haven't. And I won't." He said.

"Thank you. Lord William would unleash hell if he-"

"You don't have to give me all that." He said grumpily. Sibyl nodded.

"I'm going to have the powder delivered to me from now on..." She continued.

"I don't want to know!" Robin snapped. "I hate the powder and want nothing to do with the trade. That's Dad's doing, not mine." He added emphatically, slamming the sacks down and grabbing up a shovel.

There was silence. She wasn't quite sure what she was waiting for, but she was reluctant to leave. Maybe it was being spoken to as an equal for the first time in so long...

"I was only letting you know that I won't be bothering you anymore. If my powder's delivered, I have no reason to leave the tower at all!" She said the last with a little fake laugh that sounded sadder than she'd meant it to. Robin stopped. He was suddenly curious.

"Why do you do it?" He asked.

"Do what?"

"The powder?" He said as though humouring a child and losing patience.

"Well..." Sibyl gave a little nervous laugh and a shrug and

looked at her feet. She knew why of course, but hadn't articulated it to herself, let alone another person.

"I mean, I can see why most of us do it, the people who only have a hut to house twelve people, who live in constant fear of not being able to fill their bellies. They're desperate for a release I guess, but you - you have everything." He gestured angrily at her.

Suddenly Sibyl felt enraged. She'd been sad and quiet for so long, wondering what plan God had for her (wasting away in that tower forever?) and now here she was, being told she should be grateful and being made to feel small for indulging in one pleasure in this life!

"Everything? Robin I have nothing!" She raised her voice. Robin pulled a skeptical face. "You think my life is in any way enviable?" She asked. Robin didn't know how to answer. "Let me tell you about my life. The husband I loved is dead. We had no children. My father died, asking me to look after the family lands and name for him, but I haven't done a very good job of that because I was forced to marry the man I've always hated, who took my land and pulled down my home. That same man ruined my life so he could have me as a prize, comes and uses me when he feels like it, yet has tired of me and has disappeared to court to parade about with other mistresses no doubt - I'm not ignorant, Robin - while he keeps me a prisoner in his tower. I have no family, my brother was murd-" She abruptly stopped, breathing hard, tears springing in her eyes and clamped a hand over her mouth. Robin was stood stock still, looking uncomfortable and wary of what he had unleashed.

"Murdered?" He asked. "We were told he disappeared...who-" Sibyl saw as the realisation hit him. "William?"

"Nobody else knows!" Sibyl hissed, momentarily taking her hand away from her mouth.

"That's...that's unlawful! You could have him hung for that!"

"No! No...he is very friendly with the King. I used to

have protection, under Edward, but that's all gone now, he has it all his way. I have no proof anyway. It's better not to talk about it." She shook her head sadly.

Robin was beginning to understand why someone with all the fancy clothes and food they wanted could be so unhappy. Sibyl was a pawn, a lonely pawn, pushed around in the games of those more powerful and then forgotten in the dust when she'd rolled under the table. She was bound by the duty all felt to their families, something he could identify with as that was all that kept him at the mill. He could have happily left the mill, but he knew it would be the ruin of his family. He supposed Sibyl felt the same, but she had already lost it all. He'd moved a little closer, bare dusty forearms held uneasily at his sides, his fists almost clenched with the tension running through him because he felt he wanted to fight William there and then.

"So, what, you're just going to rot away in there forever, getting out of your mind on that devilish powder, Mother Helston growing fatter at your expense?" He channelled his aggression into encouraging Sibyl to fight against her fate. He wanted her to have some spirit about it all, to not let William win.

"I suppose so?" She shrugged, then added brightly: "I'll be fine, if something changes I'll stop with the powder and be off in the blink of an eye!"

"That's not how it works Sibyl." Robin shook his head pityingly, his blue eyes sad.

"What do you mean?" She frowned with annoyance.

"When you get on that stuff, you can't stop. You can't stop until every penny is spent so you beg in the mud at the side of the road and when you're given a coin you don't go and buy bread, you go running to the mill to get a little measure of powder. Then the next thing we know you never turn up again and we hear you were found curled up dead somewhere." Robin poured out the fate he had seen befall the locals time and again while Mother Helston and her crew escaped the noose and lived well.

"That wouldn't happen to me!" Sibyl said defiantly.

"No?" Robin cocked his head to one side and breached the gap between them, holding out a hand. "Pass me that powder - I'll throw it in the pond and give the fishes a treat."

Sibyl's hand tightened on the purse she held. She hated it, but something stopped her handing it over. Robin's shoulders slumped and he shook his head. Then he roared and slammed the door shut. Sibyl jumped, suddenly afraid of this profoundly angry man, thinking that this had all been a grave mistake.

"See?" He growled through clenched teeth.

"What can I do?" She asked in a tiny voice, watching him warily. He advanced on her and she flinched as he gripped her shoulders and glared into her terrified eyes.

"Don't let him win." He urged. "Give me the powder, go back to the tower. Tell someone you trust to lock you in. Tell them not to let you out until you're better. You'll get ill, you'll scream to be let out, but they have to hold for your sake. It's not easy, but you must do it Sibyl." He'd come closer; put his hand on the one she had clamped onto the purse. His rough fingers were now prying hers apart. "When you've come through, come and find me."

He was now looking into her eyes, and Sibyl realised with numb shock that he wasn't angry with her, he was angry with the powder and he was now intending to kiss her. She kept looking at him, frozen, unable to stop anything he was doing and felt his lips on hers. His stubble scratched her skin but his lips were soft and she could feel the passion and depth of feeling in him and it felt nice that it was directed her way. She found herself responding and letting go of the pouch.

She felt him throw it to the other side of the room and his hands return to her body, him kissing her harder, their lips now parted. Then they heard a voice outside - Walter's voice. Robin ripped himself away from her and returned to the stone, leaning on a beam with one hand, staring at it going round and round. Sibyl hurriedly straightened her clothes and stood, then opened the door herself and called Au Revoir! cheerily before politely dipping out of the way of Walter's knowing face and hurrying off.

Walter stepped into the milling room and looked about. He could instantly tell Robin was guilty, and furious with him for seeing it.

"The French girl again?" Walter began to laugh. Robin wiped his mouth and advanced on the old man, grabbing up a fistful of his shirt.

"Don't sell any more to her." He said before roughly dropping the fabric and barging past, leaving Walter stuttering in the doorway.

~

Back in the Tower Sibyl tore off her peasant clothing and thrust it untidily to the bottom of the chest. She was trembling with the shock of what had happened, feeling like she needed the powder to calm herself and not have to think about it, and then raging with herself for thinking that. Imagining Mother Helston cackling as she succumbed and suffered the fate Robin had told her of. She stuck her head out of her chamber door and wailed to the nearest passing person.

"Send for Emma!"

The man was shocked into action at the sight of Sibyl's unkempt hair and wild eyes and hurried off with a nod. Shortly afterwards Emma hesitantly arrived in the chamber, and Sibyl left her place by the fire to fall to her knees before her.

"Emma, Emma!" She wept. "You have to help me, you have to lock me in here and not let me out no matter how much I beg or wail!"

"Sibyl, why?!" Emma looked fraught.

"I take the powder!" Sibyl confessed, thinking that Emma would probably know of it.

Emma was silent. She had heard dark tales about this powder, and had been warned by her mother to stay away from it. She was glad she had, if this was what you were reduced to whilst taking it.

"Can't you just...not do it anymore?" Emma asked.

"No..." Sibyl sobbed. "It grips you with the Devil's talons! I will do anything to get at it at the moment, and I'm told this can only get worse. I have to be purged of it; I have to starve the demon out!"

"I see..." Emma said thoughtfully, now understanding what Sibyl's business at the mill was.

"It will be an unpleasant experience I think, we must both be strong." Sibyl said forcefully, gripping fistfuls of Emma's skirts, trying to convince herself as much as Emma.

"We'll do it Sibyl. I'll let everyone know." Emma nodded fearfully.

"We must get this done before William gets back. I don't want him to see me like that, I don't want him to interrupt. We must start immediately." Sibyl said, calmer now, rising to her feet. "Help me undress."

~

The next day Robin was back at Hapton Tower in the bakehouse with Beatrice. Beatrice worked quietly, as did everyone in the eerily subdued grounds. Robin grimly chewed a sweet bun and winced when a muffled scream of rage rent the air around the tower above. Beatrice glanced across apologetically and whispered:

"Lady Sibyl's having another of her...episodes..."

Robin nodded in acknowledgement of this. He had heard enough. He rose and walked out without a word.

~

Lord William marched into Sibyl's chamber and looked around suspiciously. The bright February sunlight streamed through her window, making her glow as she sat sewing happily, humming to herself. She looked up as he entered with a look of....defiance? He looked around suspiciously.

"Hello Sibyl." He said carefully.

"Good morning William!" She returned cheerfully.

"Everything well while I was away?" He enquired.

"I had some bad moments. But I'm fine now." She beamed at him.

"Good." He said, clearly still wrong-footed by finding everything so orderly and her in such a good mood.

"Did you have a nice time at court dear?" She said chattily, examining her stitching.

"Yes."

"Meet anyone nice?" She said pointedly, unable to help herself.

William said nothing, knowing he didn't need to. He was pleased to see Sibyl back to her old sharp self if anything. He was refreshed by his break at court, enjoying the lifestyle he always thought he should have. He left the room to arrange for he and Sibyl to dine together that evening and went to change out of his heavy, dirty travelling clothes.

Over their supper they made idle chit chat and Sibyl heard all about what was happening further South and wondered to herself what Edward was doing at that moment. They had heard that he was not idle and intended to take back the crown, but that he had left England penniless and help was not forthcoming. Few gave any credence to the idea he would win back the crown. Sibyl had long since decided to adapt to the new regime though, and not waste time mourning for Edward's rule.

In this new spirit she accepted a cup from William and toasted the King's good health with a tight smile. William sat back in his chair, his boots kicked off, and Sibyl saw his large bejewelled hand fall on the armrest, his fingers drumming a nonsensical tune happily to himself. He seemed content. Sibyl saw her chance to strike.

"William." She said seriously. "I need to ask something of you."

"Hm?" William looked up with interest.

"I need to get out." She said pleadingly. "I've been in this tower obediently since you left; I've seen only these grounds. I've changed my ways now, I promise, the demons are gone - please, please let me out. Just a little, just to see something different?" She begged.

"I've trusted you before..." He began

"It's different now."

"Hmm how can I know that? Sibyl, I am charged with keeping order here and that powder trade is a troublesome business. How do you think it looks if the Lord's wife herself is taking it? Acting crazed? It erodes my authority."

"I promise, I'm finished with it now - are you proposing to keep me in here forever?"

"No..." He admitted, struggling under her intensity.

"William, really, I promise, I will bring no more shame on Hapton." She said earnestly, sensing hope that he would relent. She allowed him to mull it over.

"We'll ride together tomorrow." He said, raising his cup to hers. It was disappointing he had stipulated that they would go out together, but Sibyl knew better than to childishly throw his gift back in his face at this stage. She would just have to be patient.

BEARNSHAW

10

False Promise

Her patience paid off. After a few days of being kept firmly at William's side by day and night he allowed her out without him, delighted with her new attitude. He told her he had planned to get back to court almost straight away but had now decided to stay with her for a while longer. Her heart sank, she had secretly hoped he would go again - he had enjoyed his Christmas so much - but at least she was making progress.

Of course, Sibyl chose Emma to accompany her on her first ride out 'alone', promising they were just making the short ride into Burnley for the day and would be fine without a male guard. Emma was sent into Burnley to visit family alone however and Sibyl turned her horse and urged it at a smart pace all the way to Cornholme in just an hour. Her heart was beating fit to burst with joy and excitement by the time she reached the mill. She had to stop short however, knowing she could not be seen as herself near the mill or the gossip would be back at Hapton before she herself was. She was only wearing her plain grey travel kirtle but she was still clearly recognisable.

She ducked off the road and made her way through the trees, her new dun pony following obediently. She made a wide circle around the mill and came to a stop in a spot overlooking the doorway to the stone room where she was hoping Robin would be. There she anxiously waited, hoping against hope that he would not be making deliveries today. The door was shut, but that could have been to keep the cold out.

Soon she saw a couple of young men arrive down the path, struggling through the mud with a pack pony. To her joy she saw that the pony carried no load, meaning they had come to collect and Robin would likely help them see the sacks onto the animals' back, having just finished grinding their corn.

Sure enough Robin was out of the door to greet the men before they had even knocked and then they all began hauling the sacks onto the pony. Robin then waved them off and patted himself down for a moment. Sibyl took her chance and made a loud hissing noise, then when Robin glanced over began waving her arm in a wide arc over her head. Robin looked baffled for a moment, and then Sibyl grinned as he recognised her and sprinted over the path, leaping into the trees.

"Sibyl!" He was with her in moments, taking up her chilly hands in his dusty ones and looking at her face with amazement. "You made it!"

"Yes!" She laughed.

"You look so much better..." He looked her up and down.

It was true; she had put weight back on and lost that grey pallour. Now her milky skin had a rosy flush to it in the appropriate places. He mused to himself on how nice she looked in her Lady's clothing compared to the rough peasant's clothes. He saw she had a luxurious fur-lined cloak over her slender shoulders and marvelled at how much it must have cost, having rarely come so close to such finery.

"You're not in disguise today?" He said.

"No, Lord William is letting me out - he thinks I'm in Burnley with my maid!" She beamed.

"See? It is getting better." He hugged her to him and she

realised it felt so good to be gathered up into his arms like that. She felt his chest move against her as he took a deep breath. Reluctantly, he pulled away.

"Have you the day with me then?" He asked with a hopeful smile.

"Yes!" She nodded vigourously.

"Let me retrieve my doublet...and Pilgrim if we're riding?" He nodded to the pony.

"Oh, er, yes of course." Sibyl had not known what to expect when she came to see Robin, probably just talking in the stone room again, but she was excited at the prospect of riding out with him. She had seen Robin's mule though and was unsure as to whether it would keep up with her sparky young palfrey. She had assumed they would both ride hers, but on reflection she thought perhaps Robin wasn't an experienced rider. He only ever led that mule as far as she had seen; the Millers didn't own a horse, so he would feel unsure on hers perhaps?

He returned from the stable at the rear of the mill, studiously leading Pilgrim into the trees back there out of the sight of the kitchens where he knew his family would be watching.

"Robin, we...we can't be seen on the road together, you know that?" Sibyl asked anxiously, hoping he would understand the risk. "How can we go anywhere together?"

"No one will see the way we're going!" He said with a wink, and bent to help her mount.

Eagerly she set her foot in the dainty little stirrup and vaulted up, settling herself in her skirts in the saddle. Then she watched with interest as Robin placed a hand on Pilgrim's wither and gave a little bounce which propelled him up onto the animal's back in one smooth movement. Then he motioned for her to follow and she saw that he was aiming straight up the steep, rocky valleyside.

Pilgrim evidently knew this route and was very sure footed compared to her horse. Robin periodically hopped off to lead her over a particularly slippery bit and effortlessly remounted when he could. She realised he was in fact an excellent rider, more than a match for her. Up and up they climbed and with delight she realised they were heading towards Eagle Crag. They followed the top of the valley, and she saw that familiar proud shape bursting from the rocks of the ground. She took a deep breath of the clean air and smiled in the sunshine, which gave the early promise of spring.

Robin looked at her happily as he rode along, seeing that some strands of her hair, a buttery colour, had flown free in the brisk wind. His heart beat faster as he imagined it all flying free, silky and shining. He had never seen a woman so beautiful. Then his thoughts were brought back down to earth.

"We'll be visible on the skyline to anyone happening to look up here." He said, knowing that many looked to the magnificent Eagle Crag when they could as they went about their business in the valley below. "We should move onto the tops a little."

He steered Pilgrim towards the open moor and Sibyl followed his example, equally enjoying the wide open view afforded to her up there. They headed for a particular clump of trees right next to the crag and Robin hopped down and took her reins, indicating she should get down by holding out his hand for her. She watched as he led the two animals, deflecting their nips at each other with an expert hand, tying them to the twisted, tortured branches of the windswept hawthorns clinging to the edge of the valley.

Then he turned and walked back to her and held out his hand for hers, eagerly towing her back towards the crag.

"I don't think we can sit on the rocks themselves - someone would see." He said apologetically.

"Do you think they would recognise us from this distance?" Sibyl queried, disappointed.

"I think so...we'll still have a good view though!" He led her to a spot just behind the crag, and when they sat down they saw the landscape stretching out before them with the crag jutting up in the middle of it all, so the effect was similar to standing on the top of it anyway.

"Ah it's beautiful." Sibyl said with a sigh. "Thank you, for bringing me here." She said.

"You're most welcome my Lady." Robin said with mock formality, allowing himself to play the role of obedient vassal for once, enjoying the thrill of having this elegant highborn Lady on his arm - how often did this happen in the lifetime of a man such as he?

"Why did you bring me here?" Sibyl asked.

"I just thought you'd like it. I like it. Everybody knows it. I knew you'd grown up round here and I always heard the tales about Lord Bearnshaw's wild young daughter riding about on her own, without a mother to keep her in check." He explained, rubbing the back of his neck shyly as he related the gossip to her.

"Really?" Sibyl scoffed.

"Yeah...I used to come up here too, wondered if I'd get a glimpse of this famous impish girl everybody talked about. I never did though; always had to be back at the mill really." He mentioned the mill with a kind of gloominess.

"You seem to hate that place." Sibyl said. Robin screwed up his face and took time to think.

"I think that's true." He said at last.

"Why?" Sibyl asked, not liking his unhappiness.

"I just don't like feeling that everything was mapped out for me before I was even born I suppose?" He said with obvious discomfort. Nobody had ever spoken to him about this before.

"What do you mean?" Sibyl said, familiar with the notion of wanting to buck against your decided fate.

"Well, I was born a miller and I was forced into milling early due to dad's health, and I'll likely die a miller. What's the point?" He shrugged. Sibyl didn't know what to say, so he carried on to fill the silence. "To top it all off, dad's taken up with Helston and Avice. The commons have a bad enough life as it is, always scraping around to fend off starvation. Now they have a new master. So many get drawn to it. We eat well thanks to it, but it doesn't make it right." He finished.

"Can't you change any of this?" She asked, her immediate instinct to rebellion surfacing.

"Nah." He said dismissively. "Dad makes the decisions. I'm the only lad, I have eight mouths to feed once he's gone, if I'm not milling whoever's the Lord of the Manor'll just move in a new family who will do it."

"Couldn't you move? Maybe become a soldier, support them that way?"

"I've thought about it," he conceded, "but it'd mean laying my life down to make some point on behalf of a Lord."

"Why do you bear your Lord such ill-will...they're not all Williams? What about the protection they offer you?" Sibyl felt slightly irked at the constant digs against her people.

"Protection from another Lord." Robin said grimly. "If we had none, it wouldn't be needed."

"But..who would own the land?" Sibyl was genuinely intrigued by this idea.

"Let's not talk about it now." Robin laid a hand on hers and transferred his gaze from the landscape to Sibyl again. "I'll admit, I had another reason to bring you here." A corner of his mouth lifted in a half smile.

"What's that?" Sibyl asked with a smile.

"I was hoping you'd be so impressed and grateful you'd kiss me." He confessed.

"You did? Well sir, you are sorely mistaken!" Sibyl closed her eyes and stuck her nose in the air in the haughtiest manner she could manage.

"Oh dear..." said Robin quietly but Sibyl could hear that he had moved closer, and then he was kissing her.

Sibyl enjoyed the feeling of that kiss, but her mind was transported elsewhere. Memories of the view of the glittering sea up at Swallowhurst, many images of snatched and lingering kisses with John, that image of him trotting off to battle for the last time, leaving her gazing after him. Lying above him on his grave slab. She felt a sob rising in her throat, but merely kissed Robin more desperately to suppress it.

Robin responded by gently pressing her backwards onto the damp grass, wrapping one edge of her furred cloak around himself and pulling the other over until they were cocooned together, him lying across her and reaching up to reverently touch the ribbons of her hair. Sibyl smiled through the kiss - the hair, they always wanted to touch the hair. Then her thoughts darkened when an image of William rolling into bed and grabbing at her wandered in.

She knew full well that William would be enraged beyond measure at what she was doing now and she gained a fierce satisfaction from that, making her reach up with both hands and grab Robin's hair in handfuls, then running her hands down his neck and across his powerful shoulders. He arched his back in response, pressing his hips against her to let her know he loved her enthusiastic touch.

He broke from the kiss and looked into her eyes. She gazed back at him; his breathing quickened when he saw that fervent, vehement, dangerous look in her eyes. He seemed to sense that this was a vengeful act and it made him burn for her even more. He'd had fumbles with the village girls before, but Sibyl promised so much more...he knew she had a colourful past, full of the intrigues of court, violence and glamour. He wanted a little taste of that.

Sibyl pulled his head back down so that their lips could meet again, using her spare hand to clutch at one of his and direct it down towards her hip. He took the hint and his hand kept travelling as far as it could without breaking the kiss again, then began hooking up the swathes of fabric of her skirts until he touched the wool of her hose and began tracing the leg back up until he could feel the warm, soft skin of her thigh and Sibyl could feel the slight trembling of his hand.

He ran his hand right up under her kirtle, feeling the curve of her hip, then returned to the thin linen of her underwear. Sibyl had little patience for the idea of wriggling free of the cloak and him fiddling with pulling them down, so she gripped his shoulder slightly and bucked her hips to hopefully indicate that he should just tear them - she'd get another pair. She felt his fingers curl around the fabric and then he grinned, giving a sharp tug and they both heard the ripping sound.

He lifted off her for a moment, pressing his forehead against hers, wordlessly begging her to undo his clothing, sensing she would know exactly what to do. She set about freeing him, all thoughts of being accidentally seen forgotten by both and once it was done he settled between her thighs and she gripped his hips, hard, pressing her heels into his buttocks. Then she was reaching around to cling on to his shoulders, digging in her fingers and knowing he would take the pain easily, pressing her face into the rough cloth of his doublet, biting into it, loving the thrill of revenge, the ecstasy of a mutual experience like this after so many years of being, essentially, alone.

~

Lord William was going away. Sibyl hadn't really bothered to listen to the details; it had been weeks since her day with Robin and she was literally desperate to see him again, forgoing food and sleep in favour of simply thinking about him. It was a source of wonder to her how he had neatly filled the gap left by the powder and she really didn't need it anymore. She could simply while away her days daydreaming about what she would do with Robin. It also made William so much more tolerable, like she was in a protective bubble and whatever he did just bounced off the surface of it.

It was excruciating, trying to find a way to get the message to Robin - this was their chance! She wondered how he was finding the separation? Was he as on edge as she? Finding it hard to concentrate on his work and find interest in the people around him? Or, she thought more gloomily, was he thinking very little about her after all? Regardless, she leapt at the chance to go hunting with Lord William, thinking that if she was clever she could find a chance to slip away.

William took his hunting extremely seriously and she

knew that once his bloodlust was up he would pay only minimal attention to her. If she made a conscious effort to fall behind and not chat overly much to the others in the party, and her pony stayed quiet, she could probably slip away into the thicker trees....Then she could head off to Cornholme and pretend to have gotten lost, having successfully delivered the message to Robin with any luck.

The plan worked brilliantly. The rest of the party was focussed on the activity of Lord William's hawk and Sibyl took her chance to carefully walk away. When she felt she was safely out of earshot she dug her heels into her pony's side and the speedy little thing relished the chance to kick up his own heels, weaving between the trees on a direct course to the mill.

Once there Sibyl faced an agonising wait in the trees as before, checking who was around before she could make a move. Of course, most of the family was present - where else would they be, Sibyl reflected. Travel was a rare part of a rustic's life; they didn't have a host of staff to keep their houses, crops and animals in order while they were away.

She grimaced to herself - she could hear the grinding of the stone but for quite a while there had been no sign of him leaving the room. She shivered in the grey, damp February afternoon, thinking perhaps she was mad to be stood here waiting to catch a glimpse of a man when she could be heading back to Hapton for a warming alcoholic drink with the others shortly....

Then she completely forgot all that when Robin emerged from the door heading briskly for the stables. With a rising sense of joy, Sibyl saw him return a moment later with Pilgrim and his pack saddle, whereupon he began placing sacks on his back and prepared to leave. Sibyl watched him as he walked, one hand tucked into his doublet, lead rope slack in the other, head lowered against the grey day.

After a while she saw him frown thoughtfully, and then he tipped his head to the side as though listening while he walked. With a grin she realised that he had recognised that she was following him and then he was transformed, pelting into the trees with Pilgrim dragging along on the other end of the rope. He bounced up to her and swept her up into his arms, kissing her delightedly and Sibyl felt that it wasn't really possible to be any happier than this, surely?

"Robin I haven't got long!" She said with a twinge of regret.

"Oh?" He looked terribly disappointed and she thought then that her fears that she was alone in her feelings were unfounded.

"I absconded from a hunting party, I need to get back before William sends his men out to scour the whole country for me..." She sneaked another quick kiss to cheer him up. "But I came to deliver good news - he's going away the day after the morrow!"

"So, you'll be able to see me?!" He gripped her arms tighter and searched her face eagerly for the answer.

"Well, I was hoping you would come to see me this time?" She said shyly, tracing a finger up his arm. "The crag was nice, but a little chilly...my chamber offers more comfort and privacy...."

He looked at her quizzically - this was something he'd never dared to consider, serving Lord William's wife in his own nest!

"You could deliver some flour, and then ask for Emma. She'll bring you to me. Everyone will think you've come to see her!"

Robin took a moment to think, his eyes full of concern. She could understand that; she didn't know how William would punish her if he found out, but she knew for certain the consequences for Robin would be far worse. She suffered a twist of worry about the future in her gut. This was clearly how things would be forever...secrecy or suffering. She brushed the dark thoughts from her mind when Robin gave his answer.

"I'll come to you." He nodded, butterflies beginning to flutter in his stomach at the thought of this, the most daring thing he had done in his life so far.

They shared a hurried embrace and then Sibyl mounted and urged her pony into a flying pace, her cloak flying out behind her and Robin watching her go. Before long Sibyl noted a couple of figures on the road ahead. They were both mounted on fine horses and could only really be from the hunting party from Hapton. Sure enough as she drew closer she recognised Robert and one of the other men.

"Apologies, I got lost!" She chuckled, happily joining them. "I do hope you haven't had to abandon the hunting on my behalf?"

Robert said nothing but regarded Sibyl with cynicism, pondering how a woman famous for traversing all around this country could get lost here?

~

Robin had washed and put on his good clothes. Even Pilgrim had had a brush and now the pair set off into the afternoon together. Thankfully it was dry if still chilly so he arrived in the courtyard around Hapton in good order, not like a drowned rat. He avoided eye contact with all those who spotted him and wondered what such a spruced-up looking Robin was doing, riding his mule into the grounds without a sack of flour in sight.

He headed straight for the bakehouse, unable to stop the shake in his hands as he tied Pilgrim to it. What if some knew already? Could this Emma be trusted? He could easily be walking to his doom. Beatrice knew all the gossip however and he relaxed when she looked up with genuine surprise at his entrance, without a trace of knowledge of what was really going on. He stood formally with his hands behind his back and cleared his throat.

"Good day, Robin..." Beatrice greeted him with open amusement and curiosity.

"Good day Beatrice. I, er, I've come to see Emma....she's a maid. I'd like to see her." He winced inwardly, knowing he was a poor deceiver.

"Emma?" Beatrice looked confused. "Is she your 'French' girl then?"

It took Robin a few moments to remember that and consider an answer.

"Oh, yes, that was a joke, it turns out." He put in a nervous laugh.

"Well, I can take you into the tower, though someone else will have to find her for you as I don't have much contact with her." Beatrice began dusting off her hands on her apron and heading for the door.

"Thanks." Robin nodded his gratitude and followed her back out into the busy courtyard to more stares as they made their way to a minor entrance. Beatrice wanted to hoot with laughter at the sight of Robin, usually so confident and indifferent to others in such an agitated, awkward state. She stopped herself though because she remembered the pain of young love herself, and did so desperately want Robin to settle down with a nice girl and Emma was a sweet one, so she wished him the best of luck and posted him into the tower with directions to the great hall, where he would have to be brave and ask someone to find her for him.

Robin didn't feel very brave, he was almost so uptight he couldn't croak out his request to see Emma, but somehow he did and before long he could see that familiar short form bustling towards him.

"Hello." He said with a shy smile, thinking that the people watching would be expecting some kind of affectionate greeting between a young couple.

"Hello." Emma gave him an equally shy smile, without any joy in it, perhaps even a note of disapproval, Robin thought with trepidation. She wordlessly led him away though and he dumbly followed her through the dark maze of chambers until he was deposited at the door and Emma said bitterly:

"I'll just make myself scarce until you're done then." And briskly disappeared into a chamber nearby with a slam of the door.

Robin exhaled noisily and knocked quietly on the door. Sibyl opened the door hesitantly and peeped around it, then all his thoughts of worry at how unhappy Emma had seemed were forgotten when Sibyl threw the door open and grabbed his doublet collar, dragging him into the room. He just had time to dimly take in the roaring fire, furniture finer than he had ever seen; walls lined with colourful tapestries and of course, a sumptuous bed before Sibyl had dragged him into it.

He tumbled onto her in a kind of daze but she was soon kissing him, warming his chilly lips with her own and his mind slowly collected itself and he relaxed and concentrated on what he was evidently expected to do. He opened his eyes and took in the gorgeous sight before him - Sibyl, clad only in her shirt, her long, pale fawn hair brushed out and spread around her face on the pillows as he had imagined so many times...

Sibyl was grinning delightedly and already helping him remove his doublet.

"You bolted the door or something?" He asked breathlessly as he knelt upright over her and began ripping off his clothes.

"Of course, now do your job Robin Miller!" She giggled, unable to resist openly watching as he undressed, getting her first glimpse of him unclothed and seeing the pale but hard body, no trace of the slight flabbiness settling on the hulking mass of William's form thesedays.

"Good job you've got a good fire going!" He said, thinking of how they'd had to remain clothed against the chill spring air on Eagle Crag, before diving under the covers with her, tugging off her shirt and greedily running his hands all over her smooth, warm body as he pleased.

Sibyl exalted in his reverent touch, knowing that never in his life would he have experienced anything like this. It felt good to be appreciated properly; nobles would always take a good bed and a soft, groomed woman for granted, but Robin was clearly cherishing her every move, drinking in her beauty, amazed by her long slender limbs.

He gently cupped one of her small breasts in his hand and

carefully brushed his cheek against it before running his tongue softly over the rosy nipple, smiling to himself at the sharp intake of breath he'd elicited. Sibyl responded by running her hand down his hard belly and deftly stroking as gently as she could around the edges of the thick glossy hair below, knowing full well he would only be able to stand that so long before wanting more...

~

"You must be hungry, love!" Sibyl raised her head from its resting place on Robin's sparsely-haired chest.

"Hm?" Robin replied dreamily.

"Food, Robin - do you remember such a thing?" She said with a slight laugh. "I'll get you some."

She rose to poke at the fire and select some things from the little table which he now noticed laden with foods which, admittedly, did set his mouth to watering despite not even recognising some of the things. Sibyl was aware his eyes were on her and she hoped the pre-coital magic was still there and he would like what he saw as much. She did bear a few scars from her past thesedays. She chanced a quick glance and saw that he'd sat up in bed, hands behind his head casually. He was frowning thoughtfully though.

"What be you thinking about?" She asked curiously.

"I was thinking that I don't want this to end." He replied, Sibyl catching a slight unexpected note of despair in his voice. He continued before she had chance to reply. "I can't stand it Sibyl." He said more firmly.

"Stand what?" She asked, returning to the bed and handing him the food, starting to worry. Robin was such a mercurial character, slipping from happiness to anger with ease.

"I'm going to have to go back to that mill, and wait, watching that stone go round and round, knowing that he is coming back here and taking this spot." He said bitterly, taking a mouthful of a little fancy which Sibyl knew would be delicious with a look of disgust on his face.

"Wh...well, yes, but-" She floundered.

"Run away with me." He said.

The room fell silent as the words hung between them, Sibyl blinked with shock and struggled to form a coherent thought. Robin for once offered nothing to fill the gap; he had plenty to say, but wanted Sibyl's pure, instinctive answer.

She looked at him unhappily. How could she possibly answer that? Naturally the idea of running away and living a simple life, getting to enjoy Robin whenever she liked and being far from William was appealing on the face of it, but she knew the reality was far more difficult.

"He'd find me." She said eventually.

"We'd go very far away. We could change our names." He shot back, and Sibyl realised he had actually thought about this and was deadly serious.

"What about the mill?"

"To hell with the mill!" He scowled.

"Your family?"

"I'll send money. I'll mill somewhere else if I have to."

"Robin...it's not possible, is it?" She began sadly.

"Sibyl, you're not arguing to stay here are you? With your brother's murderer? Surely if we care about each other, and we help each other, we can make it work? I've already helped you so much." He'd stopped eating and placed the plate down on the floor by the bed carefully, even though he would have dearly loved to throw it at the wall and watch the food slither down the tapestry, ruining it.

"You have, you have!" Sibyl latched on to the positive. "But...if you will think about it, this would be a huge step into the wilderness for me - I do not live among the commons, I would have no resources for survival!"

Sibyl thought of herself as worldly compared to Robin, who had never travelled further than Derby, just once. She had travelled extensively, been married twice, lain with a king, danced with foreign dignitaries, run an estate single handedly, could read and write, regularly hunted, and hawked and was a fine horsewoman. But the nearest she had been to a peasant's life was watching it from her litter, or riding through on a palfrey from manor to manor. The powder had sucked her down into it, but she felt ill-prepared to launch herself off the edge of a cliff into it for good. She could see her words had been poorly received.

"So, what is our future then Sibyl? I creep up and scratch on the door of your fancy house like a cur wanting to be let in to eat crumbs under the banquet table? Until you tire of me or someone whispers in William's ear and he has me hung?" His voice was rising.

"No, of course not, I don't know - please keep your voice down!" Sibyl was distraught at the turn things had taken, from the heights of pleasure to bewildering pain in just a few moments.

"I should have known it!" Robin spat as he tugged on his clothes with fury. "I am merely your plaything, and you would rather receive a man you hate every night than give up your finery!"

"Robin, no!" Sibyl was crying now, also pulling on her shirt and intending to follow as he was plainly intending to leave. It was too late though by the time she had pulled it on and picked up her kirtle, fearful of leaving the room part-dressed, he was gone and she was alone with the plate of uneaten food and the chill settling over her skin.

~

At least with Lord William away Sibyl had time to sicken herself from crying that night, bitterly telling Emma that it was all over and she would not have to be a part of any of her schemes anymore. Emma scurried away, chastened, and Sibyl stayed awake well past dark, knowing that the only chink of light in her life was gone and feeling like she could not take any more of this. She had no future at all and no control. With Robin she had briefly felt she had a modicum of power over her fate, but that had been snatched away as a reminder that no, she was no better than one of the sheep in the pastures.

Around midnight she made the decision to leave. She needed a way out of feeling this and felt no need to fight it. She angrily snatched up her jewellery casket and stormed out of the room. There was no one to challenge her and she whirled through the silent, dark and cold chambers in a swirl of skirts and cloak, a small orb of candlelight making its way to a side door.

She pounded purposefully over the courtyard and could hear the guards on the gate coming alive with interest as she approached.

"M'lady, where are you going? Lord William-"

"Silence!" She barked, a cloud of steam curling up from her mouth in the moonlit darkness. The man complied out of shock. Sibyl reached into her box and pulled out a handsome ring.

"Take this and keep your peace." She looked across at him furiously and he saw the whites of her eyes clearly. He took a moment to weigh up the situation, then held out his hand. Sibyl stuffed the ring into it with disdain and stalked out of the gates, onto the darkened lane.

Not caring about what might become of her in the dark, alone on the roads she marched unheedingly all the way to Mother Helston's door. With grim satisfaction she noticed a little glow of light in the window. She knocked on the door. The old woman took a while to come to the door and opened it very hesitantly, but changed the second she saw Sibyl.

"Sibyl!" She exclaimed with delight. "Come in, come in - Mother Helston's missed you..." The hissing voice said.

"I need something strong!" Sibyl wailed, bursting into tears as she threw herself down in one of the chairs. "Here, take this!" She held out the jewellery box.

"Oh dear..." Mother Helston warily took the box, but her excitement grew when she felt the intricate detailing on the surface and realised it was a casket, likely to contain valuables. She fought to control her glee when she opened it and the pile of gold and jewels glinted back at her in the candlelight.

"I have just the thing." She said, hurriedly secreting the casket in a cupboard and bustling over to rekindle the dying fire and light more candles.

11
The Hand of Fate

It was dark by the time Robin arrived back at the mill. He'd had plenty of time to stamp off his anger and furiously smear away his tears and was in a state of blank, numb confusion. He was surprised to see activity in the domestic part of the mill, but prioritised settling Pilgrim back in the stable before going to see what was happening. Truthfully he had hoped all would be in bed and he would not have to face anyone until morning - maybe later if he sneaked out to the stone room early?

When he let himself back in the door he immediately saw what the excitement within was about as he was faced with his father's corpse laid out on the table. For a moment he was stunned and looked from face to face, seeing his mother and sisters weeping all around the room. Eventually Margery seemed to notice his presence.

"He's dead Robin!" She wailed, taking her hands from her face.

"I can see that." Robin said seating himself at the table, staring at the portion of leg laid out directly before his eyes with disbelief. "How? When?"

"Not long after you left, just clutched his chest and keeled over!" Margery replied.

Robin didn't know what to say, he just felt cold.

"What will we do?!" Margery appealed to the heavens.

"We won't miss him. What did he provide?" Robin said quietly but firmly, knowing that this was poor timing, that his words were never going to go down well but that this very moment would elicit a particularly impressive reaction from his mother. Robin was unafraid however; he thought far too much emphasis was placed on keeping quiet and accepting things in this world. It was better to battle it out and clear the air.

"What did he provide?" Margery asked quietly, then repeated the exact words in a shout. *"What did he provide?!"*

Robin looked his mother in the eye perfectly calmly.

"That's what I said." He replied but Margery ignored the danger in his voice, relishing the chance to pour out her distress.

"*This* is what he provided Robin!" She gestured around at the girls seated around the room. "All these clothes, do you think they merely sprouted out of the very ground? We eat well and we look well thanks to *him!*" She pointed fiercely at the ugly corpse on the table. "Let me tell you something Robin, milling will never pay for all this!"

"Let me tell *you* something, mother." He rose to his feet. "You're going to have to get used to living on a miller's income, because all he provided was extra for us at the expense of others! I will not be a part of that; sucking money from the common people who can't spare it so that I can eat a little better, that would make me no better than the worst noble!" He slammed his fist against the wall.

"Life is not a game, Robin! It is hard, it is unfair! Any advantage we gain makes the difference between our children living or dying! We cannot be responsible for the weakness in others, we can only do our best for our own, and that's what your father was always trying to do!"

Margery was not going to cower from her son's temper this time, this time she had to fight back in order to maintain the living standards they had all become accustomed to, which had allowed seven of her children to survive where other women had only two.

"I know how hard life is mother, have I not worked hard for you?" He said accusingly.

"Of course you have Robin..."

Margery softened, knowing that Robin had been the one to step into the breach when Walter began to struggle with the milling, and the mill was the front which enabled Walter to carry on without attracting attention. Robin, despite his anger, had milled doggedly for almost twenty years, no doubt sacrificing much. He didn't have much time for courting with no brothers or uncles to help him and now of course he had the sole responsibility for feeding them all.

"I'm going round to Avice's place right now to let her know that as of this very moment the powder trade stops at Cornholme Mill." He made to leave.

"Robin! No! Please give it some thought - at least wait until your sisters have fledged, then I will be happy to live how you like!" She wept afresh.

"I don't need any time to think about the safety of our souls and stopping the misery in the village." He growled.

"You won't!" Margery snapped. "They will just get it from somewhere else and we will lose our cut! Nothing will change, except we will be poorer!"

"And God will be pleased with us. I'm always told God is important." Robin slammed the door behind him and headed to Avice's cottage.

~

Avice was abed, but Robin's constant battering and shouting brought her to the door quickly. Avice lived in a similar manner to Mother Helston. A discreet location away from others, a humble cottage that gave little sign of her lifestyle except for the fact that it looked smarter than it should, given she was a lone widow apparently without outside income.

Robin knew that years ago her husband had been a mere labourer with only this garden to his name. It was impossible he had paid her keep in such comfort long after his death. He knew she made a lot of money from what she did but all the women involved were careful not to live too lavishly and raise suspicions. At first glance they were harmless old ladies, selling the odd tincture or two to get by. To the observant however, things did not make sense - why were they always fed when their neighbours went hungry due to crop failure in the district?

Avice was used to nocturnal visits from customers, though she had tried in recent years to place Walter between her and the most of them. She was a little dubious about opening the door at this hour but also confident in her preparations, knowing that her two strapping sons, both aged approximately twenty, were woken and alert in the room ready to leap to the defence of their mother at any hour in exchange for a handsome stipend from her.

"Robin?" Avice said, her thin face registering complete confusion as she clutched her shawl about her shoulders.

"I've a message for you." Robin said without niceties.

"Go on?" Avice was ready for bad news.

"Dad's dead and I'm in charge at the mill now. That means no more powder going through it." He said. Avice sighed, she had envisaged this day coming for some time.

"What will you do?" She asked matter of factly. "Your mother would still sell for me, would you punish her?"

"I'd go straight to Lord William and report you and he'd be round here in a trice only too happy to put ropes around all your necks, you know that." He replied.

"*You'd* go running to Lord William?" Avice laughed. "You hate him, you hate all nobles, yet when it suits you would call for them to save you?"

"Not to save me. To save you, from what I would do to you if I found out you were conspiring with mother." He said simply, walking off into the darkness feeling a sense of triumphant calm. He had waited for this moment for a long time and it was sweet. No reply came from the direction of Avice's gloomy doorway.

~

Within the hour Avice was at Mother Helston's door and was surprised to see the light glowing at the windows. She let herself in without knocking and Mother Helston looked up with shock, her hand on a dagger she always had to hand. She visibly relaxed when she saw her friend but noticed that Avice was looking pensively at Sibyl, who was slumped in the chair, her mouth slack and her eyes unseeing.

"What's she doing here?" Avice enquired with a frown.

"I gave her the powerful one. She asked me to...and paid well." Mother Helston shrugged as she too looked at Sibyl's unresponsive form.

"In your own house?" Avice did not approve.

"It's that or lose her as a customer. She has less freedom than most...but more money!" Helston cackled. "Dare I ask why you are here?" She sobered quickly.

"I've just had a visit from Robin." Avice said grimly. "Walter's dead." She knew Helston would realise the implications of this without further details.

"He has acted as we supposed?" Helston shot back, already knowing the answer. Avice simply nodded once in reply. "We need him out of the way." Helston concluded.

"How can we do that?" Avice did not relish any of the obvious options - Margery would not take kindly to someone killing her son or any such tactics. It all had the potential to become very messy.

"I believe we have been given our answer." Helston nodded towards Sibyl. Avice narrowed her eyes and cocked her head to the side in enquiry. Mother Helston's face broke into a gleeful, toothless grin. "Mother Helston gets to know things and I happen to know that young Robin has been courting a French girl nobody's ever heard of."

"Yes I'd heard about that..." Avice muttered in reply, not

seeing the connection.

"Who would even speak French around here?" Helston asked, waiting for the penny to drop. Avice kept her silence, unwilling to make silly assumptions. She hated to look foolish. "Out of all the people who would speak French - the nobles - which of them, the female ones, would have cause to visit the mill?" Helston watched as Avice finally committed to the idea that Robin and Sibyl were romantically entangled.

Avice's eyes widened and she allowed a smile to creep over her face.

"So...we have the leverage we need right here!"

Mother Helston nodded.

~

The next evening Robin was working hard at the mill, exactly as Mother Helston predicted he would be. Everyone involved was aware that he would have to work hard, perhaps buy up surplus grain and take the sacks further afield to markets to sell, in order to support his family now. He thought over it all furiously as the stone went round and he shovelled.

That day his mother had made a deliberately thin soup for supper and told him he had better get used to that kind of fare. He was insulted his mother would think he would be swayed by such petty things and ate it with relish to spite her. Now he was aching and his eyelids were beginning to droop; he was considering finishing up for the day and joining the others in the bed.

Then the door burst open and he only had time to make out the form of Nicholas, one of Avice's sons. Nicholas did not pause but bore down on Robin and grasped his throat with one of his hands, the momentum of his bulk continuing until Robin was driven up against the wall. With dismay, Robin realised he could not fight back. He was fighting for breath, his kicks bouncing off Nicholas's muscular thighs ineffectually.

This was it. Avice would easily best him, and no doubt sweet talk and bribe his replacement into being the face of her business. Mother Helston would win. So easily! He was furious, but impotent. Then Simon was walking in, equally as huge as Nicholas, helping to peel him off the wall and wrenching his arm up behind his back, placing his own bearlike paw around his throat and holding him so. Neither said anything and Robin began to wonder what they were waiting for. His throat was held so tightly however that he could only hiss and squeak and they ignored him completely.

Then he stopped struggling, for he saw Mother Helston and Avice coming through the doorway and between them they held Sibyl, who was obviously sick in some way. His struggling started afresh in his outrage - what had they done to her? Their spat yesterday was forgotten; he felt only the need to liberate her.

"Now then Robin." Mother Helston began, not looking at him but patting Sibyl's slack face after Nicholas took over the task of holding her on her feet. Sibyl's eyes lolled unseeingly and did not register the touch of the old crone. "Mother Helston needs to speak to you I hear, about how things will run from now on."

The old woman reached into a little bag she had placed on a surface nearby as she entered. With great ceremony she produced a little goblet and a tiny blue jug with a little stopper, which she popped as she spoke.

"You have proven yourself dangerous to our cause and I'm afraid, as we cannot trust you not to run simpering to the nobles, you must be silenced. For good." She said calmly, pouring a thick, black ominous-looking liquid out of the jug.

Robin, outraged, gurgled his furious reply. Helston nodded to Simon to lessen the neck hold so he could speak.

"It'll be obvious you've murdered me you odious vecke! All know you work by poison, and it would be too suspicious for me to die the day after my father - my mother may love her trinkets, but would not trade them for her son! She would have no qualms about running to Lord William, or do you plan to poison the lot of them as well? Do you think that would go unnoticed!?" He cried, spitting all his fear into a fearsome tirade. "And what do you hope to achieve by poisoning your Lord's wife?!"

He had a suspicion Sibyl's presence had something to do with their recent activities and was trying to distance himself, to pretend she was no kind of leverage on him and perhaps spare her? Mother Helston seemed tellingly unmoved by his speech however.

"Mother Helston knows all about your romance with the Lady Sibyl Robin." She held the goblet up to inspect it, motioning to Simon to clamp down on Robin's throat again. "Who mentioned murder? I only said silence."

Robin's eyes flickered back and forth in confusion. Silence? Helston had produced a shiny dagger from the bag; did she mean to cut his tongue out? She handed the thing to Nicholas, who held it to Sibyl's pale throat, pulling her head back by the hair. Sibyl heard Robin's anguished cry. She was not completely unconscious, the world was just terribly thick and slow around her. Her limbs felt like lead, every movement took a monumental effort that she could not summon up the conviction to complete. Voices were slurred and echoey, her eyesight blurred. Mother Helston's voice slowly trickled into her brain now:

"When you have drunk this you will live Robin, you just won't be able to speak. Or move. Or communicate your unhappiness in any way. You will be frozen, irreversibly, forever. You will not be able to mill, your mother will have to attend to your every need...if she will. There will be no outward sign of poisoning; all will merely assume you were struck down with an appalling affliction. Unlucky."

Robin took a few moments to digest what he was being told, his hands clenched on Simon's forearm.

"That....is pure evil?!" He squawked pathetically, the fear now being given free rein as he squirmed against Simon.

Mother Helston advanced on him with the goblet and like a child refusing to eat its food Robin clamped his lips shut and forced his head from side to side to avoid it. The old woman quickly lost patience.

"Come Robin, it's surely obvious - if you don't drink this like a good boy, we slit Sibyl's throat. We don't want to bruise or cut you, so it would be better for you to drink this willingly." She calmly waited, one hand around the rim of the goblet, the other holding it gently on her palm as though at a banquet serving him wine, ready to help him take a sip. Robin had a look of despair on his face as he wrestled with the horrendous decision he had to make now.

Sibyl had heard the words. They had bounced around the inside of her skull, sharply underlined by the cold blade at her throat. She was aware she should panic, she should fight...but she could not. One eye lazily rolled down though, peeped at the scene before her with vague interest and saw Mother Helston's back moving away, towards Robin. There was no further sound now save the rain that was drumming the ground outside and Sibyl knew he had acquiesced, on her behalf.

She was enraged, upset, desperate. She had played with Robin and placed him in harm's way. Her actions had directly attributed to this fate, though it was more devilish and cruel than she could ever have considered. A rope around the neck, or a sword through the chest if Lord William had stumbled upon them, sure - but this? Spending his life trapped mutely in his own body, unable to respond to the world? Just as she was now, she realised, but with no hope of recovery whereas she knew that, provided he supped that concoction, she would snap out of it in a few hours. She knew however that if that did play out, if she woke to full alertness and Robin was paralysed due to her, she could not live with herself. She willed herself to think of something and to her intense joy, she did. It was a slim hope, but at least she would have tried.

Robin too was having the same thoughts. He knew that one or both of them were doomed one way or another so he may as well try something. As Mother Helston had been talking, his hands had been punching and grabbing at Simon as though he was still vainly struggling to get away. In fact, he was subtly building up to grabbing the billhook he knew was hanging on a pair of nails on the wall next to them.

Mother Helston's piggy little eyes were still as sharp as ever though and he saw with disappointment that her eyebrows rose as his hand quickly grabbed the handle of the hook. Her mouth opened to warn Simon but before she could say a word the room was plunged into darkness. Everyone was stunned, but Robin took only a second to gather his wits and begin fighting Simon, who could only dumbly maintain his hold as Robin tugged the billhook from the wall.

Sibyl had remained calm, firmly talking to herself in her mind, gathering the energy for one big push. When she felt she had built up enough momentum she let fly with a leg, clumsily kicking the lamp next to her off the worktop. Nicholas had not seen that coming, she had been limp and heavy in his arms without a problem this whole time. Now she slumped forwards with all her weight and that, coupled with his shock at suddenly becoming blind, made him cry out and drop her.

She lurched forwards crazily, unable to stop herself falling but her legs still working to try to get across the room to where she knew Robin had stood. She ricocheted off Mother Helston's puffy side and plunged forwards, clutching at fabric as she fell. She landed on the hard floor and lay, unable to move further, dimly feeling trampling feet on her in the confusion above. People were speaking but she could not make out the words. She was focussing on something she felt she should be paying attention to - a sensation in her arm that she knew was sharp, though it was not painful.

Vision returned. A red glow, flickering, growing stronger and brighter with each passing second. Now she saw the blurred figures above her, and Mother Helston barking:

"Go Simon, now! Dump her at Hapton; we don't need the murder of William's wife on our hands!" With more urgency than she had ever heard in that woman's voice before, which perplexed her. Murder? What was she talking about? She'd only fallen?

~

Robin looked around in a horrified daze. Was that just a bad dream? Had he fallen asleep at the stone? His pounding head and the echoey noises of voices disappearing into the night said different. As he looked around he saw the flames licking across the floor and suddenly felt the heat on his skin and he realised the whole room was about to burn and that he had to get out. He looked down and saw the hook soaked with blood from his frantic slashing at Simon who had thankfully fled after punching him on the temple, knocking him to the ground for a moment.

He threw down the hook with revulsion and turned to leave, until an alien sight caught his eye and stopped him in his tracks. It was startling, because it should not be. There on the floorboards next to the dropped goblet and splash of black liquid was a human hand, without an arm attached to it. Robin immediately saw that it was a small hand with smooth, white skin and slender fingers - it was not the hand of Simon, who he had been slashing at. He bent quickly to pick it up before it was burnt and fled out of the door to stand in the glow of the fire and examine it in order to confirm his suspicions.

His mother and sisters were clustered a little distance away, hugging each other and screaming as they watched their home burn with terrifying speed despite the heavy rain, the quantity of perfectly dry wood and thatch helping it burn. Now his voice joined theirs as he recognised Lord William's badge stamped into the gold of the ring and realised that he had made this grievous error and separated Sibyl's hand from the rest of her, which would surely kill her?

He fell to his knees in the orange light and clutched the hand to his chest, sobbing up at the sky which poured down onto his head, dripping steadily in so many tiny waterfalls from the end of each dark curl. Sibyl was not here though he realized; they had taken her, and he remembered what they had said - to Hapton Tower, back to Lord William, to 'dump' her because she was no longer useful. He had to get to her - who knew where they would leave her - if he could speed up her receiving help, maybe there was a chance? He knew nothing of medicine - perhaps all was not lost?

He set off in the dark, staggering along through the sticky mud, waving off the traumatised calls of his mother and sisters for his help, for him to do something. He heard a mule's strange hybrid bray, raised into a pitched shriek and then the mill boomed as the dust from years of milling caused an explosion and all went quiet, save for the crackle of the flames.

~

Robin pelted up to the gatehouse of Hapton Tower, soaking wet and caked in mud from the knees down, whereupon the Porter barred his entrance. Robin was so crazed by this stage he could not manage a coherent argument for his entry; instead he barrelled into the other man and struggled in his exhausted and weakened state to get past him by force. The soldier deftly held him back.

"Sibyyyyl!" He screamed into the tower grounds, unsure of what he hoped to achieve by this, as Sibyl, wherever she was, was unlikely to answer.

"Speak man, what is your business!" The guard had been joined by others, who held Robin back and gave their senior the chance to question the hysterical rustic in their hands.

"Sibyl! This is Lady Sibyl's hand! See the ring, man!" Robin brandished the hand and choked out the words desperately.

The porter recoiled in horror and was clearly caught in indecision. This was unprecedented in his career; earlier that evening Lady Sibyl had been dumped off the back of a horse at the gates - the rider, clothed all in black with a heavy hood, failing to stop. Of course he had hurried to get her to her chambers and find help, and now this? The feminine hand did indeed bear a ring with Lord William's crest on it.

"That's Robin Miller sir, I know him, he's the miller from Cornholme down the road." One of the soldiers thought this piece of information would be useful.

The porter quickly decided that as Robin was alone, known to his men as a local and clearly unarmed, it would be acceptable to let him in and see to this hand business, with an escort to supervise of course.

"I'll take you to them." He said, motioning for one of the other men to take over the gate duty.

"Hurry, hurry!" Robin nodded, roughly shoving the man forwards, relieved that Sibyl had found her way back here after all, maybe there was hope? The porter threw off Robin's arm and begrudgingly broke into a businesslike jog, head bent against the rain. They traversed the courtyard, Robin stumbling and slipping in the wet and dark, the porter faring better as he knew the ground well. Suddenly the rain ceased and they were running through the labyrinth of chambers in the tower which were dimly lit by the candles and lanterns held by various residents, woken by the noise of Lady Sibyl's arrival and now interested in this new development. Robin paid no attention to them, or the route, clutching Sibyl's cool, wet hand to his chest as he ran.

Then the porter stopped abruptly and Robin almost piled into the back of him. The man pushed the door with his gloved hand, thinking that under the circumstances speed was probably more important than manners. Robin leapt through the door, instantly seeing Sibyl stretched out on the bed which, just a day or so ago, he was enjoying her in. Now she was again laid out on it, her hair spread about the pillows in a strikingly similar manner except now it was damp and matted. Sibyl herself had taken on a grey pallour and her eyes seemed glazed. For a moment he thought she was dead and he approached the bed slowly, with mounting horror, not at all noticing the stares and gasps of the people in the chamber.

"Robin..." Sibyl whispered, a corner of her mouth curling up into a weak smile, her left hand making a tiny movement towards him.

Robin collapsed onto his knees at the edge of the bed, dimly aware that he was elbowing some old man out of the way and sobbed as he reached for Sibyl's hand with his own, smearing it with blood and mud.

"Explain yourself young man!" Boomed the surgeon angrily.

Robin ignored the man and simply tossed the severed hand on the coverlet before him in answer, maintaining his focus on Sibyl.

"Sibyl?" He spoke her name.

"Oh, you brought the hand." The surgeon said.

"Yes I brought the hand," Robin said over his shoulder, "can you reaffix it? Will she live?"

"I will try." The man replied, having never tried such a thing before but being loathe to admit he did not think it likely the hand could be reattached, as it was unhelpful to say such things to paying customers. "I will clean it and do my best - the rest is up to the Lady." He said sagely.

Robin watched with vague interest as the poultice of comfrey was removed from the stump of Sibyl's arm by the women present, at the request of the surgeon who was delicately cleaning the hand in a basin, thinking it to perhaps be a task beyond the delicate constitutions of servingwomen.

"I'm sorry Sibyl...I am so, so very sorry!" Robin sobbed.

"You could not see." Sibyl looked at him, smiling softly.

"...Does it hurt?" Robin could not understand Sibyl being so calm.

"No..." She shook her head slowly. "I am still under the effects of Helston's potion I think...it was strong stuff." Robin simply looked back at her, a deeply unhappy expression on his face as the hand was bandaged onto the stump with a fresh application of the knitbone paste. Then the corners of Sibyl's mouth sank and her face crumpled a little. "Robin, I am afraid."

"Why Sibyl? You can see the surgeon is reattaching your hand, you'll be as new soon!" Robin tried to reassure himself as much as her. Sibyl shook her head again in reply, looking away from Robin as though disappointed in his attempts.

"No." She said simply.

"Yes Sibyl, you heard the man, you have to do this!"

"I had a son, Robin." Sibyl looked back at him.

"What?" Robin frowned...Sibyl was childless, she had told him so herself.

"I had a son, and I never knew him, not even his name....and now I will die and I never will know." Sibyl was weeping faintly now. "I want to see my baby..."

Robin was stunned into silence, pained to see Sibyl's heartbreak, feeling his own breaking in two at her words, knowing they would soon be parted, feeling bewildered at this new turn of their brief, intense liaison.

"Who...by?" He croaked.

"Edward." Sibyl replied.

"Edward?" Robin did not know that name.

"King, Edward." Sibyl clarified, carrying on when no reply came from Robin. "There is not the time to find him now..." The work on her stump was finished and Robin stared dumbly at the bandaged ball on the end of her arm, the cloths beneath stained with the blood which seeped from the wound despite the attentions of the surgeon.

"I wanted you to know." Sibyl continued to explain. The others in the room listened intently and discreetly. "I buried it. I regret that now, cannot even remember why." Her voice broke, then she transferred her tired gaze back to Robin's stormy blue eyes. "But now you know - you know I uncovered him and remembered." She smiled through the tears and faintly squeezed his hand.

At that moment Lord William entered the room. He had returned home from his visitation to find Sibyl missing and with a cold, resigned anger had ridden straight back out again to scour the area for her. He had found Mother Helston's cottage dark and empty, the ruin of Bearnshaw a bleak skeleton devoid of life, the builders having moved on to construction of the new hall elsewhere now. Eventually he had admitted defeat and he and his men had walked back to Hapton to rest and continue the search later, only to find the tower in turmoil; everyone awake and mumbling incoherently about Sibyl and a miller and a surgeon?

Sibyl did not react at all to William's entry, had expected it, but Robin jumped up and whirled around to face him, defiant. William stood stock still in open confusion; the only movement from him was of his eyes as he scanned the room, trying to interpret who all the people were and what their place in this was.

"Robin Miller?" He said questioningly. Robin nodded. "What are you doing here?" He asked, but all could see that he was clearly figuring out what must be going on as he spoke. "What is your business in *my wife's chambers*?" He said darkly.

Before Robin could answer Lord William bellowed to the tired, wet men behind him.

"Lock him up! *Lock him up!*"

Robin fought uselessly as two men hefted him up by the armpits and prepared to march him out of the room.

"I will deal with you later," William snarled at Robin, allowing all his confusion and anger to pour out on him, "but now, my wife is sick and I must attend to her!"

William turned away from Robin and made to kneel next to Sibyl's bed. Robin dug his heels into the floor and blurted out;

"Your wife is dying sir, and she wants me! And I want her!"

"*Get out!*" Lord William roared.

"This is your fault!" Robin screamed as he was dragged out of the door. "You did this William!"

He was attempting to make himself feel better about his role in Sibyl's impending death, to blame someone. He knew it was true to an extent; if Lord William hadn't pursued Sibyl so terribly and had placed her feelings above his own she would have had no reason to get entangled with Mother Helston, and would never have been at the mill. As the words left his mouth though he felt the stab of recognition that he was also responsible, that maybe he had even exploited Sibyl for his own ends? Struck when she was vulnerable and conveniently run when she balked at the cliff edge he subsequently offered her...and then...and then...cut off her hand and killed her! Robin went slack in the men's arms and allowed himself to be carried away.

"Go get some sleep Robert." Lord William called over his shoulder to the man hovering uncertainly in the doorway, his voice cracking as he did so. Robert obediently hurried away, eager to distance himself from yet more of the turmoil that that woman brought to Hapton.

"Sibyl....what has happened?" William enquired with genuine concern.

Previously he had been furious with her for going back to her old ways, and of course the new revelation that she had been carrying on with the miller had triggered a monumental rage in him but that was all temporarily shelved now, walled off in the face of how awful Sibyl looked. He was faced with the undeniable realisation that she was going to die and he was going to be a childless widower and would never see Sibyl Bearnshaw again after a lifetime of being absorbed by her.

Sibyl did not answer, just glowered at him from her pillows.

"My Lord, the Lady's hand has been...cut off." The surgeon took it upon himself to answer, gesturing at the mass of bloodied bandages on the end of her white arm. "I am giving her the very best of my knowledge, though I will admit this is not something I've attempted before...." He sounded dubious.

William took a long, dry swallow. He was no fool, he had seen similar injuries from battle before and never had he seen someone survive it, let alone heal the limb back on.

"Sibyl, Sibyl please, speak to me!" He pleaded.

"Robin set me free." She said simply.

She knew it was a vain hope, but she hoped nonetheless that Robin would not be punished too severely. She was trying to explain that she bore him no ill will, that she even thought of him as having done her a favour in all this. Now she would be free and although she felt things had been left undone and some of her life had been snatched away, she also saw little hope in the future overall and was cheered by the prospect of being reunited with John, Tom, her mother and father.

"Sibyl," William's jaw worked as he choked out her name, "please, don't talk about that now! Don't you understand? You are dying, and I will...miss you. You are still my wife, please, please can you think about me now?"

Sibyl's face contorted. William could feel the hot fury emanating from her even though she did not move a muscle and he imagined himself burnt by it. He physically flinched under her gaze.

"No William." She said firmly. "I will not think on you again. I am going to join my husband now. You, however, can think of me whenever you hunt around Eagle Crag. You can think of me hoping your horse stumbles at speed and your neck breaks!" She visibly calmed after making her speech, then added: "Now fetch me a priest," dismissively.

William took a deep breath and Sibyl saw him blink back tears. Then he sniffed and nodded to himself before looking back at her.

"I know not why you need a priest, when you be so clearly of the Devil!" Was all he said, before turning on his heel and storming out of the room.

William sent for Sibyl's priest and headed straight back out to the stables and had the marshal re-saddle his favourite bay, whereupon he rode into Burnley alone to lose himself in the inns for a few days. The priest dutifully came and performed the necessary rites to ease Sibyl's passage into the next world, listening patiently and with interest to her story, her fears and confessions. Sibyl felt calmed and lasted until sunset when she slipped away peacefully. When Lord William came home he faced the decision of what to do with the body, which had been prepared and then held, his staff unsure of what to do in his absence.

"Bury her at Eagle Crag." He said, unwilling to put her in his family chapel, intending to find himself a new, obedient wife and put her in there instead, to pretend that this whole disastrous marriage had never happened. "And I will never set foot on Bearnshaw land again." He added, before riding off to meet Warwick as requested.

~

Edward was aware only of the rhythmic snorting of his destrier as they pounded heavily over the ground together, aimed squarely at Warwick's forces. All around roared the battle cry of his men with him but Edward was concentrating, alone with his thoughts, holding his sword raised and steady in one hand and his reins in the other, his eyes trained ahead through the slit of his visor.

He experienced a heady concoction of emotions. The burning indignation of Warwick's audacity, the chilling worry of his poor reception in Yorkshire after sailing from the continent to take back his kingdom, which he had swiftly managed to reverse by personally charming the city of York into supporting him. This was quickly backed up by a joyful reunion with his fickle brother Clarence who had hopefully learnt his lesson this time. Having Clarence and his endlessly loyal little brother the Duke of Gloucester at his back, together once more, gave him the courage to take back what they had won and punish their overbearing, treacherous cousin once and for all.

London had evidently caught the air of promise and invincibility in the reunited Yorkist force and quickly accepted Edward back, handing Henry over. Even Henry himself had been happy to see Edward, refusing his hand and instead favouring him with a hug, Edward remembered with bafflement - proof if ever it were needed that God was with him!

Yet more confirmation that things were now working in his favour arrived when he rushed to see his wife and the face of his first legitimate heir, happy and healthy despite months spent living in sanctuary. It was an unspeakable joy to liberate his family and spend time with them, but now he had unfinished business to attend to, knowing that he could never rest easy while the formidable Earl of Warwick was loose.

Warwick had been evading a battle for a long time, but Edward was now pursuing mercilessly, and had finally caught up with him at Barnet near St. Albans, silently creeping up to within half a mile of the 'Lancastrian' forces under the cover of darkness, which would surely force Warwick to fight? Edward thought back with glee on how Warwick's guns had fired fully over his army, Warwick evidently completely unaware he had crept quite so close.

Edward wanted to make full use of his advantage and prepared to strike as soon as there was light to see by. It was Easter Sunday, but if God had not wanted blood spilled that day, he surely would not have handed Edward this glorious opportunity now? It was unfortunate that there was heavy fog which would confuse things for both sides, he knew, but there was no way he was going to let this chance slip by, so he galloped onwards to see what was planned for he and his cousin.

~

All was confusion in the Lancastrian ranks. William had been awake all night with the others, listening to the guns firing and hearing only sinister silence back. All awaited dawn with trepidation and then suddenly he, Edward, was upon them. In the fog it was difficult to see how many they were up against, but Warwick had assured them that his was a mighty army and it was unlikely Edward could match it, therefore all they could do was stand and fight and see.

William was tiring, the battle had seemed endless - he guessed they were evenly matched after all. A whole raft of confusing shouts had gone up though as the two armies outflanked each other at either end, each without knowledge of what was going on further upfield. It was difficult to tell who was for whom and many were beginning to think about extricating themselves from this terrible situation.

Then came the dreaded cry - Warwick was dead.

Suddenly William became actively fearful; with their strong leader cut down, confusion would reign and many would desert. William decided he would be among them and turned his mount to the nearest clear space behind him, flailing his sword arm at any who would pursue behind. With relief he broke from the main mass and his mount could lengthen its stride.

~

Behind him Edmund was in the mass of the fighting, raising a triumphant cheer when the cry went out that Warwick was dead. Even though he knew that Edward had given orders that Warwick be captured it was better that they won the battle than worrying too much on that: this was a decisive moment as all knew. The resistance was now rudderless and Edward was truly King once again, with only Henry's wife and pup to seek out and remove now.

With satisfaction Edmund saw that sure enough the Lancastrians who could were beginning to flee and he determined to chase them. A group caught his eye - a blood red and black livery with a badge depicting a black hound. He recognised that badge; it was the badge of the chap Sibyl had not wanted to marry. He had heard since being back in England that he had indeed forced her to marry him while Edward was safely out of the way and Edmund now saw the perfect way to make amends to Sibyl.

~

"I caught this one fleeing - it's Hapton." Edmund said proudly to his King as the haul of prisoners was paraded for him, adding: "The one Sibyl Bearnshaw didn't want to marry." He hoped that Edward would remember the story despite having been heavily distracted by recent events.

William was stripped of his armour and valuables and kneeling, his hands tied behind his back, staring into the middle distance as the men discussed him. He probed the bloody hole in his gum where a tooth used to be with his tongue, formed after Edmund had dealt him a few back handers with a gloved hand during his capture.

"Oh yes." Edward nodded, his head now free of the helmet, his armour blood spattered and dirty, the bright colours of the fabric about his person dulled with the filth of battle. He had chosen to do this now, despite having gone without sleep for many hours, as he wanted this job finished for good with no chances for any escapes. "That one is certainly for the chop." He added grimly, nodding to the men with the improvised tree stump of a block to do their work.

"Edward." William quietly muttered, "Edward. Of course, of course." Nodding to himself and thinking not of Edward at all but of Sibyl as he was led in only his shirt and hose to the block to lay his head down calmly, but wincing and shuddering as the swordsman raised his arm.

Legend of the Whyte Doe

Postscript:

The most common question I have been asked by people who have read my story is where does the original legend end and my story begin? There is also of course, a third element stirred in - actual history. To save anybody hours of research, I'll talk about it here.

There is a 'Bearnshaw Tower Farm' in existence today on the edge of Todmorden moor, and nearby are 'Tower Causeway', 'Tower Wood' and 'Tower Clough' so it stands to reason that there must have been a towerlike structure there at some point! Tales and legends abound in the area and Bearnshaw Tower has two to its name that I know of. The Legend of the Milk White Doe, about Sibyl, and the story of how it came down in the 1860s as a result of digging beneath it for a fabled stash of gold.

It's unclear whether the 'Doe' legend was entirely made up by a chap named Roby, or whether he heard the legend locally and merely wrote it down, perhaps with a few embellishments. No hard evidence of a Sibyl or a William has been found. However, to my mind this proves little; it seems entirely feasible that these characters may have existed further into the past than the records we have unearthed go, and although the details may have changed in the retellings, there is probably a seed of truth in there somewhere, if Roby didn't completely make it up himself!

Regardless, in the popular tale all we know about Sibyl/Sybil/Sibell is that she was an intelligent, beautiful and uncommonly independent young woman with a love of nature. She was betrothed to 'Lord William' but didn't want to be, and turned to the local witches for help. The witches helped her to sell her soul to the Devil and she became one of them, taking the form of a white doe to bound around the moors and avoid William.

William himself went to Mother Helston for help and she gave him an enchanted silken rope to get around Sibyl's neck in order to trap her. William went out on horseback one night and the chase went all around Eagle's Cragg (which is most definitely real) and William was joined by a black hound - Mother Helston's familiar - which helped him to trap Sibyl in the end. Apparently the hunstman and the black hound going after the milk white doe can be seen if you visit the moors on a moonlit night...

Once trapped the soul-selling was reversed and Sibyl married William, agreeing to give up witchcraft for good. She was soon back to her old tricks however, joining the other witches at the mill in the form of a white cat this time. They caused so much trouble Robin the miller was moved to lop off the paw of the white cat, which promptly turned into a hand. Sibyl had fled, but the telltale ring bearing William's crest was on the finger of the remaining hand and Robin took it to William.

Sibyl was found in bed with only one hand and all knew what she had been up to. The hand was reattached with witchcraft, but she sickened and died anyway and is reputedly buried at Eagle Cragg.

I am not one to tinker too much with history or real people. Edward IV existed and his deeds and movements should be accurate except for his night with Sibyl, which is obviously extremely unlikely to have happened with her! However, Edward was known for being a ladies' man and fathered illegitimate children. He also did indeed marry Elizabeth Woodville who was virtually 'a commoner' aswell as being an older widow and it did cause great scandal at the time, going some way to sparking the rift between he and his erstwhile ally Warwick.

The scandal continued after Edward's death when his children by Elizabeth were pronounced illegitimate because he had secretly married yet another older widow before he had married Elizabeth. Given these shennanigans it did not feel unfair to put Edward and Sibyl in bed together!

John Arnold and Edmund are fictional, as is Robert. The Towneley family however are real, and were the true owners of

Hapton Tower which is now gone. Towneley Hall near Burnley is well worth a visit, and I hope the Towneley family are not offended by my representation of their real ancestor John.

The incredible story of the final capture of King Henry and the characters involved (except Lord William, Tom and Edmund) is true but another little-known example of the national significance of this beautiful part of the country that deserves more tourism!

The drug is entirely fictional. I am quite sure that people would have had access to various substances in the past but I have no idea what exactly they would have been. This one is supposed to be some kind of herbal concoction from what Mother Helston could have acquired, most likely revolving around magic mushrooms but probably with extra potent imported ingredients too.

The results really stem from what I've seen of the whole shamanic side of other cultures. The visions and rituals all seem to revolve around animals – talking to animals, through animals, taking on the form of animals. Nature and animals were still a big part of life in medieval times, they would have literally lived cheek by jowl. In the absence of all the other stimulations we have today I think it's likely that any hallucinations Sibyl had would focus on animals and the heraldic symbols that dominated her life perhaps.

It has been pointed out to me that it would be wrong to refer to Sibyl as 'Lady Sibyl', she would be Mistress Sibyl. I made a conscious decision to keep the terms Lady Sibyl and Lord William however as they are the names from the original legend and are virtually all we have of these characters and to remove them felt like too much of a removal from the original for me.

I realise also that the characters' familiar use of first names is also technically 'wrong', particularly in the case of Sibyl referring to her elders and betters, however I stand by this as I do believe that in real circumstances people would have deviated from the terms they were 'supposed' to use if they felt comfortable to do so. Titled people are probably not obsessed with pressing home the correct use of their title at all times with their friends and in private - imagine how exhausting that would be!

Some have found Sibyl hard to warm to. I'll let you into a little secret - me too! I don't think there's much to like about her in the original legend or this adaptation. In the original she is nothing but a troublemaker in league with witches, making false promises and pleasing herself. In my story she's quick witted and gutsy which is admirable, but she is at heart just another Wars of the Roses ambitious climber, willing to throw everything, even her own child, under the bus in order to keep her family's wealth and property. Was she even so sorry when Tom was lost and she had to take the reins herself I wonder?

I see her as something like a female George of Clarence (Edward IVs brother) - disadvantaged due to being the second son/a woman, but always grasping for more regardless and ultimately paying the price. George was executed for his scheming having never worn a crown and Sibyl endured plenty of emotional pain and died having lost everything. I feel dreadfully sorry for her but I don't think she'd be a good friend!

Made in the USA
Charleston, SC
18 November 2014